Tim Cope is an adventurer, author and film-maker who is passionate about inspiring young people to explore the world that exists beyond their doorstep. He has studied as a wilderness guide in the Finnish and Russian subarctic, ridden a bicycle across Russia to China and rowed a boat along the Yenisey River through Siberia to the Arctic Ocean. He is the author of *Off the Rails: Moscow to Beijing on Recumbent Bikes,* and *On the Trail of Genghis Khan: An Epic Journey Through the Land of the Nomads.* He is also the creator of several documentary films, including the award-winning series 'The Trail of Genghis Khan', which covers the journey of this book. He currently splits his time between Melbourne, Australia, where he is a regular speaker in schools, and remote Mongolia, where he takes people on nomadic adventures annually.

www.timcopejourneys.com

ALSO BY TIM COPE

Off the Rails: Moscow to Beijing on Recumbent Bikes
(with Chris Hatherly)

*On the Trail of Genghis Khan: An Epic Journey
Through the Land of the Nomads*

TIM & TIGON

TIM COPE

PAN
Pan Macmillan Australia

First published 2019 in Pan by Pan Macmillan Australia Pty Ltd
1 Market Street, Sydney, New South Wales, Australia, 2000

Cataloguing-in-Publication entry is available
from the National Library of Australia
http://catalogue.nla.gov.au

Typeset in Minion Pro by Midland Typesetters, Australia
Printed by McPherson's Printing Group
Maps courtesy of Will Pringle.
Cover photographs courtesy of Cara Poulton and Tim Cope.
Internal photographs courtesy of Tim Cope or as otherwise credited.

The author and the publisher have made every effort to contact copyright
holders for material used in this book. Any person or organisation that may
have been overlooked should contact the publisher.

Aboriginal and Torres Strait Islander people should be aware that this book
may contain images or names of people now deceased.

MIX
Paper from
responsible sources
FSC® C001695

The paper in this book is FSC® certified.
FSC® promotes environmentally responsible,
socially beneficial and economically viable
management of the world's forests.

*To Tigon, my dear companion who turned hostility
into friendship, fear into love, danger into curiosity,
and faraway places into our home.*

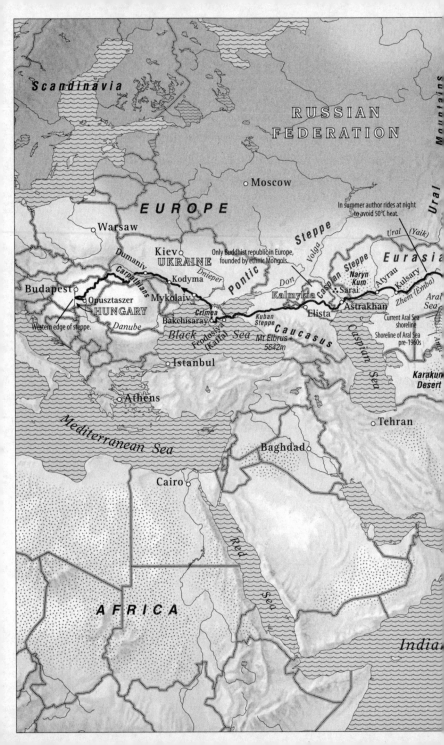

Scandinavia

RUSSIAN FEDERATION

EUROPE

o Moscow

Warsaw

Dumaniv

Carpathians

Kiev o
UKRAINE

Only Buddhist republic in Europe,
founded by ethnic Mongols.

Steppe

Ural

Ural (Yaik)

In summer author rides at night
to avoid 50°C heat.

Eurasia

Budapest o

Opusztaszer

HUNGARY

Danube

Western edge of steppe.

Kodyma

Dnieper

Mykolaiv

Crimea

Bakhchisaray

Black

Feodosiya
(Kaffa)

Pontic

Sea

Don

Volga

Kalmykia

Elista

*Kuban
Steppe*

Sea

Caspian Steppe

*Naryn
Kum*

Sarai

Astrakhan

Caucasus

Mt Elbrus +
5642m

Caspian Sea

Atyrau

Zhem (Emba)

Kulsary

Current Aral Sea
shoreline

Shoreline of Aral Sea
pre-1960s

*Aral
Sea*

Karakum
Desert

o Istanbul

o Athens

Mediterranean Sea

Baghdad o

o Tehran

Red

Cairo o

Sea

AFRICA

India

Mountains

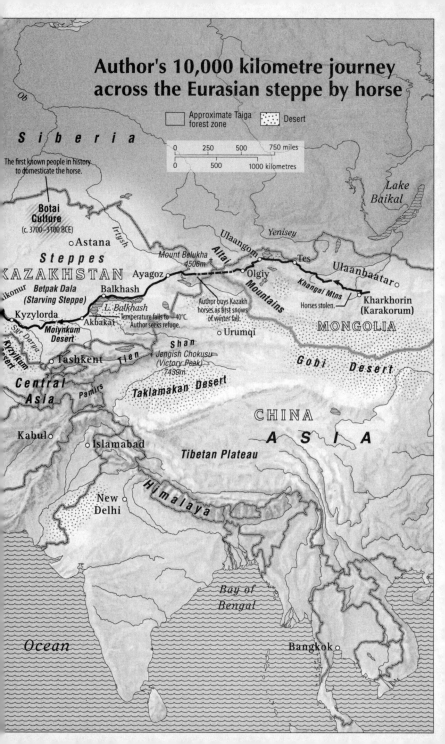

Author's 10,000 kilometre journey across the Eurasian steppe by horse

Approximate Taiga forest zone   Desert

| 0 | 250 | 500 | 750 miles |
| 0 | | 500 | 1000 kilometres |

Ob

S i b e r i a

The first known people in history to domesticate the horse.

Botai Culture (c. 3700–3100 BCE)

Astana

Irtysh

Yenisey

Lake Baikal

S t e p p e s

KAZAKHSTAN

Ulaangom

Mount Belukha 4506m

Altai

Ayagoz

Olgiy

Tes

Ulaanbaatar

Khangai Mtns

Horses stolen.

Kharkhorin (Karakorum)

Baikonur

Betpak Dala (Starving Steppe)

Balkhash

L. Balkhash
Temperature falls to –40°C.
Author seeks refuge.

Author buys Kazakh horses as first snows of winter fall.

Kyzylorda

Akbakai

Moiynkum Desert

Sur Darya

Kyzylkum Desert

Tashkent

Urumqi

MONGOLIA

G o b i   D e s e r t

Tien   Shan

Jengish Chokusu (Victory Peak) 7439m

C e n t r a l   A s i a

Pamirs

Taklamakan Desert

CHINA

Kabul

Islamabad

Tibetan Plateau

A S I A

New Delhi

H i m a l a y a

Bay of Bengal

Ocean

Bangkok

Contents

When in the steppe I stand alone
With far horizons clear to view,
Ambrosia on the breezes blown
And skies above me crystal blue,
I sense my own true human height
And in eternity delight.
The obstacles to all my dreams
Now shrink, appear absurd, inept,
And nothing either is or seems
Except myself, these birds, this steppe . . .
What joy it is to feel all round
Wide open space that knows no bounds!

     —Unknown Kalmyk poet

Foreword

Sometimes I catch myself thinking: if only I could have known where this journey would lead me. All those nights I spent lying by a campfire, ears pricked and axe by my side, listening for the terrifying sound of a wolf. Of clinging to the warm fur of my dog in the dead of night while snowstorms howled at my tent. The times when I thought all was lost until strangers came from nowhere to help me. Sipping camel milk tea together with nomadic people in the middle of the desert in Kazakhstan. Eating boiled lamb scalp – and loving it – with horsemen and horsewomen high in the mountains of Mongolia. I could never have imagined that I would experience those moments, in the unlikeliest of places, making friends with the unlikeliest of strangers.

If only it were possible to go back in time. I would return to my younger self and tell tales I would hardly believe. I would encourage myself to keep going, and prepare myself for what was to come. But then again, isn't that the beautiful thing about adventure? The tingles and sweat snaking down the spine, hair on end, not knowing what is around the corner? None of us knows where life will take us, and we don't know where we will lead it, either.

This book is about a dream that I turned into reality. That dream has set my life on a path that my former self definitely would not believe. It has been difficult, and sometimes it has felt as though I wasn't on a path at all – and sometimes, quite literally, I wasn't – yet I wouldn't change a thing.

In the hardest times, what got me through was trying to keep belief in myself. And where that failed, the belief of family and friends – of both the furry and human kind – carried me on.

This is a story for you, so that you too can step into the saddle and ride towards your dreams. But it is also for the young boy in me, who still struggles daily with fear of the unknown, who still wonders whether I can get over the next hurdle, or if things might go wrong if I take a risk.

I want to remind myself to be brave, to have patience, to never stop making new friends or nurturing old ones, and to never let go of dreams. And to have fun! Every day is a chance to learn something new, and it's best to live vividly, to feel every moment of every day, rather than sleepwalk through life (even though I still love sleep-ins). And at the end of this book, perhaps you, like me, will have shared some of the friendships and loneliness, the tears and laughs, sheep eyeballs, scalding summers and freezing winters that made my journey so special.

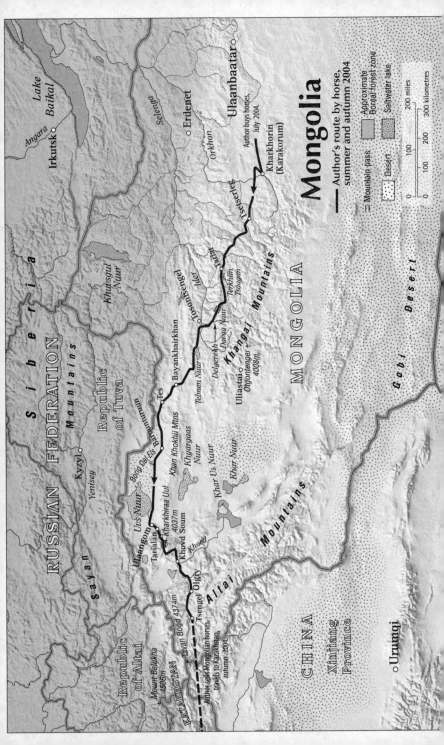

1

Mongolian Dreaming

Ten minutes earlier I had been hunched over my saddle, leaning into the horizontal rain and hail. The storm, which had begun with a whirlwind of dust and sand, had hit like a train. But just as quickly as it had appeared, it had gone. Now the afternoon sun was shining and the wind had stopped. I gazed at the storm cloud that sailed over the land to my left. It crossed a valley plain and continued on to distant hills.

When I was younger I had watched clouds such as this, envious of their freedom. Here in the wide, open land of Mongolia the boundless sky was mirrored on the land. Herds of horses and flocks of sheep and goats moved about like cloud shadows. For the nomads who looked after these animals, nowhere, it seemed, was off-limits. Their round, white felt-walled tents, known as *gers*, were perched on hilltops, by streams, and tucked into distant slopes. Horsemen and horsewomen were everywhere, and not a tree, fence, or road was in sight. This was a world without boundaries.

Gripping the reins of my riding horse, Bor, I felt my heart skip a beat. My surroundings might have looked like something from a dream, but the sour taste of goat curd in my mouth, the feeling of the wet leather saddle on my sore bum, and the pull of the lead rope from my packhorse were undeniable – this was real.

Six days earlier, after a lot of bargaining, I had bought three Mongolian horses. Now I was setting off to ride 10,000 kilometres across the nomad lands of the Eurasian steppe, from Mongolia to Hungary. Ten thousand? It might as well have been a million, it seemed so far. Ahead lay deserts, ice-capped mountains, and sprawling plains.

In theory, the idea was simple. I would ride one horse and lead two packhorses to carry all my belongings. Each night I would camp out under the stars with my horses for company, until finally one day I would reach Europe. One friend had even assured me: 'Get on your horse, point it to the west, and when people start speaking French, it means you have gone too far.'

In reality I had always known it would be a bit more

complicated. One of the nomads who had sold me a horse looked at me like I was crazy.

'You are going to ride to Hungary . . . and you are not carrying a gun?'

People kept reminding me about the usual dangers – wolves and thieves, not to mention deathly cold, high mountains, and scorching-hot summers where, it was rumoured, you could become dried out and mummified in a single day. But that wasn't what really frightened me.

What frightened me was that I could barely ride a horse. In fact, prior to this journey, my only experience as a horseman was when I was seven years old. On that occasion, I was bucked to the ground and shipped to hospital with a badly broken arm. Despite some training in Australia in recent months, and a handful of days in the saddle, I was still terrified of these big powerful creatures.

My fear of horses had kept me awake many a night. I imagined being thrown off, kicked, bitten, and not being able to control a wild, bolting horse. But somehow I had convinced myself that the difficulties ahead were mostly beyond my imagination. Besides, who could possibly be better horseriding teachers than the nomads of the steppe?

But I was here now, and there was no turning back. Ahead of me lay 10,000 kilometres of open land, and across all of these empty horizons, not a soul knew I was coming. At this stage, in fact, no one even knew I existed.

Or so I thought . . .

When the sun began to edge towards the horizon I watered the horses, then chose a campsite halfway up a hillside. As would become my nightly routine, I set about hobbling the horses' legs and tying them up. As dinner boiled, and I rested against my pack boxes, I watched flocks of sheep and goats come swarming over the hills. To me they almost looked like schools of fish, moving this way and that over the land. The breeze carried the sweet smell of burning animal dung – from the cooking stoves in nearby gers – mixed with the sounds of bleating and baaing and cries of distant horsemen and horsewomen. When my dinner pot had been scraped clean I lay down on a mattress of horse blankets, listening to the crunch of horses chewing grass.

I must have fallen into a deep sleep, for when I opened my eyes the idyllic scenes had gone. It was pitch black and the tent clapped and bucked around me in a roaring wind.

Something had woken me. I crawled out of my sleeping bag and clutched blindly for my torch. When I failed to find it I lay still, held my breath and strained to listen for my horses.

Minutes passed.

There was no jingle of the horse bell, no sound of the horses grazing. But then beyond camp, above the roaring wind and my thumping heartbeat, I heard muffled voices and the thunder of hooves. I forced my way out of the tent and ran barefoot to where I had tied the animals. There, madly neighing into the night and pulling at his rope, was Bor – all alone. Somewhere beyond camp the sound of galloping was fading fast.

Holding Bor's tether rope tight, I stumbled further until I felt the other two ropes between my toes. All that remained of my two other horses were the bell that had been tied around the packhorse's neck and a pair of hobbles.

Warnings from nomads flooded back: *What are you going to do when the wolves attack? What about when the thieves steal your horses?*

I had brushed these questions away. Wolves? Surely that was just a story to scare me. And even if thieves did exist, I had a plan. Sheila Greenwell, a vet in Australia, had suggested that if I put the bell on my horses at night I would wake up if thieves approached, because the horses would become nervous and the bell would ring loudly.

In reality, the sound of the bell had probably led the thieves straight to my camp.

I kept searching, hoping I might have missed something, but by the time I returned to the tent, frozen, there was no denying it: on only the sixth day of my journey I had lost two of my horses.

*

For a couple of hours I lay paralysed, more from fear than cold. Was this the end of the expedition? What would I do? My dream was in tatters.

From the very beginning I had lived with the uncertainty of how long it would take to get to Hungary, and when I would get to see my family again. But that night the question on my mind was not when, but *if* I would make it to Hungary. And even worse – *would* I get to see my family again?

It wasn't until light began bleeding into the early morning sky that my mood began to lift.

This wasn't the first time that I had found myself scared and vulnerable, and I was pretty sure that it wouldn't be the last. For now, I was safe. I still had a full belly and I had one horse. Adventures are not meant to go to plan, are they?

I needed to get the horses back.

After thinking hard, I did what any modern adventurer might do in a bad situation: I picked up the satellite phone and called for advice.

My long time Mongolian friend, Tseren, picked up the phone.

'Well, Tim,' she said, 'here in Mongolia we say that if you don't solve your problems before sunrise, then you will never solve them. You better get on that last remaining horse of yours and start looking!'

There was still time.

At five am I saddled up and pointed Bor into the pale blues and reds of the eastern sky.

Smoke was curling its way up from the nearest ger as I rode forwards. People would soon be getting up to milk their goats and yaks. Sitting high in the saddle I put on the angriest look I could muster and imagined galloping into the camp to demand answers. But I could not make the horse move any faster than a walk. As I drew near, what I thought was a pile of old mangy fur, leapt to life with the fangs and growl of a giant guard dog. Bor reared up, I struggled to hold on, and together we went trotting back the way we had come.

When I finally got close to this nomad family camp, the only answers were shrugs and looks of confusion from sleepy herders. I was beginning to realise that the chances of finding my horses in a country where millions of animals graze freely, and there are no fences, was very, very slim.

Bor and I calmed down a little. As I rode I stroked his neck and watched his big hairy ears twitch this way and that. When the sun began reaching into the sky I watched his summer coat light up like a shiny full moon. In Mongolia nomads always name their horses by their colour, and Bor meant 'white'. Thank goodness the thieves had been kind enough to leave him for me.

I had begun to accept that I would never see my horses again when my luck changed.

From over a rise came the sound of thundering hooves, followed by an entire herd of galloping horses. Squinting hard against the sun I could just make out the shape of two horses trailing behind. I looked closer.

My horses!

A horseman who had been herding them approached me and stepped out of the saddle. He stood proudly in his long Mongolian cloak, called a *deel*, and wearing his knee-high riding boots. A lasso was strung over his shoulder.

'I know,' he said, before I could say anything. 'They came to me themselves this morning. You must have tied them *really* badly.'

I was invited into the man's nearby ger where I was handed a bowl of fermented mare's milk. It had a couple of blowflies floating belly up on the surface. I didn't mind at all. As I felt the fizzy, sour taste trickle down my throat, the herder sat on the dirt floor looking me and said: *'Tanilgui hun algiin chinee. Taniltai hun taliin chinee.'*

With the help of a pocket dictionary I was able to translate this: A man without friends is as small as a palm. A man with friends is as big as the steppe.

It was an old Mongolian saying. I didn't know it yet, but it would rescue the horses and me on many occasions in the years ahead.

There was an important lesson in this nomad saying. If I was to have any hope of making it another 100 kilometres, let alone 10,000 kilometres, I needed to break out of my own little dream world and start getting to know the people, learning their ways, and above all, making friends.

2

Nomad Apprenticeship

A few days later I woke to the early morning sun glowing red through my eyelids. Beyond the rising chorus of cicadas came the reassuring sound of swishing tails, the odd stamp of a hoof, and a 'brrrrr' that I was beginning to recognise as the clearing of nostrils.

When I finally pried my eyes open I could only laugh. I was still fully dressed, half in the tent, half out, and there was dried, scabby toothpaste all down my chin to my shirt. I remembered now. I had passed out while brushing my teeth, then woken several times during the night to check on the horses.

This was starting to become a pattern. In my exhausted yet wired state I didn't seem able to reach my sleeping bag at night before passing out. Then I would wake countless times with my mind racing: 'Why are the horses silent?' 'Is that a thief I hear?' 'Where are they?!'

It wasn't just the thought of thieves that gnawed at me. I was a novice at just about everything. Whether it was learning how to ride, fit saddles, pack my horses, navigate, or find the right grass, every task demanded all my effort.

I hadn't even begun to figure out how to cope with the everyday things like feeding myself and washing my clothes. Then again, I only had two pairs of trousers, two shirts, and a couple of pairs of underwear to get me through the next couple of years – surely that was the least of my worries. I had to accept that it would be months before I would learn enough to take these everyday challenges in my stride.

But that was all in the future. For now, I was learning to take it one hoofstep at a time.

After packing up and finishing off my morning porridge I cast off into vast plains of luminous, olive-green steppe. It appeared empty until the sun revealed distant animals grazing in herds, and the white flecks of gers at the base of far-flung mountains. I pointed my horses roughly in their direction, guessing that I might reach them by nightfall.

I had developed a very simple technique for protecting my animals. In the evening, just as darkness was closing in, I would approach nomads and request permission to camp near their gers. Everyone seemed welcoming, and by the unwritten laws of the steppe they would see me as a guest of the family and protect me. If trouble did occur in the night I had someone to go to for help. It wasn't a perfect solution, though. The grass tended to be eaten down to the ground around nomad camps, which meant my horses wouldn't have enough to eat if I stayed with nomads every night. But for the time being, this strategy gave me just enough room to breathe, and to focus on the terrain ahead.

Mongolia stretched for the next 1500 kilometres, a vast plateau of wild steppe, mountains and desert that was wedged between the dense forest of Siberia and the even denser population of China. At roughly the size of Queensland – or of Great Britain, France, Spain and Germany combined – Mongolia is home to just three million people, making it the most sparsely populated country on the planet. Despite the raw natural beauty, it was the traditional nomadic life that Mongolians still live that had drawn me here.

My dream to ride across the steppes was first conceived four years ago, when I was twenty-one years old and approaching the end of a very different journey: riding a bicycle across Russia, through Mongolia to China. Together with my friend, Chris, I had been pedalling through the Gobi Desert, admiring the sand dunes and dry crusty plains that stretched in every direction. We had been riding for a year, experiencing everything from frost-bitten toes to metre-deep snow and swarms of mosquitoes so thick you could swallow a breakfast of them in a single breath. We had a few easy weeks to go before crossing out of Mongolia into China to the finish line.

But then, from the horizon came a sight that stopped both of us in our tracks. A small black dot rapidly grew until I could make out the clear shape of a horse rider galloping in our direction. He was sitting supremely still as his horse's legs worked in a furious blur. No sooner had I begun to focus in on the details than he pulled up on the reins and came to a halt right before me.

The horse transfixed me. It stood still, but sucked in air with immense power, its nostrils flaring and its ribs expanding and contracting like giant bellows. I could feel its breath on my skin, and smell the sweat that ran down its shiny, pulsating chest.

By contrast the rider was calm and breathing easy. He sat looking at me curiously. His face was sun-blackened, and his hands were as tough and wiry as old tree roots. Kind, smiling eyes beamed out through this rough exterior. Without saying a word he reached deep inside his deel and handed me some hard dried cheesy-looking food that I later learnt was called *aarul*. For a while the three of us sat on the sand trying to communicate. Then, as abruptly as he had appeared, I watched him gallop off into the distance.

I'd always thought of my bicycle as a freedom machine, allowing me to break away and explore well beyond the main roads. I also liked to think that I was an adventurer. But by comparison to this nomad, and many others we had seen on horseback, Chris and I were just tourists. Mongolian nomads lived year in, year out in an environment where it could reach −50°C in the winter, and sometimes almost 50°C in the summer. And unlike the house where I grew up, with thick walls, electric heating and a wood stove, they had just a couple of inches of wool felt and some dried dung for fuel in their stoves to protect them from extremes. But what really struck me was that they lived in a world without fences, and only owned as much as could fit on the back of their animals. With the turn of each season, they would pack up their home and move together to new, fresher pasture.

Nomad life offered a type of freedom that I had never imagined. I felt the beginnings of a deep yearning to know what it was like.

When I returned to Australia I began to read about the history of the Mongols. Eight centuries before, under warrior and leader Genghis Khan, the Mongols had used horses to charge out across Eurasia and create the largest ever land empire. At the height of Mongol power, nomad herders ruled an empire that included some of the most populous cities on earth and stretched from

Korea and the Pacific Ocean in the east to Hungary in the west, Indonesia in the south, and the sub-Arctic in the north. Genghis Khan himself was legendary. He had a terrifying reputation as a kind of royal Mongolian pirate, but was an incredible emperor whose former empire is now home to half the world's population. It is said that Khan's soldiers would routinely saddle up in −50°C and march onwards with sheep and marmot oil smeared all over their faces to protect them from frostbite. When they were low on food supplies they would even drink blood from the necks of their horses, sew up the wound, and keep moving.

I tried to imagine what it would have been like for young Mongolian men and women of my age to saddle up and leave their homes behind. What was it like to live day and night in friendship with such powerful, graceful animals? What kind of people did they meet along the way?

I decided that the only way to experience this land, its people and history, was to climb onto a horse myself. I wanted to begin from Mongolia in the summer and make my way across the steppes, through Kazakhstan, Russia and Ukraine and as far as the Danube River in Hungary – the western edge of the steppe, and one of the westernmost boundaries of the Mongol Empire.

I thought long and hard about the journey.

I wanted to travel by horse, not only because it is still the main mode of transport for nomads of Mongolia, but

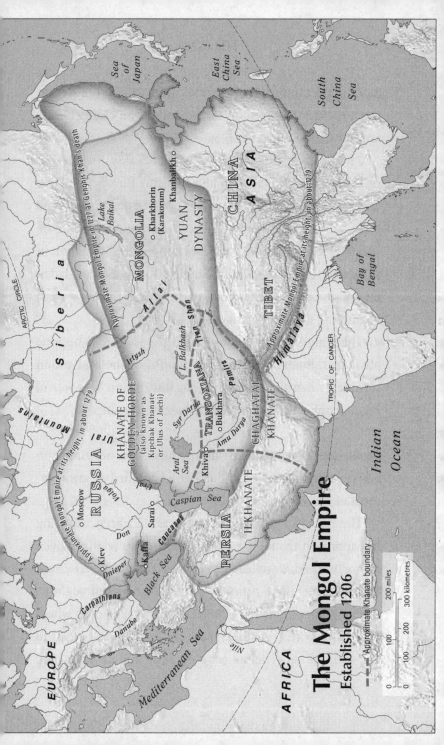

The Mongol Empire
Established 1206

- - - Approximate Khanate boundary

Sea of Japan

East China Sea

South China Sea

Bay of Bengal

ARCTIC CIRCLE

Siberia

Ural Mountains

Approximate Mongol Empire at its height, in about 1279

Approximate Mongol Empire in 1227 at Genghis Khan's death

Lake Baikal

MONGOLIA

o Kharkhorin (Karakorum)

Khanbalkh o

YUAN DYNASTY

CHINA

ASIA

TIBET

Himalaya

Altai

Irtysh

L. Balkhash

Tien Shan

KHANATE OF GOLDEN HORDE
(also known as Kipchak Khanate or Ulus of Jochi)

Pamirs

Syr Darya

TRANSOXIANA

o Bukhara

CHAGHATAI KHANATE

Aral Sea

Khiva o

Amu Darya

Approximate Mongol Empire at its height, in about 1279

Moscow o

RUSSIA

Volga

Ural

Caspian Sea

Sarai o

Don

ILKHANATE

PERSIA

Indian Ocean

Kiev o

Dnieper

o Kaffa

Black Sea

Caucasus

TROPIC OF CANCER

Carpathians

Danube

EUROPE

Mediterranean Sea

Nile

AFRICA

| 0 | 100 | 200 miles |
| 0 | 100 | 200 | 300 kilometres |

more importantly, because horses are native to the steppe. It is believed that nomads tamed and began riding horses around six thousand years ago.

I had chosen to start in Mongolia because I wanted to ride from traditional nomadic life into Europe, and see how settled life looked through the eyes of the nomad. And I wanted to start in summer because although it could be very hot, the conditions were much more forgiving than in winter. Beyond Mongolia lay challenges such as snow-laden mountain passes where one slip would send the horses and I tumbling to meet our makers.

Thinking it all over now, from the saddle, it became obvious: the next two or three months of the Mongolian summer, when the days were long and the air was warm, was my opportunity for a nomad apprenticeship.

Come late afternoon, just as the land was beginning to bask in thick shades of golden light, I reached an encampment of three gers.

The nomad families camped here had been watching me approach through a spyglass and were waiting. Even before I could introduce myself, let alone ask if I could stay, children came running with fresh bowls of yoghurt, my horses were taken to water, and I was shown where to set up my tent. A team of young and old descended to help unpack, and before long my tent was up and three generations of family piled in. An elderly man wearing a silky green deel fetched some crooked spectacles – held together with Band-Aids – and lay down inside my tent for an inspection. He seemed to approve, and moved on to my Australian-made saddle, planting it on his horse and taking turns with his sons to gallop this way and that. By the end of the session he came to me with a great big toothless grin and the first of many offers to buy the saddle.

The party at my tent was eventually cut short when the grandmother – the wife of the man in the green deel – came out firing orders. I couldn't understand what she said, but the tone was clear, and within seconds everyone had scattered. In the long winter months nomad children live in boarding schools, but for now school was out, the days were long and the grass was green, which meant lots of milk and plenty of helpers.

Prior to my arrival immense herds of sheep, goats and yaks had been driven back to camp for milking. The fanfare of setting up my tent had interrupted their work, but now the nightly milk production got into full swing. Little children began rounding up the most mischievous goats. They sprinted after the animals, diving to catch legs, ears, or even tails. Sometimes they just ended up face-planting in the dust, grimacing at first but then brushing themselves off with a laugh. When one particularly large and courageous goat made a break for the open steppe one of the boys, probably no older than ten, swung up onto a horse bareback and went galloping off with a shriek.

One by one the goats were tied head to head with ropes made from yak- and horse-hair. Girls moved from animal to animal, milking away until the pail was full, when it would be taken to a ready pot for boiling. The milk would be turned into a whole range of food products from yoghurt to cheese, cream, butter, alcoholic fermented drinks and of course the dried curd known as aarul. By carrying a bag of this bitter, rock-hard snack – which to me smelt like old mouldy yoghurt – warriors in Genghis's day were said to be able to survive ten days without any other food.

Before the milking was over I was beckoned into a ger where one of the mothers, a bandy-legged woman with an angelic face but worn hands, passed me a cup of salty, milky green tea.

While the woman retired to cradle her baby, I took in the details of the ger. The frame was constructed with six collapsible wall sections that could be swiftly dismantled and tied to the back of a camel or, as was the tradition in this region, strapped to a yak-drawn cart. From the top of the walls more than seventy painted wooden roof poles – much like wheel spokes – angled up to the circular opening at the apex of the ceiling. Wrapped around this wooden frame were thick sheets of felt, insulating against the cold and the heat.

When the milking was finished, it was dark outside and everyone crowded into one ger. Outside there came the muffled sound of bleating and farting as the sheep, goats and yaks settled in around the gers.

When I finally retired to my tent I sank into a feeling of completeness. This was nomadic life, virtually unchanged from the days of Genghis Khan eight hundred years before.

3

The Land has Eyes

From the nomad camp I rode northwest through a mountain range known as the Khangai. It was a knotted maze of snowy peaks, deep valleys and broad steppe in Mongolia's central heartland. As I rode, I found myself absorbed by the unfolding terrain.

The higher mountain peaks were generally sleek, round-edged and emerald green. Down below in the valleys, rivers threaded their way through a series of bony hills that looked like the backs of skinny old horses. Sometimes I camped on the edge of wide, shallow lakes. I would get up early and watch the dawn mist roll across the glassy water.

Each day flecks of white on the horizon grew into gers, filling my day with characters, sound and colour, then melted over my shoulders just as the taste of fermented milk and dried curd faded. I began to mark out my days through feelings and events rather than time or place. In one valley I was mesmerised by a vulture that was pecking away the rotting flesh of a dead yak under the burning sun. A whole afternoon was marked out by a storm that came roaring through, breaking the heat and slamming me with a barrage of hail. For an hour I stood, like the horses, tail to the wind, shivering, but within half an hour the black wall had given way to blue, and I was soon searching the sky for shade-giving clouds.

With each night that I stayed in the protection of a nomad family my confidence grew. As I had predicted, however, there was not enough grass for my horses, and they began to lose weight. I had to start branching out on my own into more remote country.

And so it was that I found myself riding away from the main valleys to cross a wild mountain pass known as Davaa Nuur, which means 'mountain pass lake'.

Upon hearing my plan, the family I had camped with became alarmed. A gruff toothless herder in a torn, threadbare deel shook his head and repeated, 'It's dangerous up there!' The bowlegged elderly grandmother loaded me up with dried curd and yak cheese and flicked three ladles of fresh milk to the sky. *'Ayan zamdaa sain yavaarai!'* she called, wishing me luck on my journey. This was a ritual that had been preserved from ancient times, even before the era of Genghis Khan. White represented luck and purity, and painting the road with this sacrifice of milk asked the gods to favour me with safe travels.

Several hours later, the family ger was nothing more than a glint of white below. I had lost any hint of a trail, and followed a stream that cascaded down a gully through swamp and loose rock.

By evening the scrub and scattered trees gave way to dense, alpine grass and the wind-ruffled surface of the lake – Davaa Nuur. Davaa Nuur was located just below the pass I was aiming for, but muscular black storm clouds had already cut the sunlight short. I made camp on a grassy slope just before the storm broke.

I planned to continue on in the morning, but woke to waves of rain and hail that drove into the tent so fiercely the tent threatened to tear apart. I sat hard up against the fabric, feeling the blows pepper my spine. I delayed my departure until lunch, hoping for better weather, then put it off until the next day. But the fog and rain kept coming.

Come my third day, my food supplies and fuel for my petrol stove were running low. There was no choice but to make a break for it.

I bundled out of the tent at five am, and by seven was skirting around the edge of the lake. A hint of sunlight broke through the moody clouds, but even so, my toes turned to ice.

As I contemplated dismounting to warm up my toes, Bor fell knee-deep through a frozen crust into a bog and we were forced to continue on foot. Time and time again I backtracked from bogs with panicked horses, or became blockaded by fields of jagged rocks.

The past few weeks had been a steep learning curve as I struggled to come to terms with the nature of the horse, and now more than ever I felt pushed to the edge. At one stage one of my packhorses, a fiery chestnut horse called Sartai Zeerd pushed past me then flew at me with his back legs, his hooves clearing my head by a hairsbreadth. I stopped and sat down for a time, my hands trembling with adrenaline, and my vision blurred from hunger.

Mongolian horses are stocky animals that survive the winters by digging through the snow to find feed, but they fall into two broad categories: horses with a calm temperament, known as *nomkhon*, and wild, untamed horses that can nevertheless tolerate humans. Two of my horses – Bor and Sartai Zeerd – were definitely of the latter variety. Just the touch of a brush or a blanket could send them into a wild display of bucking and rearing. Fortunately I also had Kheer, a bay gelding who didn't seem to be bothered by anything. Quite the opposite, in fact. He seemed to roll his eyes at my own skittish behaviour, and would eat and fart breezily while I tried to get the other horses under control.

As I took some time out to sip tea from a thermos, I noticed something that rekindled hope. Delicately marked out between two rocks was the unmistakable shape of a hoofprint. Sensing the significance, I stood up and only a little further on found a similar indentation. Then I laid eyes on something that told me all I needed to know: the butt of a cigarette.

Over the next three or four hours I lost the horse tracks several times, but just when I was convinced I had gone astray, they would materialise again. The companionship I felt from the sight of these hoofprints was something I would come to experience time and time again. In remote areas, the tracks of wild animals, horses, or humans provided comfort and clues to the lie of the land. They helped me ignore my fears as I tried to guess where the tracks might be headed and why. When I finally departed from one set of tracks, it was always like saying farewell to an old friend.

After six hours of heavy trudging the mist dissipated slightly and the triangular silhouette of a cairn, known as an *ovoo*, came into view. It was a humble pile of rocks scattered with fragments of dried curd and a tattered blue silk scarf known as a *khadag*. A few craggy tree branches were planted in the middle of the pile, bandaged by another sash, this one white and yellow. Ovoos like this had been a familiar sight on mountaintops and passes across

Mongolia for centuries, if not thousands of years, possibly as marker cairns for navigation but also as sites of worship where travellers paused to say a prayer to *tengri*, the eternal blue sky.

I dismounted and, following tradition, walked around the ovoo in a clockwise direction three times, offering a new rock to the pile with each circle.

Just below the ovoo I dropped down a crumbly slope of clay and rock and emerged from a curtain of mist into daylight. It was another world.

Boggy permafrost gave way to sturdy ground, and the sun's rays gently filtered down. The only sign of storms here were wispy trickles of mist that boiled over the lip of the pass I had just crossed. While the other side had been treeless and windswept, the slopes here were thickly carpeted with forest. Following the tracks of the horseman, I descended at a good pace, until the cold and storms had become a distant memory.

For the next few hours I followed the twists and turns of the stream as it led me into a forested valley. The horses pushed through the waist-high grass and I fell into rhythm with my horse, imagining that the mountain pass had delivered us into another time.

Genghis Khan had grown up in this kind of high, forested backcountry. Hunting was a mainstay of his small tribe's survival, and whenever there was trouble in his life he would retreat to the forest, where nature afforded him food and protection. In one legendary story, at the age of sixteen he managed to narrowly escape a raid on his family by fleeing to the forested Khentii Mountains, not far from his birthplace in northeast Mongolia. There, surviving on marmots, rats and whatever else he could find, he managed to evade capture.

Just as the yellow disc of the sun began to touch the jagged skyline, my mood swung. I had lost the horseman's tracks, and the slopes of the valley side had become so steep I was forced to lead the horses along narrow ledges and crisscross from one riverbank to the other. The forest had been gutted by a bushfire, and where trees had once bloomed with colour and crawled with birds and squirrels, only bare, sooty trunks remained. No nomads had lived here for a long time.

By the time dusk came on I was feeling a bit more positive. After negotiating the steepest section of the valley, I had reached a broad, open meadow on the riverbank, and set about making camp. Just as I was tying down the guy ropes, there came a howl from down the valley.

'There must a be a nomad family down there after all,' I thought, peering downstream. As I strained to focus in the fading light, the only white tinge to the landscape came from a ghostly rock that glowed from a slope of blackened, dead trees.

The howl came again, long and hound-like. From up the valley a similar cry echoed, then another from high in the forest on the far bank. My panicked eyes skirted the forest. Nothing moved, and again things fell silent – too silent.

When I was nineteen I had studied as a wilderness guide in Finland. I had been taught that despite all the rumours and fear about wolves, there had only been a handful of recorded attacks on humans, and even then the victims had been babies or young children.

It was only now that the real threat dawned on me. The wolves weren't interested in me – they wanted my horses! If the horses were frightened enough to break free of their tether ropes and escape, what would I do?!

Night flooded in fast as I chopped away at nearby trees, the axe smashing its way through charcoal before hitting a core of dead, dry wood that was as hard as steel. After an hour's work I barely had enough wood to fill my arms, but I hurried back to camp.

Without a gun, I only had two courses of action. First, I peed near each of the three horses – a trick suggested to me by veterinarian Sheila Greenwell. Second, I lit a fire and rationed out the meagre wood supplies that would need to see us out until dawn. According to Mongolians, a fire would keep the wolves at bay.

Once the fire was going I relaxed a little and sat gazing into the flames, eating a mash of rice and rehydrated meat.

The flames licked the night air and cast a circle of flickering light that just reached the horses. All three of them had eaten themselves silly in the afternoon and now stood like statues, their heads hanging. The sky was giant above, yet as we nestled in this tall grass, there was an intimacy that cradled us.

By three o'clock an invisible heaviness tugged at my arms and legs. I rested my head on a rolled-up coat and drifted off.

When I felt the thudding of hooves vibrate through the soil beneath me, at first I thought sleepily that I was in the tent. But then I heard furious pounding coming towards me from all directions.

My eyes had just blinked open when a howl shot through the darkness. It was from somewhere right behind us, perhaps no more than 100 metres away, on the edge of the forest. I lay low, not daring to breathe. It was black all around – I had let the fire burn down to just a few glowing coals.

When the fire was again ablaze I picked up the axe and checked on the ropes and metal tethering stakes. The horses' necks and withers were tense and their heads were raised high, ears twitching. Over thousands of years they had evolved a supreme ability to outrun predators, able to reach top speed within seconds. By hobbling them I had turned them into easy prey.

For the next few hours I sat, axe at hand, convinced our lives hung in the balance. When the fire sputtered and it seemed my meagre pile of wood wasn't going to make it to dawn, I was sure I could make out the furry outline of wolves prowling the edge of camp. I even began to think there might be hundreds of them, half crazed by starvation in the cremated remains of the forest. Feeding my remaining branches into the fire piece by piece, I prayed for dawn. There was something deeply petrifying about these howls in the dark.

The wolf holds great significance for Mongolians. There was a legend that the ancient Mongolian people had been born from a union between the blue-grey wolf and a deer. Wolves carried the spirit of the Mongolian ancestors. It was also understood that when a wolf howled, it was praying to the sky, making it the only other living being that paid homage to sacred tengri.

Perhaps most important for nomads was the belief that wolves, although dangerous, helped keep the balance of nature, stopping plagues of rabbits and rodents from breaking out. This in turn protected the all-important pasture for the nomads' herds. It was also true that wolves mostly attacked the injured and the weak, meaning that only the strongest horses lived on to breed. There was a Mongolian belief that only through wolves could the spirit of a person who had died be set free to go to heaven. When a person passed away, his or her body would be taken to a mountain and left for the wolves to eat. A good person would be eaten by wolves quickly, while a bad person would be left to rot for days. According to legend, wolves would fly up to the sky with the ingested human flesh and release the person's spirit.

As I would later discover, this 'sky burial' was a practice still carried out among some nomads today. In Uvs province, only a day's ride from Ulaangom, I came across the skeleton of a young man on the steppe with only a few remaining pieces of sun-dried flesh and a torn khadag lying nearby.

In the safety and comfort of a nomad ger this whole philosophy might have sounded magical. But as the fire wavered it was difficult to feel gratitude towards the wolf. How could I respect and love the wolves that were surely about to attack my horses, and perhaps even me? And how was it that Mongolians could worship the wolf, yet kill it and eat it too?

The answer was staring me in the face, although I would not realise that for years. Survival on the steppe was a fine balance, and wolves, like humans, were no crueller than was required to survive.

In the end, the race between night and my fire was very close, and there were times when I was sure the fire would not hold out. When finally the night began to wilt away, however, there had been no howls for hours. I placed the last morsel of wood on the flames and lay until the sun's glow was brighter than that of the coals. Soon the fire was nothing more than a grey bed of ashes.

By the time I was ready to go, the sun had painted out the shadows, and the threat of the wolves seemed exaggerated. Had it all been a bad dream? But a stone's throw from camp I passed the fresh tracks of a wolf on the muddy banks of the river. The land did indeed have eyes, and at this point they saw me a long time before I even recognised what was around me.

4

A Fine Line to the West

It was late afternoon when I emerged from the wild, forested valley. The lower valley opened up into gentle, sunlit slopes dotted with the reassuring sight of nomad camps. I squeezed Bor's sides with my heels, willing him on. I wanted to put as much distance as possible between my little crew and the prowling dangers of that valley before sundown.

There was still a lesson or two in store, however. As they say, the most dangerous wolf is actually the one that walks on *two* legs.

I had just set up my tent next to a ger when the distant grumble of a four-wheel drive from down the valley rapidly grew into a roar. I was tending to a pot of boiling water when the headlights found me. The beaten-up old van motored in and jerked to a halt next to my stove. The engine cut out, a door opened and, silhouetted against the glare of headlights, a man stumbled straight at me.

'I take two of your horses now! They are mine!' the man screamed, digging his index finger into my chest. His breath hit me like a wave, thick with the stench of vodka and meat. I said nothing and suddenly he lunged for the knife on my belt. I resisted, keeping it out of his reach, and he clenched his fist and drew it back as if preparing to punch. I froze, and the man lunged again, this time not for my knife, but for something far more important: my maps. With one fell swoop he took my only means of navigation. I watched helplessly as he bundled back into his car and drove away.

My first priority was my own safety, so I moved inside the nearby ger to sleep with the protection of a family. Come morning two young men came to me and announced that they had found my stolen maps. Just as promptly, however, they threatened to rip them to pieces unless I paid for their help. After negotiating a fee of $10 – which for me was a whole day of spending budget – I carried on.

I was now scared, angry, and in desperate need of sleep. One thing was crystal clear, however: one of the main challenges on this journey would be treading the fine line between the dangers of the wilds and those of a human kind. There would never be a day when I could let my guard down completely. In the days and weeks to come, I would realise that navigating these challenges was also the daily reality for the nomads.

After two days' rest with a nomad family I headed north-west, away from the Khangai Mountains towards the drier, wider horizons of northwest Mongolia. The mountains gave way to open, barren plains and sleepy hills, the weather mellowed, and for a while nomad camps, like my troubles, grew sparse.

On the shores of a lake known as Telmen Nuur, I bought a new horse and was able to give Bor the chance to rest and travel load-free. The new addition was a calm eighteen-year-old gelding, bigger than most Mongol horses, with a sharp odour and unusual colouring. His torso was white, speckled with rusty flecks of chestnut, while his hind-quarters were splashed with large chestnut spots. Rusty, as I named him, led from the front with a fast pace, which, coupled with the wide-open land, enabled me to cover around 40 kilometres a day.

Just over a week after leaving the Khangai Mountains behind, the land began to test me once more. The north-west of Mongolia was a place dominated by desert, shallow saline lakes and salt flats, where the distance between watering points for the horses was further than I could cover in a day.

I weaved my way between a rocky range known as the Khan Khokhii and the southern fringe of a sprawling sand dune system called the Borig Del Els – a place renowned as the northernmost sandy desert in the world. For two days I saw no one, and was only able to water the horses thanks to a chance thunderstorm that left a handful of puddles.

Three days on, it was the heat that was taking its toll. The temperature was soaring well into the thirties, and I had lost my sunglasses. After days staring into the raging sun, my pupils felt burnt. I, like my horses, was also weary and dehydrated.

Desperate for water, food and rest, I stumbled into an isolated camp of two gers. Although my Mongolian language skills were still only basic, I was in a land where the language of the horse held sway, and the rigours of horseback travel were universally understood. Without uttering a word, a mother and her children took me to a well in a dry riverbed, then invited me to join them in picking apart the boiled head, liver, kidneys, heart, intestines and even the trotters of a freshly slaughtered goat. It was tradition for the boiled organs and head to be put in one central bowl and for the host to cut and offer portions for guests. Only a few weeks earlier, the sight of these animal innards, offered to me on the end of a pointy knife, had been a little nauseating – especially when served cold at breakfast caked in fat. In my ravenous state now, however, the rubbery boiled scalp, lips, ears and intestines, which were filled with boiled blood, slid down with ease.

For all the sanctuary this family offered me they were in a difficult situation themselves. In the summer months they would normally migrate to the cooler air of the Khan Khokhii Mountains, but their remote pastures there had been overrun with wolves, so they had recently migrated to the slightly more populated lands down here between the mountains and the desert. As I would come to learn, life on these baking-hot plains between the wolves and the dunes was by no means a perfect solution.

Early in the morning I woke with my eyelids glued shut by gunk and dust and a terrible throbbing at the back of my eyes. Trying to ignore the pain, I lay listening to the sound of a thousand goats and sheep being herded out. The long gruelling summer days were what nomads dreaded most – it was important to take the sheep and goats as far as possible to graze between dawn and dusk so that they would grow enough muscle and fat to see them through the winter. In some respects winter was an easier life – long dark nights meant lots of sleeping, and during blizzards the animals would not leave the pens.

On the second morning of my stay I woke feeling overcome by nausea. The semi-broken-down goat innards from the arrival feast seemed to be inching their way through my bowels like some slowly dying creature. Soon enough the sun surfaced with a vengeance. Stripped down to my underwear in the tent, I looked in horror at my bloated stomach. As my belly grew taut and round, it seemed to highlight just how bony my arms and legs had become. After just seven weeks on the road, the muscle and fat appeared to have shrivelled away, leaving my knees and elbows – knobby at the best of times – more skeletal than I had ever seen them.

By midmorning the temperature was 40°C. I staggered into the shade of the main ger and joined the family, who were lying on the dirt floor. To keep the ger as cool as possible, the felt was hitched up from the ground, allowing airflow. Just beyond the wall in the sliver of shade of the ger, the mother of the family lay in dry dust and animal dung on her side, her baby cradled in her arms.

For the rest of the day I lay where I had fallen, taking in the world from ground level. Every detail suggested that even in the paralysing heat, surviving winter was at the forefront of the nomads' minds. Directly above me hung a curtain of meat strips being dried to produce what is known as *borts*. When dry, the strips would be cut into pieces, then ground into a powder, meaning the meat would be light, easy to carry, and would keep for months. During Genghis Khan's time it was said that by carrying borts, warriors could carry a whole sheep in their pocket as they rode.

Next to me in the ger, under a bed, lay a cow stomach freshly filled with the cream known as *urum*, and beyond the door outside sat a pile of dried manure – the only fuel for cooking and heating in a land where the temperature could drop as low as –50°C.

As difficult as it was on these searingly hot plains, where the pastures were thin, at least the herds weren't in as much danger as they had been in the mountains. To lose animals, whether it be to wolves, frost, or drought, was a matter of life and death for any nomad family.

When finally I emerged in the cool of evening the herds had returned from another day of grazing, and children were busily tying up the goats for milking.

By dawn the next morning I was up and moving.

The toughest part of my crossing into the northwest corner of Mongolia still lay ahead of me. Before having to tackle this, however, I was fortunate to have two days' rest in an unlikely desert oasis.

After one long day's ride west from the previous ger, I reached a nomad camp on the silky green banks of a delicate little brook. Children splashed about in the water, and the women lay out their washing on a carpet of grass. I was welcomed by five adult brothers and their families, who lived in five or six gers strung out along the stream.

By the time I had set up camp and watched the family's herd of eighteen fat camels thunder down the surrounding dunes for a drink, I knew this place would make a deserving home for my horses. Despite my attempts to find enough grass, Bor was beginning to look a little thin, and Kheer – my loyal packhorse – was tired. I couldn't bear the thought of pushing either of them on longer than necessary, especially across the thirsty land ahead. Quarantine laws forbade the export of Mongolian horses because they are a 'national treasure', so I would have had to sell them before leaving the country anyway. And besides, with Rusty I had four horses, which was one more than I needed.

There was great excitement among the families when they realised I was offering two horses in exchange for one, and by dusk children came galloping bareback into camp. The first horse I checked was tame but had a fresh injury on its back hoof, and the second tore away and bolted before I had even looked him over. The third horse stole my heart. A small bay gelding with a long, matted mane and dark eyes, he was young but calm. To prove he was nomkhon – quiet-natured and tame – six children climbed onto his back, while another clambered underneath and gripped his penis. Through all of this the poor horse stood looking resigned. The only sign of impatience was the trembling of his rubbery lower lip.

The following day we celebrated the exchange. In an old tradition, the herder took his horse out onto the steppe with his children, where they plucked hairs from its tail and mane. I too took my horses aside, pulling out a few strands, while stroking them and whispering heartfelt thanks.

Mongolians believe the spirit of a horse can live on in its hair, even long after death. In the past, nomad warriors collected the hair from their best stallions to weave into a *sulde* or 'spirit banner', to bring good luck and harness the spirit of nature. Genghis Khan had famously used a white spirit banner in times of peace and a black banner during war, and it was thought that after death the soul of the warrior was preserved in these tufts of stallion hair.

On this occasion, the herder selling us his horse simply strung up the hair in the ger so that a part of the horse's spirit would forever be with the family.

'You should keep the hair from your horses close to you as well, especially when in danger, for it will protect you from bad people,' he explained. I promised to keep hair from all the horses I used until the Danube.

After the ceremony, we retired to the ger of the elderly parents, where we feasted on a meal of noodles and mutton and sat watching a Korean soap opera on their shoe-box-sized black-and-white TV. They had a satellite dish parked outside and a solar panel on the roof charging a

12-volt car battery, which powered the TV. Using this set-up earlier in the day I had been able to recharge my video camera, satellite phone and laptop computer.

Unfortunately, I had almost completely flattened the family's battery. It wasn't long before the TV went dead.

The family sighed and moaned, but the disappointment was short-lived. An elderly woman as thin and creased as an old bedsheet pulled out a stringed instrument known as the *morin khuur*, or horsehead fiddle. As this old woman moved the bow back and forth, the shaky, bony fingers of her left hand pressed on its two strings at the top of the stem, just below a carved horsehead. The sound coming from the wooden box was like a scratchy, drawn-out cry, but nevertheless her husband, a bandy-legged old man, began swaying back and forth. I found my eyes wandering to various points around the ger: the horsehair ropes that tied it together, the fermented horse milk in the corner, and a piece of horse dung dangling from the ceiling for good luck. According to one Mongolian legend, the morin khuur had originated from a boy whose slain horse came to him in a dream and instructed him to make the fiddle using its body so that they would forever be together. In the present day, the morin khuur was a celebration of this union between horse and humankind – a relationship that not only made life possible but which, like string instruments, had been adopted worldwide.

When I was saddled up the next morning, the man I had bought the horse from came to my tent with his ten-year-old son. If leaving my horses behind was difficult for me, it was hard to imagine how it was for them. The horse we had bought, named Bokus, was the boy's favourite, and had been raised from birth by the family. Now Bokus was about to leave for good.

Just before riding out, the boy's father pressed a gift into my hand – a wolf's ankle bone tied onto a necklace. 'Keep it with you for luck,' he whispered.

The boy cried at first, but by the time we had crossed the brook, I turned to see that everything was returning to normal. The camels had been released for a day of herding, and the boy was moving them out on a different horse. A woman was wandering down to collect water, and a sheep was being slaughtered in the morning cool. Bor and Kheer were mingling with the family's herd and didn't raise their heads as I moved away.

A day from the oasis camp the land between the Borig Del Els desert and the Khan Khokhii mountains widened to a thirsty plain. Nomads had warned me that there might not be fresh water for at least 100 kilometres. The only solution I could think of was to ride through the cool of night when the horses weren't as thirsty, and keep going for as long as it took to find water. My horses usually needed a minimum of 20 litres a day.

In theory, night riding was something that excited me. In practice, it became a comedy of errors.

I started late in the dark and soon became disoriented and rode into a swamp. Rusty sank up to his chest in mud, and it was a good half an hour before he could pull himself out. When I did get riding, the soupy black of night seemed to give me motion sickness. Then my torch batteries went dead and I spent an hour searching for my compass after I accidentally dropped it. The only way to stay warm, awake, and nausea-free was to get off Rusty and walk.

When fragments of morning sunlight began to reappear I watched the mountains grow from the south, and to the north a slim flicker of silvery grey – the waters of a giant saline lake called Uvs Nuur.

Come midmorning, the blazing sun was upon me. The horizons all seemed impossibly distant and dry, and the lake somehow seemed further away than it had during the night. By keeping my head down and focusing on the end goal of each day, I was usually able to avoid feeling overwhelmed, but not today. The great plain that rolled out into a heat haze directly ahead was inescapable, and too big to fathom. Sleep tugged at me from every direction, but remembering the distances the Mongols once travelled kept me upright.

For Mongol cavalry just to *reach* the enemy typically took weeks, if not months. The number of horses available to Mongols during long campaigns was a key to their success. Every Mongol soldier travelled with at least one spare horse, and up to three or four. This way they could constantly rotate the horses and ride fresh mounts.

I plodded on until late evening, at which point I had been moving without a break for more than thirty hours, but had covered little more than 50 kilometres. I made camp and collapsed.

Come morning the horses were thirsty but alive, and through my spyglass I spotted something that dramatically lifted my spirits: a handful of gers along the edge of the lake shore!

By evening we had reached the lake, the horses had gulped down bucket after bucket of fresh water from wells, and I had filled my belly with fresh yoghurt.

Somehow, we had made it – we had crossed the divide from central Mongolia to the remote northwest corner.

In the next few days, there would be grass, water, and nomads at every turn. But I was already captivated by the next challenging chapter. Rising like white, wavy clouds on the western horizon lay the ice- and snow-encrusted peaks of the Altai – the 'Golden Mountains'.

5

Roaring River Mountain

Reaching the Altai Mountains was a milestone. Not only did it mark my first 1000 kilometres in the saddle, but it coincided with the end of August, meaning summer had come to a close. Ahead, the mountains beckoned with the crisp and cold of autumn, and even the possibility of an early winter storm. The Altai themselves stand as a range of peaks that stretch for hundreds of kilometres and rise more than 4000 metres, encrusted by the ice of glaciers that are millions of years old. They also mark the crossroads between Mongolia, Russia, Kazakhstan and China.

Immediately before me lay a series of peaks called the Kharkhiraa, which means 'roaring river' – a place where snow leopards, mountain goats and deer roam, and where motorbikes and four-wheel drives could not tread. My task was to somehow find a way over these peaks to the far side, where my chapter in Mongolia would come to an end.

The only way to get into the mountains was through a narrow river gorge. It was at the mouth of this gorge, where the road for motorised vehicles ended, that I found Dashnyam – a local nomad who I had been told knew the trails across the mountains and could possibly help me.

As soon as I dismounted at Dashnyam's ger, his children waved me inside and slid a bowl of dried curd and stale pieces of deep-fried dough (known as *boortsog*) under my nose. While children from neighbouring gers stood in the open doorway poking their heads in – some of them pulling funny faces for good measure – Dashnyam's wife ladled boiling tea into a cup, then passed it to me.

'Drink tea, eat boortsog,' Dashnyam said.

He looked different from other Mongolians I had met. His eyes were deepset, wide and almond-shaped, thoughtful and kind. His cheeks were hollow and his nose hooked and craggy.

When the tea had begun to revive me I pulled out the map and asked whether he could help me. At first he scanned the map with narrowed eyes and a look of confusion – he had never seen a map of his own lands before. But when I made myself clearer in broken Mongolian, he pushed the map aside.

'When do you want to leave? Today? Tomorrow? I need to fetch a camel!'

He told me that he would travel with me for eight days – time enough to make it over the highest passes. A camel, he explained, was essential for carrying my heavy load – my horses, after all, were tired, and the way ahead was challenging at the best of times. We needed to leave as soon as possible, before the high passes were blanketed with snow.

Dashnyam was in his late forties and had the stiff, stringy body of someone ten years older, but he launched himself into action like a young man. After shopping for supplies in the village, he sent me home. 'Take the bag of flour back to my wife and tell her to make boortsog. I am going to find a camel!'

I spent the day preparing, and getting to know Dashnyam's family, who, it became clear, were very poor.

Dashnyam had five children all under the age of fourteen, but owned just one old horse and seventeen goats. Milking was over within twenty minutes, and the little pail it filled held barely enough for a day's worth of milky tea.

When Dashnyam returned with a small female camel in the evening, I decided I wanted to help him. I didn't need a third horse anymore, and Saartai Zeerd, who wasn't happy walking on rocks at the best of times, was not suited to the mountains.

When I first placed the horse's lead rope in his hands, Dashnyam looked at me blankly. But then a nervous smile spread across his face, revealing a not quite full set of yellow, crooked teeth.

At dawn Dashnyam gave Saartai Zeerd to his son and told him to take the animal away to pasture. Then we packed the camel, Dashnyam's wife threw a single spoonful of milk in the air, and we were off.

As we entered the river gorge, mountains drew like curtains over the sky, and the steppe shrank to a puddle behind. The river tumbled through, carving out a gap through an otherwise impassable wall of rock.

At first, the riding was easy and pleasant as we followed the riverbank beneath the shade of tall, elegant trees. Where the trees ended, however, the gorge's walls drew in tight and we were forced to ride along a precarious ledge. I was beginning to lose confidence in Rusty, whose hooves slipped about on the loose rock, but then, as abruptly as the canyon had begun, the cliffs parted.

Before us lay a wide glacier-carved valley, and through

the middle of it, weaving through a maze of river boulders, came a camel train. From a distance they seemed to move in slow motion, their long, curved necks extending and shortening with each step forward. But by the time my eyes had focused on the men and women who led the caravan, they were right before us.

'Good journey!' cried Dashnyam with such a smile that his pointy chin reached out to greet them.

'Good journey to you!' they replied, dismounting to join Dashnyam cross-legged on the earth.

Excited, I stayed on Rusty and rode to the woman who controlled the lead camel. She smiled with pride and gestured towards the five camels behind. Like all camels of the steppe, they were *bactrians* – a type of camel best known for its distinctive double hump. Sometimes I had seen children riding snugly in the dip between these humps, luxuriating in the animal's shaggy hair. Now, however, I marvelled at the way in which the parts for two gers were slung and tied over the humps. The load on each animal apparently weighed around 300 kilograms.

It wasn't long before the woman dismounted and encouraged the lead camel to its knees. It was then that I realised that the cane baskets tied to the sides of this camel contained more than mere possessions. From the far basket a young girl, perhaps three years old, raised her head shyly above the humps.

The woman lifted a sheet covering another basket, and there, gazing up at the sky from the cocoon of sheepskin, was a newborn baby.

For much of the morning I had clung to Rusty's mane, fearing that he might misstep on one of the narrow ledges, but this woman trusted her animals with the precious lives of her loved ones.

After farewelling the family and riding on, Dashnyam seemed pleased that I had witnessed the camel train.

'Up there in the mountain they live in the summer camp.' He pointed to the high mountains. 'Very, very good grass!' he said, then leant down from the saddle, picked some grass, and brought it to his mouth.

It was clear that the nomads' migration was all about the needs of their animals. They spent summer in the high mountains where the grass was rich and the animals could avoid the heat and insects of lower down. Some families would stay on the lowlands for winter, but many would return to camps here in the mountains, where it was a little warmer. This drive to search out the best conditions saw families move hundreds of kilometres in a single year, and had caused nomads to spread far and wide across Eurasia. My journey was not only on the path of Mongol warriors, but those nomads who had ridden from Asia into Europe many thousands of years before.

As the sun began to fall, we rode far above the river

on a grassy shelf, marvelling at cliffs on the far side. The shifting columns of light lit up a series of rock circles and some tall standing stones – nomad grave markers. Among them were the figures of men carved from granite. Each man held a cup in one hand and the dagger on his belt with the other. What really drew my attention though were the perfect circles of stone, which each had four straight lines of stones spreading out from the centre to the perimeter like the spokes of a wheel. They were *khirigsuurs* – graves from around 2700 years ago, where nomads and their horses were known to be buried together. I had read that up to forty-five horses had been discovered in a single grave – a sign of the belief that the horse carried nomads into life when they were born, then through the struggles of life, and, they hoped, through the afterlife as well.

Over the next two days and nights the mountains grew taller and the valley sank. The nights were frosty, and Dashnyam was keen to stay close to the few isolated families that remained in the mountains. On the first night I discovered why – from sundown till dawn the mountains were alive with the sound of howling wolves. We were safely camped right next to a family ger, but all night the nomads came and went to check on their animals. Every time I seemed to be falling asleep the ger door would creak open and bang closed again, usually followed by the echo of gunshots.

One of the only people we met during daylight hours was an old man out watching his yaks. Dashnyam sat down beside him and offered his stone snuff bottle, filled with spices and tobacco. In return, the man produced his. The two men sniffed each other's bottles in a sign of respect – sometimes known as the nomad handshake – then sat back to drink tea and smoke from long pipes. As this unfolded I sat and watched as the man's horse leaned in with its bottom lip quivering and pushed its nose affectionately over its master's forehead – another gesture of friendship that I was starting to get used to.

On the second night we stayed with Dashnyam's friend, Davaa. I lay in the ger with a belly full of boiled goat's head, gazing up at antique rifles, a fresh wolf skin, and rows of drying goat that hung from the ceiling and walls. It was a night of warmth and safety that I would come to savour in the days to come – there would be no more nomad families until we had crossed the mountains.

On the third morning after the gravestones the spectacle of Kharkhiraa Mountain slid into view. At 4037 metres, it stood like a giant entombed in a sarcophagus of ice.

As we began climbing towards the high passes I felt a surge of excitement. I leant forward, gripping Rusty's mane, and followed Dashnyam along a zigzag of narrow ledges. The camel cried every time its soft, wide feet became wedged between rocks. The horses wheezed, and I felt the air grow thin in my lungs too. As we reached higher, chains of turquoise lakes appeared, tailing off at the end of the glaciers that snaked their way down from the peaks.

The following day I decided to hike to the top of the mountain ridges while Dashnyam looked after the horses at camp. The weather was so still that the sound of my heart beating and my lungs almost seizing up were deafening. I peered into the silent never-never land that spread out in all directions. Although the horizons of desert, mountains and plains seemed long and unending, I knew that this was a mere dot on the map compared to how much further I had to ride.

The next morning we woke to clouds like floating battle-ships, and wind tugged and pulled at our tents. The snow soon came thick and hard. Dashnyam was worried.

'The camel's pads will slip on this snow, and we will have a very bad accident if we continue. Better wait till tomorrow, when the snow might have melted,' he explained.

I was more than happy to spend the day in the tent, using the time to catch up on my diary and rest my tired body. It soon became clear, however, that we were not as alone as we thought.

After breakfast there came the standard Mongolian door knock – the clearing of the throat and a loud spit – before three men carrying rifles and bearing frozen, chapped cheeks clambered into Dashnyam's tent.

'How is your journey going? Good?' they asked.

'How is yours?' asked Dashnyam, offering them tea.

I sat squeezed up against the tent wall, watching the tea breathe life back into the men. Their rigid expressions soon melted and the tent became abuzz with chatter.

The men – one middle-aged, the others in their twenties – were marmot hunters who had been living for a week in a rock shelter nearby. Their aim was to collect as many marmot pelts as possible, which they would sell to traders on the plains. All was going well, so they planned to stay another week.

In the late afternoon when the weather cleared we joined the hunters as they checked their marmot traps. With little emotion they hauled out their victims and snapped their necks, then we returned to the cave. The carcasses were skinned and tossed into a pot of boiling water, then vodka was passed around. Before drinking, each man flicked a drop to the sky and one to the earth, then rubbed a little on his forehead.

As the vodka set in I leant up against the rock wall and studied my hosts. Their deels were shredded and stunk of oil, dung and soil. They had nothing to sleep on, and no food except for the marmots they caught and a few morsels of stale boortsog.

When the meat was done, a single knife was offered up and fatty chunks carved out and eaten. The older hunter chewed on a jawbone, then picked pieces up and slurped on them before licking his fingers and hands clean of the rich marmot oil. Marmot oil is valued as a treatment for burns and wounds, although eating marmots, as these men were doing, is frowned upon. A rodent, the marmot had been one of the first known carriers of the Black Death – a disease of catastrophic proportions that threatened entire civilisations from China to Africa, and in part was to blame for the fall of the Mongol Empire.

'What about the Black Death? Are you scared?' I asked them in broken Mongolian. Although the hunters looked back blankly at first, Dashnyam, who had developed an uncanny ability to read me, soon translated.

Their laughter said it all. I bent forward and accepted a piece of the fatty meat. As it slipped down my throat, I had no doubt these were the hardest men I had ever met. On the steppe when the grass was rich and thick, herds flourished, and the people rejoiced and gave thanks to tengri. When there was no rain or they were stung by a bitter winter, their herds shrunk and the people accepted it. Life and death were at the mercy of the earth and the sky.

These men had an uncomplaining attitude that I would have liked to think I could carry with me to Hungary – but which I knew was probably beyond me.

*

Two days from the hunters' cave, we paused by an ovoo where the mountains dropped away to a vast crater-shaped valley. A wrinkle of a stream flowed through the valley to the west and out onto a distant plain, where it spilled into a wide shallow lake. We were about to drop down to a rugged landscape of sand and rock where alpine grasses gave way to hardy desert bushes.

I rode behind Dashnyam, admiring the way he held the camel's lead rope with one hand and smoked with the other, still managing to tap gently at his horse's rear when necessary. 'Aha aha,' he called every time the camel threatened to slow or panic. I didn't have the heart to tell him that for days he had been wearing my backpack upside down.

In the evening we reached the abandoned summer community of Khovd Brigad, where a few old shoes and round circles of yellow grass indicated that the community had recently packed up and gone. It was here that our journey together would come to an end. Dashnyam needed to return before the winter snows blocked the pass, and with only one serving of porridge, a handful of pasta and some dried strips of meat remaining, one more day together meant that our food stocks would run out completely.

Given our humble prospects for dinner, my heart sank when two men on motorbikes came to us at dusk. They were hunters, had been riding all day, and had no food or shelter. Dashnyam offered them half of our meal, and we went to bed ravenous. The hunters lay down on the earth and pulled their deels over their heads. In the morning they stood up, dusted off the frost, and climbed back on their bikes.

Over breakfast, I took the time to appreciate Dashnyam's character one last time. As always, he ate his share of semolina by dunking his head into the buckled old pot and licking until it was shiny clean, his hooked nose needing a wipe afterwards. I still couldn't work out whether he had forgotten to bring a spoon and was too proud to borrow mine, or simply thought it unnecessary.

Without all my equipment the packing that had taken us over an hour took Dashnyam just ten minutes. The distance had taken us seven days to cover together, but he said he could manage the return in two and a half – and noting his light load, I could partly understand how. I would never master the art of travelling light the way he did.

When he was ready to go I gave him a packet of Russian cigarettes and paid him for an extra couple of days. He presented me with a packet of matches, which I accepted with two hands and brought to my forehead, according to custom. The packet hit my headlamp and went tumbling to the ground, much to my embarrassment. In Mongolian culture dropping a gift was a grave sign of disrespect.

Lastly, I split our meagre rations – a few pieces of curd and some old sand-encrusted jellybeans from the bottom of the boxes. Then Dashnyam mounted up and swung his arm in an arc to the northwest, indicating the way I was to travel.

I watched him shrink into the distance until he disappeared beyond a ridge. The sad cry of his camel lingered for a few moments, then I was alone.

It was about 250 kilometres from Kharkiraa mountain to the point where the borders of Mongolia, China, Kazakhstan and Russia converge in the heart of the Altai Mountains – a two-week journey. Just two days after saying goodbye to Dashnyam, however, I crossed the Khovd River, and my Mongolian journey effectively came to an end. I had reached Bayan-Olgiy Aimag, at Mongolia's westernmost extent – a Kazakh province of Mongolia that was more related to my next destination, Kazakhstan.

I decided to finish up my journey not far past the village of Tsengel, just short of the border itself. I sold my horses to a Tuvan schoolteacher who promised to use Rusty and Bokus as work animals and not slaughter them for winter meat. Then I was horseless, and Mongolia was truly behind me.

6

Winter Falling

At the top of a craggy rock that was plastered with snow I flung my backpack down and felt my lungs suck hungrily at the freezing air. Doubled over with my hands on my knees, I stared at the fresh, knee-deep snow below me and marvelled at how dry and powdery it was. This could only mean one thing: the snow was here to stay.

When I had caught my breath, I lifted my gaze. To the east and north lay slopes and pyramid peaks of the Altai, cloaked in white. I thought about my horses, who I had farewelled only two weeks ago. Would I ever see them again? I remembered the fistful of tail and mane hair that I carried with me in my backpack. I was determined to never forget the horses, and to take the Mongolian spirit with me to Europe.

I swung around to the west, where there was a very different view. Winter had taken hold up here in the high mountains, but down below the white gave way to a mash of autumn browns. It was bigger, flatter and emptier than anything I had ever seen. For the next three or four thousand kilometres lay this country of Kazakhstan – a vast land of open steppe, desert and nomads at the heart of Eurasia.

For me Kazakhstan was a place steeped in mystery. During my bicycle journey across Siberia, local people told of a place so hot in summer that nomads wore heavy sheepskin coats and hats to protect from the sun. In winter, the wind and the cold could freeze entire herds of animals to death – and there were no forests for shelter or firewood to keep warm. Perhaps because of its isolation and extremes, I was also told that it had been the favoured place of the Soviet Union and the Russian empire for gulags – terrifying prisons where if inmates didn't die of overwork, violence, or disease, they would freeze or bake to death.

Kazakhstan was not only a place of extremes, and huge – almost twice the size of Mongolia, and the tenth largest country on the planet – it was also home to the oldest horseback culture in history. The word Kazakh is thought to mean 'free rider'. Somewhere out there, around

5500 years ago, humans had first climbed onto the backs of horses and begun to tame them.

I'd always known that Kazakhstan would be the longest and most challenging part of my journey. What I couldn't know then, as I stood gazing out to where the sky blended with the steppe, was just how hard it would become. The coldest winter in almost forty years was about to descend on this corner of Kazakhstan. And that was only the beginning of my difficulties. In the years to come I would look back and see Mongolia as the honeymoon. But while Kazakhstan would be unimaginably hard, it would also teach me about the incredible kindness of strangers. And then, of course, I would never be truly alone. I would make friends of the furry kind that would be by my side for the next three years. One of them in particular would change my life forever . . .

As I tilted my eyes down to the snowline at the bottom of the ridge I could just make out my two new horses, which I had tied to a tree before climbing up. Buying these horses had been quite the journey.

On arrival in the *aul* – meaning village – of Pugachevo a week earlier, word had quickly spread that an Australian had come to buy horses. Everyone, it seemed, wanted to try their luck. There was an old white horse that I was told was nine years old and would 'gallop all the way to the Danube

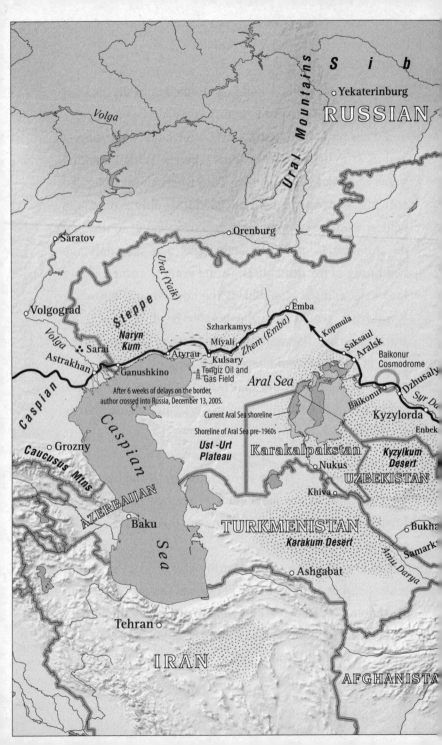

Kazakhstan

— Author's route by horse, autumn 2004 through winter 2005/2006

Taiga Forest · Desert · Saltwater lake

| 0 | 100 | 200 | 300 miles |
| 0 | 200 | 400 | 600 kilometres |

i *a*

FEDERATION

○ Omsk

Botai Culture
(c. 3700–3100 BCE)
e first known people in history
to domesticate the horse.

○ Astana

Irtysh

○ Karaganda

KAZAKHSTAN

ezkazgan

Semipalatinsk ○

Oskemen ○

Mount Belukha
4506m

Zhana Zhol

Azunbulak

Kindikti

Ayagoz ○

Balkhash · Ortaderisin

Tasaral

Betpak Dala
arving Steppe)

Lake Balkhash

Kopa

L. Zaisan

Terektbulak

Pugachevo *Lake Markakol*

Tsengel

Altai

Mtns

Tarbagatai Mtns

MONGOLIA

Author buys Kazakh horses in
October 2004 and begins near Lake Markakol.

Ili

Tasty ○
huantobe
aratau Mtns

Moiynkum
Desert
Ulanbel

Akbakai

Chu

trar

○ Shymkent

Bishkek ○

○ Almaty

○ Urumqi

Tashkent ○

KYRGYZSTAN

Tien

Shan

Jengish Chokusu
(Victory Peak)
7439m

Ismoil Somoni
ommunism Peak)
7495m

Pamir Mountains

TAJIKISTAN

CHINA
Xinjiang
Province

Taklamakan Desert

○ Kabul

PAKISTAN

Karakoram Range

○ Islamabad

INDIA

River', which turned out to be twenty years old and only a few hoofsteps from the grave. One man had assured me that his horse was the 'calmest I would ever find', but it was so wild that to safely put a saddle on it, its four legs were first tied up and the horse was pushed over.

Eventually I had been offered a large chestnut horse named 'Ogonyok', which means 'small flame' in Russian. He was a large, heavyset, almost rhino-shaped guy with a barrel-like body, short stocky legs, and a mane that flew like red flames in the wind. I could tell at once that his strength would make him a great packhorse, so over a meal of vodka and horsemeat, I agreed to buy him for $500. I later learnt that the owner had sold him because Ogonyok had stumbled one day during a hunting trip and fallen over, breaking the owner's leg. Kazakhs believed it was bad luck to keep a horse that you had been injured on, and so he had decided to sell. So far Ogonyok had proven strong, but he had untrusting eyes, and would often shiver in panic even when I attempted to rub his back. He was so paranoid and jumpy, in fact, sometimes he would rear up and then run away at the sound of his own fart.

Fortunately for me I had also been offered a horse by the name of Taskonir. He was an older horse, around twelve, and had spent his life herding animals and carting loads of fish down from a nearby mountain lake. I took him for a test ride and felt him move beneath me with only the lightest of commands. I could tell he was a hard worker, but also that he had a good heart – much like his owner, Altai.

When I asked Altai the price, he yelled back, 'Seventy thousand tenge!' – about $520 – 'But for that price I keep the horseshoes!'

'How about sixty-five thousand *with* the horseshoes?' I asked.

'No way!' he shouted. 'What kind of person are you? Take your saddle off my horse.' He threw my saddle into the mud and stormed off, taking the horse with him.

At first Altai had refused to come out of his house again, but eventually his son emerged, and I sent him back with an offer of seventy thousand tenge – *with* the horseshoes.

Later, I joined Altai at a small wooden table. He sat still, glistening eyes shifting back and forth from the window to the cup of tea in his weathered hands. He had removed his fur hat and coat to reveal a bald scalp and a wiry figure that was sinking with age. Sadness filled his pale brown eyes – he was selling his horse to pay for medical treatments and his daughter's education at university.

I counted the money out onto the table, where it was counted again by his wife, then by his son.

'This horse,' he boasted, 'will take you all the way to Hungary.'

We took photos together with Taskonir, and I promised to send a photo from the Danube. I realised that in buying

Taskonir, I was taking away a part of Altai's soul, and I pledged to never forget the bond between them.

It was almost dark by the time I had descended the mountain with the horses and reached a hut at the bottom of the slope. By that time the stars were out, and their reflection danced upon the snow. Inside the hut were two men who had helped me buy the horses, Nurkhan and Orolkhan. They had the fire going and were busily cooking up the heads of some wild boar they had shot while I had been on the mountain.

'Two wild pigs were guests in our home today. They left their heads behind but they themselves ran away,' said Orolkhan as he plunked the two boiled skulls on the table and raised a toast.

'To your journey through Kazkhstan!' they said, cheering and laughing in Russian.

I spent the next night in a nomad's winter hut where in the early hours of the morning I was woken by the old man of the family, who strode outside and began howling. He had been woken by a wolf and this was how he scared them away. Before leaving in the morning the man offered me a gun, which I refused. 'But what will you do about the wolves? Thieves?' he asked. I said nothing, just smiled nervously. I hadn't quite figured out what to do about wolves but I *had* decided that carrying a gun was not an option. I had never shot a gun before, and the responsibility of looking after such a weapon seemed beyond me. And besides, what if a thief was able to steal my gun . . . what then?

On the lower slopes, safely out of the creeping snowline, I bought my third horse, Zhamba – an old scarred work-horse who was much thinner and weaker than the other two horses, but which I could more easily afford. With the Altai Mountains rapidly shrinking behind me, I rode on towards that huge endless ocean of plains.

But just when it felt that my caravan of animals was complete and we were off, the most important meeting of my time in Kazakhstan – if not the entire journey – was about to unfold.

On the edge of the vast plains I reached the aul of Zhana Zhol. By chance a man called Aset, who I had met briefly on arrival in Kazakhstan, lived here. I had hurriedly scribbled his address down on the back of an old cigarette box.

It didn't take long to find Aset, and my horses were quickly taken under his care. Soon I was invited in for dinner, and Aset offered to travel with me for a couple of weeks. I agreed, and the night became one of celebration. Neighbours came from across the aul to cram inside the small timber home and share in a feast. I told them about my journey in Mongolia, about my plans to travel to Hungary, and showed them photographs from my home in Australia. Across the kitchen table Aset could not stop grinning. His face was broad and full, framed by a crop of silver hair above patchy bristles that skirted his chin below. He spoke in a husky, gentle voice that seemed poised to break into laughter.

'Ah, Tim! Tim! Don't be shy – drink, eat! This is Kazakh potato. Best in the world!' he shouted.

Next to Aset sat his ten-year-old boy, Guanz, who had cerebral palsy. When he hobbled into the kitchen, Aset lifted his buckled-looking frame into the air in an almighty hug, making Guanz giggle.

When the stars filled the night and our bellies were full we went outside to mingle on the street. Dogs from all over the aul brushed past my legs in the dark. Later, I felt two warm paws on my chest. The moist breath of a dog reached my cheek, and for a moment the animal was still. I glanced down in time to see two milky white paws vanish into the night.

'He likes you,' murmured Aset.

When the children began to tire, we returned inside and Aset told me that I needed to ask permission from his wife to have him accompany me as a guide. As I asked her, she put on a serious face: 'You can take him all the way to Hungary if you like!'

If I'd been more observant I might have noticed that watching all the happenings from the shadows with great curiosity was the unmistakable figure of a lanky skinny dog with tall black ears, and paws like snowy white socks.

I spent two days in Zhana Zhol preparing for my journey. During this time I spent many hours drinking tea with villagers and visiting the local school to tell the students about my travels. I couldn't understand Kazakh language, but most Kazakhs also know Russian – a language I'd been learning ever since my first adventures in Russia and Siberia. I began to understand that although life in Kazakhstan had been traditionally nomadic, the twentieth century had brought many changes that would make my experience here different from Mongolia.

Autumn was turning, and while in Mongolia nomadic families were no doubt preparing to migrate to winter pastures, Kazakhs here were gathering coal; firewood, and hay to see out the long months of cold. Most families had a milking cow, chickens, and even a horse or two, but none boasted the kind of herds I'd been accustomed to in Mongolia.

At the school I met young, wide-eyed children who knew about nomad life, but who had never seen the inside of a ger, or, as it is known more generally across Central Asia, a 'yurt'. Only the elderly, such as Aset's mother-in-law, could recall life moving with the seasons on horseback.

Nomadic life had largely come to an end during the seventy years of communist rule when Kazakhstan was part of the Soviet Union. In 1928, under the watch of Soviet leader Josef Stalin, authorities had begun confiscating animals and other possessions from Kazakh nomads. Families were stripped of everything they needed to survive, including blankets, clothing and cooking utensils. More than ninety per cent of livestock disappeared in the years that followed, and it was only a matter of time before the nomads themselves started to go hungry. By the spring of 1933, somewhere between 1.7 and 2.2 million Kazakhs – around a third of the Kazakh population – had starved to death, in a famine from which Kazakhs today were still recovering.

On my third day in Zhana Zhol Aset and I led the horses out onto the muddy street for a public farewell. The plan was for us to ride for two weeks, after which Aset would catch a bus home and I would continue on alone.

Many of Aset's neighbours considered the prospect of our ride a death sentence. 'The frost! The cold! It will be here soon, and it will hit you! There will be snow up to your neck,' said one man, running his hand across his throat.

'Yes, but the most dangerous of all are drunks,' an old babushka wrapped up in a shawl cackled. 'We have many of them – don't go near them!'

This was too much for Aset's wife, who broke down in tears. Despite her joke earlier about my taking him all the way to Hungary, she had been fretting for the past two days, and today she had spent all morning helping to dress and equip her husband. The poor man seemed more likely to die of constriction than cold. He wore two thick woollen sweaters, a neck warmer, and a denim jacket stretched so tight it couldn't be buttoned. His pockets had been stuffed with sunflower seeds, pig fat and garlic, and on the belt holding up his thick Russian winter overalls was a knife big enough to chop down a tree. With only minimal movement possible at the knees and elbows, he waddled with great difficulty over to Ogonyok and heaved himself up.

When finally we turned to leave, the old babushkas and children didn't know whether to laugh or cry, so most did both. The last sight I caught before leaving the village was Guanz, who was filled with pride to see his father set off on such an exciting adventure. When we pulled away from the crowd, he lifted his better arm in an attempt to wave, and called out: 'Write to us!'

We headed for the open steppe, and within half an hour the timber homes had sunk into the creases of the land. The horses charged ahead, full of energy. I went to move into a fast trot uphill, then noticed that Aset had not come alone.

Behind us, running at speed, came that black dog with those unmistakable white paws. All ribs on long match-stick legs, he had a skinny trunk and snout followed by a frenetic wagging tail. From his skeletal frame rose two large ears, rather like that of a hare.

'Aset! What is this dog?' I demanded.

'Travelling on horse without a dog is incomplete,' he replied.

'No! How will you take him home after we part?'

He said nothing, merely spitting out a few sunflower seed shells.

Aset had told me that this dog was his son's, and was in deep trouble. Ever since he was a couple of months old, the dog had made a habit of getting up really early and stealing eggs from under the bums of chickens before the old babushkas had time to collect them. By the time Guanz and Aset were up, the dog could usually be found snoozing in the hay with dried egg yolk stuck to his whiskers. Dogs like that did not have long lives in places like Zhana Zhol.

The dog now peered up at me in the saddle with innocent, loving eyes. It was hard to know who was more infuriating – him or Aset.

That evening the sky cleared, and as the last light retreated, the breeze slowed to a halt and cold fell like a heavy blanket. I loved the feeling that there was little separating us from the stars, but as the temperature dropped, Aset grew nervous.

After dinner he looked worryingly into the food pot. 'And for the dog?'

I reluctantly pulled out a can of meat. 'If he is going to eat, he has to earn his keep. He must be a guard dog and stay outside.'

The poor dog, barely six months old, was a short-haired variety of sight hound, known as a *tazi*. He looked as if he might struggle to stay upright in a stiff breeze, let alone cope with sleeping in frosty weather. Later, when Aset pulled the poor shivering dog inside the tent to sleep at our feet, I pretended to be asleep.

In the morning, my hopes of making significant headway before winter were dashed. A heavy panting from outside had woken me, and when I zipped open the door, I locked eyes with Aset, who was bundled up and jogging around the tent.

'It's freezing in there! It's much warmer out here!' he cried.

The temperature overnight had plummeted to around –15°C, and unfortunately we had just one sleeping bag and mat between us. Poor Aset had shivered through the night under my horse blankets.

When the sun rose higher we rode out into a honey-yellow sea of wild grasses and heath. To the northwest, a sliver of earth blanketed in snow rose across the horizon like a rogue wave. We met only one man during the day, a sheepherder who drifted across and away from us as if on the ocean currents.

It was the kind of autumn riding I had dreamed of, when the horses didn't overheat, there was plentiful pasture, and the air was clear. As soon as the sun began to dip again, however, there was no denying that winter was setting in. The grass howled with random, menacing strokes of wind, and the light disappeared behind a sweeping curtain of black and grey. It began to snow even before we set up camp.

Over the next two days snow painted out every last patch of autumn brown until we were shuffling through an endless blanket of white. The poor dog, who was experiencing the first winter of his short life, was suffering from frozen paws. Whenever we stopped for a break he whined and peered up with a look of bewilderment. Once, in a desperate attempt to escape the cold, he leapt up onto my back with his front paws clinging to my shoulders. I was taking a pee at the time, and he ruined my aim.

But the real cold hadn't even begun. Into our third afternoon of snow, stony clouds began swooping low over the snow, blocking the sun. We cut across a plain and climbed through a tangle of snow-laden spurs towards a plateau. My legs were beginning to ache, and I could think only of retiring in camp with dinner on the boil. Just as we were nearing the top of a gully, however, the light dimmed and there came a gust of wind. Then, without warning, the cloud and wind came tumbling down like an avalanche. Aset, who had been singing songs all day, stopped mid-verse, and within seconds the world lost all shape and form. The wind hit so hard that the ice and snow it carried felt like miniature glass shards. There was no sky or earth anymore, just a swirling, soupy sea of white. Leaning forward and clinging onto Taskonir's mane, I flicked my head back to see Aset's silhouette melting in and out of focus. When he caught up, Taskonir nudged forward, uneasily probing for solid earth. I urged him on, but for every step forward our circle of vision closed tighter.

It might have been an hour, or two, I don't know. There was no telling where we were or when this rushing cloud might pass. Several times I lost Aset, only to scream out for him, and he would reappear. Every ten minutes I checked my GPS and compass bearing. The horses plodded on up slopes, down into gullies, and up again.

Eventually we crested a hill, the wind eased and the mist parted ever so slightly. The dog caught up and all together we looked west. Dark, jagged clouds began to lift, and a purple-blue light flooded over the frozen earth. The tail end of the sun slithered over the horizon, leaving a trail of fading watercolours – blue on the clouds, purple on the ground, a hint of orange here and there.

But the truce was short-lived. Darkness fell, the wind recoiled, and cold took its grip.

'The closer to people the better!' Aset yelled over the wind.

For the hundredth time I stopped and spread the map out over the reins, studying it with the light from my headlamp. We were aiming for the aul of Kindikti, two days' ride to the southeast.

'We have food, we have a tent!' I yelled to Aset. 'We can stop now, make ourselves warm, cook dinner, sleep, and see how things are in the morning.'

'To hell with your tent! What if a snowstorm really comes in? What about wolves? We have to get to a *kstau*!' he replied, using the nomad term for a herder's winter station. Finding one would be a long shot, even with my GPS and the directions a local had given us the day before. But Aset was willing to bet his life on it.

My hands turned stone cold and stiff. The horses became so exhausted they were immune to the press of my heels. The poor dog vanished. Aset screamed for him and he appeared, a tiny black shadow at our heels – so faint that he looked like he might soon be blown away.

At half past ten we arrived where we thought the kstau might be, but there was nothing. I had given up trying to figure out the landscape.

'It's got to be somewhere here! We have to make it,' shouted Aset, his words garbled by his nearly frozen face.

As a last resort, we released the reins and let the horses guide us. This is a custom found across the steppe – when lost or in search of water, always let the horses guide you.

To my surprise, the horses seemed to know where they were going, and half an hour later we stumbled into the dark shape of something man-made. There was no one to greet us, but this was good enough for now. We crawled into the shelter, whatever it was, and passed out.

I woke in the morning with the echo of wind in my ears and the dog tightly tucked up between Aset and I, his nose hidden deep under his tail. As shadows turned to real shapes, it became clear we had camped in an abandoned concrete pumping shed littered with frozen manure and graffiti.

Outside, nothing had escaped the fury of the storm. The thick cover of small bushes and plants looked like a bleached, exposed coral reef, each twig entombed in finger-thick ice. Every blade of grass was also encased, rising from the earth in a million stalagmites. The horses stood stiffly in half sleep. As Taskonir turned his head to me, ice cracked and fell away from his mane. Ogonyok woke, automatically lowered his head, and crunched through a carrot of ice with his teeth.

When Aset woke, slit-eyed and puffy, he was worried. The storm had passed for now, but this kind of weather apparently foreshadowed the beginning of a *zhut* – a harsh winter, more universally known by the Mongolian term *zud*, that sweeps through the steppe every few years.

'At first the ice weighs down the grass, snapping it off. If this is followed by a warm period, the ice and snow will melt before freezing again to form a cap of ice. On top of this may come deep snow, which means even if the animals dig to the ground they will only find ice and won't be able to break through. If any horses survive, they will be naked by spring because as a last resort they eat each other's hair,' he told me.

There were different kinds of zuds – some caused by an impenetrable layer of ice, others by the sheer depth of the snow, and others still when there was no snow at all. I had heard of this phenomenon before. Kazakh herders would later tell me how, when the grass was particularly lean, they kept their animals alive by feeding them a combination of horse dung mixed with sheep tail fat.

After feeding the horses a bag of crushed corn, we loaded up and wrenched ourselves away from the shelter. The horses moved hesitantly, like barefoot children on sharp gravel. Ice shattered, popping and exploding under their hooves. The poor dog remained curled up in the pump shelter until it dawned on him that we were not coming back. He came whimpering, tail between his legs and whiskers all frosted up.

An hour of riding took us over a hill where another scabby piece of civilisation broke the emptiness. This time smoke tendrils rose timidly from it, and a herd of sheep and goats inched across the landscape. It was the kstau we had been searching for and, as we drew closer, a herdsman on horseback pulled away from his animals and approached.

'*As-salam aleikum*,' he said, extending his hand. The man had swollen, chapped cheeks and was struggling to control a violent shiver. He looked how I felt. The cold was inescapable.

The herdsman and his wife had only recently retreated to the winter camp. They had made it just in time before the storms hit, but they said that others might not have been so lucky. If caught out in the open, sheep could become literally encased in a heavy armour of ice, and eventually be unable to move.

When we reached the kstau I watched as the man skilfully climbed onto the roof of the shelter and with a fork peeled off hay for my hungry horses. As I sat there in the saddle, my elbows and feet freezing, I felt that I wouldn't last more than a few more weeks. I didn't know how to look after horses in such conditions, and I doubted I could manage alone with three of them.

I hoped we might turn in for the day, but after a quick cup of warming tea we were back in the cold and riding under a dark grey sky. The storm was gathering again. We pushed the horses into a trot. I had no objections to Aset's urgency – we would ride for as long as it took to find shelter.

The light was fading fast and the snow was falling horizontally when we came across the trail to Kindikti. First there came the holler of cattle and the cry of herders, then two figures materialised from the bleakness, hunched in their saddles, whips in hand. Up close I could see they were wearing *valenki*, traditional Russian knee-high felt boots, and rode atop saddles with thick cushions – the kind that Aset had recently been encouraging me to get for my own saddle to prevent haemorrhoids. Despite the conditions, the men took off the mitts they wore and reached out to shake our hands. As luck would have it, we had caught them herding their horses and cattle home to shelter for the night.

When the glow of homes emerged from the pall of snow, cattle peeled off to their owners and we followed a herder to a mud-brick house. Askhat, as he was called, dashed inside and came out with his father, a tall man named Bakhetbek. There were handshakes all around before we rushed to unload. Askhat was sent to the roof to gather hay, a young boy was given the job of preparing a barn, and Bakhetbek must have told his wife to prepare things in the house.

I was hesitant to go inside until everything was done to care for the animals. Since arriving in Kazakhstan I had learnt that it was unthinkable after a long day's ride to remove the saddle and offer the horses water and feed until they had rested for two or three hours, or until their backs were warm and dry under the blankets. This was a kind of universal law on the steppe, and possibly one that had been around since before the time of Genghis Khan.

I began to explain to Bakhetbek how important this system was for my horses, but he interrupted me.

'Tim! Tim!' he said, almost angrily. 'Don't even say it – it is offensive. Everything will be done, you don't have to worry about your horses. You are our guest!'

Aset pulled me aside. 'Trust him, and watch carefully – a sign of a Kazakh host who respects his guests is that he will feed the guest's dog before his own.'

Bakhetbek fed our ribs-on-legs dog a pot of lamb innards and stale bread, sinking his boots into his own dogs when they tried to join in.

As tired as I was, somehow I got through dinner, and a few shots of vodka too, before tumbling into sleep. At some point in the night I woke in panic from a dream: we were on a creaking ship, but where was the exit? Then I remembered where we were and surrendered to sleep, confident that the horses, like us, were under the watch and care of the family.

By the time I woke it was late. A pile of blankets lay where Aset had been, and the sounds of shuffling feet and muffled conversation drifted from the kitchen. Peeling my eyes open, I sat upright slowly. What I had assumed to be bright sunshine was the glare of a snowdrift creeping up the windowpane. Outside, the storm raged on. Heavy clouds of snowflakes were being tossed about in violent gusts, and

I could just make out the outline of an animal shelter, its timber frame encrusted by wind-driven snow.

The blizzard had all the hallmarks of a *buran*, the fierce winter windstorms of the steppe, accompanied by a whiteout, which could last for days and could bury livestock and people alive if caught in the open.

I found Aset and Askhat by the softly crackling coal stove, looking over my Australian saddle. When he noticed me, Askhat motioned to the window and joked, 'You think this is winter? You should see winter here! There is usually *two metres* of snow!'

The family and I settled down with tea. Every time I had nearly finished my cup they immediately refilled it. In the afternoon the blizzard briefly abated, and movement out a window caught my eye – a young boy riding bareback with a hypothermic sheep slung across the neck of his horse.

Bakhetbek was a tall and stately man in his fifties with leathery dark skin, green eyes and a strong jaw. He was the father of four, and both he and his wife worked as schoolteachers. His passion was geography.

'Tim, if I am correct, you are not the first foreigner to travel here. An Englishman once came prospecting for gold and other minerals. That was about eighty years ago. I am fairly sure, though, that you are the first Australian,' he said, eyes twinkling. His hands, broad and strong, shifted gently in their embrace around his cup of tea.

Bakhetbek had been born near Urumqi in China's Xinjiang province, and fled to Kazakhstan after his brothers were murdered in the 1960s. Later his nephews, who remained behind, were also murdered.

'They killed us simply because we are Kazakhs,' he said. 'Back then, and even now, Chinese authorities don't protect Kazakhs.'

After telling his story, Bakhetbek looked spent, but there was a sparkle in his wife's eye. 'Actually . . .' She looked over at her husband. 'We still have one relative alive in China. She is Bakhetbek's niece, and she is studying in Urumqi. She wrote to us one year ago, but we have never met. She gave us a phone number, but we have never been able to call.'

It was dark by the time everyone assembled outside in winter coats and fur hats. I pointed the satellite phone aerial to the sky and dialled, and a woman answered. All of Bakhetbek's family members took turns talking, struggling to hold back tears.

The occasion called for a feast, and after the phone call it was all hands on deck. Bakhetbek's brother raced to get a sheep, and the men gathered to say a prayer before its throat was cut.

Late into the night we sat around gorging on meat. A *dombra*, the traditional two-stringed mandolin of the Kazakhs, was passed around. When Bakhetbek played there was a fire in his eyes. Strong fingers moved instinctively up and down the instrument's neck. I looked across to Aset, who was welling up with pride. The last beat ended, and Bakhetbek looked at me. His eyes arched into crescents, and tears spread into the many channels of his weathered face.

Kazakhs believe that when a guest walks through the front door, luck flies in through the window. It is a good omen: the sheep will give birth to twin lambs in the spring. Looking back on this occasion, the magic of this belief was embodied by my meeting with Bakhetbek.

As we prepared to leave Kindikti, Aset was whistling and calling angrily – the dog was nowhere to be seen. I was still unhappy that Aset had brought the blasted dog along in the first place, and now it was holding us up. If we didn't get out of Kindikti today and start heading south, I risked being stranded here until spring.

'If he doesn't come, let it be that his destiny is here,' said Aset at last, trying to mask his distress. Just then there came a whoosh as a stringy heap of bones and elastic tendons leapt over the fence of a pen and came screaming towards us, eyes wild in panic, and egg yolk dripping from his chin.

For the first few hours we followed the compass through a labyrinth of deserted hills and gullies. The sky had been blown clear of clouds, but despite the white glow of the sun, cold tightened its grip. Even the slightest breeze landed heavily, forging ice crystals in my eyelashes and nose hairs.

It gathered on the horses as ice beards. The air was powder dry, and the snow exploded in puffs beneath the horses. Bakhetbek's tune strummed in my head.

When the sunlight withered we were stranded in the open. The earth froze to a standstill and the temperature dropped to around −20°C. Aset and the dog hung around my camping stove, looking unconvinced we would survive the night.

'In these conditions without vodka you won't survive. When your hands get cold, rub the vodka into your skin,' Aset said. He produced a small bottle and rubbed vodka into his hands and the paws of his poor little dog.

Food and hot tea in our bellies, we climbed into the tent. Aset bundled himself up in my down jacket under the remaining horse blankets and put on the insulated liners of my winter boots. The dog curled up at his feet.

In the morning the inside of the tent was covered in hoarfrost, and the slightest movement sent a shower of ice down on us. Overnight one end of my tent fly had suffered a rip half a metre long, and the windows had turned brittle and shattered. When Aset went for a pee he came back with worrying news – a stone's throw from the tent there were fresh wolf tracks.

Nothing, it seemed, came easy this morning. Although I had arranged for the horses to be shod with special studded metal shoes that were meant for gripping on ice, this hadn't prevented the snow from balling up under their hooves. Additionally, one of Taskonir's shoes was loose. We improvised with an axe head to solve both problems, but it took more than three hours, all told, to pack up, eat, and load the animals. By the time we settled into the saddle my feet and fingers were numb.

Not far beyond camp we passed through the tiny aul of Chubartas, a collection of twenty ramshackle homes and barns inundated by snow. Dogs came running, snarls of teeth, slobber and fur, and I watched our skinny little guy scuttle away under Taskonir, tail between his legs and his back arching up like a skinny feline's. Taskonir, who was not about to be intimidated, stomped his hoofs angrily, revealing an immense power in his muscular chest. The dogs kept their distance, but would not leave us alone. Not a soul came out onto the street.

That evening Aset insisted we camp by an old Kazakh grave. It was a tall mud-brick dome, worn away at the top like a giant, upright, cracked eggshell. It was part of a cluster of similar graves known as a 'silent aul'.

The next morning Aset turned to me hesitantly.

'We had a visitor last night. The old man from the grave. Nothing out of the ordinary; he was just here to check on us, to see what we were doing.' Then he added, 'My recommendation to you is that if you are alone, always try to find these graves. The old men of the steppe will protect you. If possible, the best thing is to even sleep inside the graves.'

For the rest of the day Aset seemed quiet but content. On a horse, on the steppe, under the sky, he was living by customs that meant so little in settled village life. Like most Kazakhs I would meet over the coming months, he clung to a belief in his nomadic heritage and the spirit of his ancestors.

In the aul of Karagash we met a man called Kazibek who was out collecting firewood on his horse. Aset had a distant relative in this aul who we were hoping to stay with, but Kazibek told us the relative had just died. The next day, just shy of Ayagoz, we received more sad news, this time by my satellite phone – another relative of Aset's had been run down by a tram in a city and killed. The funeral would be the next day.

That night near Ayagoz, Aset pulled out the city clothes he had been carrying, and suddenly I realised our adventure together was over. At the local market I bought him some basic carry bags for his belongings and a bus ticket home.

There was something Aset had been waiting to tell me.

'Tim, you need a friend on the long road, someone to keep you warm at night and protect you from wolves. His name is Tigon. Tigon means 'fast wind' or 'goshawk'. He is a hunting dog. His father was a tazi, a breed of hound that is not afraid of wolves and can run quicker than the wind.

'And in our country dogs choose their owners. Tigon is yours.'

I was not in the mood. I cut him off.

'But what will I do with him? What will happen to him when I get to the border? I won't be able to take him further. Can't you take him on the bus?' I was frightened of the commitment of having a dog, and besides, how would this skinny little ball of fur protect me?

Aset shrugged. 'I don't know. You can give him to someone if you like.' Then he looked me straight in the eye. 'But there is one thing. In my culture there are some things that you cannot receive as gifts, that you must buy or steal: dogs, knives and axes. This dog is not mine. It is Guanz's. You need to give me something for him; it doesn't have to be money.'

I paid Aset $120 for accompanying me; gave him a toy koala, some photos from Australia, and $10 for Guanz; and promised to print and send all the photos we had taken together. I needed a second packsaddle, and so he offered to sell me his own saddle, the one he had been riding in. I bought that for $50.

We tied Tigon up and waved down a car on the road into town. Then Aset was gone.

Aset had travelled only eleven days with me, but he knew so much better than I the challenges that lay ahead; it was almost uncanny. I would forever be indebted to him.

7

Alone

I broke out of the tent into a landscape that resembled a frozen sea. Above, the sky was steel blue. Below me the steppe panned out in white sheets, tussocks of grass puncturing the surface like frozen fingers. Moisture in the air had snap-frozen and now floated around me, twinkling like quartz.

I took a big breath.

Ahead of me, the rest of Kazakhstan yawned – more than 3000 kilometres of steppe. The absence of fences, borders and even mountain ranges meant I could ride in whichever direction I pleased. But if I remained this far north I would be ambushed by deep snow. Too far south, and I might find myself in a freezing desert without snow, which would be my main source of water during winter. The land ahead would be much more sparsely populated than Mongolia, and the nomads who did live out there had already retreated to their winter homes. I could expect to travel up to a week at a time without seeing other human beings.

Late the previous afternoon, I had called home on the satellite phone. I received bad news: our family dog of sixteen years, a blue heeler we called Pepper, had died. After the sun disappeared I had lain awake deep inside the cocoon of the sleeping bag, crying, and thinking of her doe-eyed, tail-wagging presence. At the same time I was aware of the curled-up ball of fur and bones pressing up against my thighs and snoring. It was hard to believe that earlier that day I had almost left him behind.

With Aset gone but Tigon yawning by my side, I stood with the morning sun on my back and gazed west. Yesterday I had worried mostly about finding water, pasture and shelter through all that emptiness. This morning I was overwhelmed by the fact that I would have to do it alone.

My plan for the next few weeks was to travel southwest towards the salty waters of eastern Lake Balkhash, before riding west along its northern shoreline into central Kazakhstan. My immediate goal was about a week's ride away – an aul called Kopa. I had been told of a man who lived there, known as Serik, who might take me in.

After sharing a pot of semolina with Tigon, I set about saddling and packing, determined to overcome my nerves. I found some solace and calm by thinking of myself as a young Kazakh child learning the ropes of life on the steppe. By nomad standards I decided I had probably reached the age of ten, the age at which boys would undergo a custom known as *tokym kagu bastan*. The boy was sent off alone on a horse for his first long journey. *Tokym kagu* means 'waiting for the boy to return', and the return home would be celebrated with a feast including the most sacred of drinks, fermented mare's milk, known in Kazakh as *kumys*. Aset had surely known that these first few days were my own *tokym kagu bastan*.

Four hours later, however, I was still in camp and struggling to get the loads tied down on the two packhorses. Perhaps it was a little optimistic to think that I had reached the skill level of a ten-year-old nomad.

When I did finally get moving, my seat had barely warmed before the load on Taskonir loosened and fell to one side. It took another half an hour to reload, but by then it was clear that the horses had their own issues. I was riding Zhamba, with Ogonyok directly behind me and Taskonir bringing up the rear. Taskonir, who had asserted himself as leader, took every opportunity to bite Ogonyok's bum. This would send Ogonyok bolting forwards, the pack boxes brushing Zhamba's side and bashing into my right leg. In his nervousness, Ogonyok would then let rip with a loud fart. Zhamba was not pleased. His ears rested flat on his head while he bit and then kicked until Ogonyok was back in his place. I tried tying Ogonyok behind Taskonir, but Taskonir continued the bullying by trying to kick Ogonyok in the head. Ogonyok pulled back until Taskonir came to a standstill and the lead rope was torn from my grasp.

Ogonyok and Zhamba weren't the only ones in Taskonir's sights. As I went to tighten a strap on the packsaddle, I felt a sudden pain in the middle of my spine. I could feel Taskonir's teeth pull a whole sheet of skin away from my bones. For weeks I would carry Taskonir's tooth marks and bruising on my back.

There were rays of enthusiasm that kept my spirits up, and they came from the most unlikely of places – Tigon. Although he was as stiff as the ice on my tent in the early morning, he waited with great impatience for our morning departure. After stretching out and yawning so wide that it looked as if he might drink in the whole morning sun, his eyes glowed, his ears twitched, and he watched my every move, waiting for signs that we were leaving. When finally it seemed we might be getting on the move he darted around camp, his tail so big and furiously circling behind that it seemed that his whole body was wagging. Beside himself with joy, he greeted each horse with a big kiss on the nose. Ogonyok didn't know what to make of this, swishing his tail and furrowing his brow suspiciously. But Taskonir was not taking any of this silliness. When Tigon went to leap up, Taskonir stamped down his hoof angrily, narrowly missing poor Tigon. Tigon turned to me with a look of great concern and bewilderment, his head bowed and tail between his legs. I tried not to smile, but I couldn't help it.

Come darkness we had travelled little more than 10 kilometres. But it was good enough that we had made it to camp alive and uninjured. With the horses staked out, the stove turned off and my stomach filled, everything felt remotely possible again. While the horses ate their daily ration of grain I rubbed their necks and felt through their manes, under their hairy chins, and along their woolly bellies. Afterwards I sank back onto my big canvas duffle bag beside the tent and watched the crescent moon travel across the sky. Tigon, who had passed out hours ago, was firmly asleep in my sleeping bag. 'Thank goodness Tim is protecting me from the wolves,' he was probably thinking.

For the next two days, the same circus with the horses continued, but a routine emerged. In the morning Tigon bravely broke the trail ahead of us, sometimes trotting along with snow up to his armpits. Whenever a small hill came into view he would dart across and climb up it, then look out over the land as if scouting our route for the day. A couple of times a hare and some wild antelope darted away and Tigon shot off in pursuit. To see him in full flight was really something. His long stick-figure legs stretched out so far ahead and behind that he doubled in length and seemed to fly above rather than through the brush. When he returned, clouds of breath heaved from his lungs and his tongue lolled about, a bright red against the snow. When he began to run out of energy in the afternoon he fell into a march behind us all, eyes to his feet, trailing along like a slinky black shadow in the hoofsteps of the horses.

In the afternoon of the third day the air thawed and the snow grew thin and patchy – signs that I was making progress south. By dusk the frozen silence had been filled with the sound of wind rustling through grass.

Free of snow, the steppe turned ashen in the sinking light, and I made camp near the ruins of mud-brick graves. During the night I woke several times with sharp pains in my chest and the terrifying feeling that the horses were gone. Ever since my horses were stolen in Mongolia I had resolved to sleep in my trousers with belt, knife and headlamp fitted. I was therefore somewhat used to this feeling of paranoia. But this night I woke to something altogether different.

I jerked awake, flicked my headlamp on and prepared to rip open the door to the tent. But no sooner had I sat up than Taskonir's head appeared right in front of me. His eyes were as dark and shiny as maple syrup. There was a sheen to the long, dark winter hair around his face and under his chin. His floppy underlip quivered like jelly on a plate. I wanted to reach out and touch him. But then I realised Taskonir was looking not at me but over me, away into the night. All the horses were in front of me, and I had their lead ropes in my hands. They were pulling hard!

I held on. My hands and shoulders felt like they were on fire. I couldn't understand why the horses were in my tent, but I knew that I couldn't let them go. It was then that I noticed the stranger. He stood in the darkness just around to my right – I could see him from the corner of my eye. He seemed old, I thought – balding, with grey hair and strong workman's hands. He walked towards me.

The rope began to slip from my grasp. The heads of the horses lifted out of the beam from my headlamp and into the shadows. Before I could catch another glimpse of this man, my legs and arms gave way with heaviness. I closed my eyes and fell into deep sleep. I had the feeling that the horses were safe.

In the morning it was hard to get up. Outside, wind lashed the tent with thick wet snow. Inside, I lay trying to understand the experience of night. Was it a dream, reality, or a mix of both? Whatever the case, it would recur every night for the next six months. Later in the journey I would find it familiar and comforting. When I told Kazakhs about it, they were sure it was the spirits of the old men of the steppe, protecting me. This morning, though, it was still raw and frightening.

By afternoon, reality hit. Melting snow dribbled down from my neck to my ankles. I sat in the saddle, head bowed and shivering, and found a trail of sorts. Hours probably passed, and when I lifted my head the track had turned to mud. It was raining, and there was no snow in sight. Ahead, Tigon had found his way to a herdsman who was out with a flock of sheep. It was the first sign of life I had witnessed for almost five days.

I could have found someone to take me in, but this was my first stretch travelling fully alone in Kazakhstan, and I wanted to prove to myself that I could cope. I camped in sight of two large dome graves and shivered through till dawn in a wet sleeping bag. Tigon did the same, curled up all soggy on a horse blanket beside me. By morning the sky had cleared. The sun brought relief, and I packed up for the first time in three weeks without mitts.

'Another half a day south to Kopa. It must be still summer down there!' I said to Tigon. The dog looked back at me, ears upright. He just wanted breakfast.

8

Light and Shadow

Tigon was the first to lay eyes on Kopa. He stood poised on a hilltop, head cocked to one side. When we caught up I stepped out of the saddle and, kneeling beside him, took in the view framed between his tall, alert ears.

The huddle of forty or so homes was nothing more than a little island dwarfed by a wild sea of brown and grey steppe. But to me, after a week alone, it was a bustling hive of life. A herd of sheep and goats was being driven home for the night, and people were emerging from their homes to welcome the animals and herders back.

The thought of warmth, food and friendship propelled me into Kopa, and I was not disappointed. My host-to-be, Serik, came out to greet me with a big meaty embrace.

'Where have you been? We have been expecting you for two days!' he boomed, clutching me with his bear-like hands.

Two of Serik's workers hauled out giant bundles of hay and laid them at the feet of my horses. Tigon was thrown some bones, and after I had been treated to a *banya* – a kind of Russian sauna – as well as a dish of meat and a couple of shots of vodka, Serik decided that I was staying for three days.

'In old times for the first three days the host did not have any right to ask the guest who they were, or what their business might be. The host must look after the guest like they are part of the family!'

Serik informed me that there was a wedding planned, and it was essential that I be there.

Two nights later, the community hall was shaking with a crowd of several hundred. Men in suits and women wearing camel-hair vests mingled on the dance floor with teenagers clad in skintight jeans. Disco music and traditional songs blasted out through old crackly speakers. I was pulled awkwardly in to join the dancing, and clopped about in my hiking boots.

To announce the beginning of the ceremony a musician entered with a dombra cradled in his arms. He roamed the hall in a long silky cloak, and as he began to sing, people left the floor. When finally the bride and groom walked in, the musician serenaded the bride before ushering the crowds into the dining room.

I paused in disbelief.

Three rows of long trestle tables were laden with a tapestry of fresh fruit, horse sausage – a Kazakh delicacy – dried curd, pastries, confectionery, salads and nuts. Serik explained that it was a small wedding – 'only three hundred guests'.

Glass after glass was raised to the newlyweds. Time and time again I somehow found room for one more piece of horse sausage, one more piece of cheese . . . one more piece of cake.

The party spilled back onto the dance floor and I hobbled in clasping my stomach, which was as tight as a drum. There were women twirling in shrieks of laughter, and grooving old men whose shirts had popped out from their belts and shook like flags in the wind. The night was far from over, but I was unsteady on my feet and my eyes were starting to close.

Before too long I was sleeping in a toasty warm house in my thermal underwear by the crackle of a fire under a heavy blanket. Tigon was in the barn snoring on a bed of hay, and the horses munched like hungry lions at food that kept getting dropped at their feet.

The only thing more overwhelming than the food, companionship and celebration of Kopa was the bleak aloneness the next morning as I rode away. The wedding echoed in my head for a while, but as soon as Kopa was behind me, the cold and wind felt more acute than ever. The steppe out the front gave way to wide cracked clay pans, between which grew tough, grey woody plants. The horizon was so flat and deserted that nothing but Tigon with his tall pointy ears bridged it with the sky.

I set up camp in a mush of fading greys and soon discovered that it wasn't just *my* tummy that had expanded after all the feasting in Kopa. I turned my back on my dinner for only a minute, but when I spun back my pot had been licked clean. Tigon was pretending to be fast asleep inside the tent on my sleeping bag, and I could see the hint of rice and meat on his lips. I was not amused – I only had a week's supply of food, and I wasn't sure where the next supply would come from.

Later that night I began throwing firecrackers out the tent door as a precaution to ward off wolves – a strategy that Aset had suggested, and which I would use until winter was all but finished. Unfortunately, as I tried to film myself doing this I forgot to open the tent door before I lit one. As I fumbled with the zip the firecracker exploded, burning a hole through the entrance.

When I finally crawled into the sleeping bag there was no denying it: things were going to get a lot harder before they became easier for me. The reality of my journey, especially in these colder months, was that I would be moving across bare empty steppe for days on end. I would need to learn how to fend for myself, only to arrive in the warmth and light of communities where every waking moment I would be surrounded by people. The isolation would make me crave company, and the company would make me feel even more alone when I set off again.

What I couldn't yet appreciate was that not all the attention from people would be welcome, and sometimes there was nothing safer and more comforting than being completely alone in the shadows – even if the wolves were looking over me.

For a week the sky remained as overcast and dim as the featureless, colour-drained steppe. The temperature was below freezing, but there was very little snow. Most mornings I collected my own drinking water by peeling ice off the exterior of the tent and melting it in my pot. There were no livestock, and only morsels of grass. At times the semi-frozen shoreline of Lake Balkhash came in and out of sight, its waters salty and undrinkable. One of the only people we met in all this time was a herder with chapped, red cheeks who came racing over to tell me that he had fended off a wolf that very morning with his whip. The wolf had attacked his sheep in broad daylight, and managed to kill one.

Despite the glum sky and the shortening daylight hours, Tigon found every day as exciting as the last – that is, after he finally got out of bed. Each morning he would hold out until the tent itself had been pulled down and I had shaken him out onto the ground. Even then, after tumbling out he would pretend to lie dead to the world, his long twiggy legs tangled up, tongue hanging out, and eyes closed. But as soon as I turned my back he would spring to life in a desperate attempt to crawl back inside. If he did manage to get back in he would once again pretend to be fast asleep.

During the day Tigon's long-ranging missions began to expand. Sometimes I could spot him as a black speck on a distant ridge line, then he would race back to check in, like a homing pigeon. At times he would appear so suddenly that the horses, Ogonyok especially, would get a fright.

A week into my journey along Lake Balkhash the troubles began. There was still no snow on the ground, I hadn't been able to find fresh water for more than a day, and there was nothing for the horses to eat. Taskonir dug at the ground with his hooves, snorting and looking increasingly unhappy. I lay awake for hours wondering what to do. Since arriving in Kazakhstan I had been carrying grain for the horses and feeding them a few kilos each night, but this was all finished.

I decided to make a break from the empty steppe to a

small workers' camp on a remote industrial railway line. Serik had told me about these small communities, where men worked on the tracks and trains would deliver fresh drinking water once or twice a week.

I soon found a room flooded with the stench of vodka and tobacco, where three men were heads down playing cards. They hadn't seen me coming. At first they thought I might be a Russian illegally fishing the lake, but upon seeing my horses, they agreed to help. I paid one of them to hitch a ride on a train to the nearby town of Sayak and bring back a sack of grain and some food supplies for me by evening.

Waiting a day amid the diesel stench, blackened earth and scattered rubbish was not pleasant, but the only other way of resting the horses and getting supplies was to ride into Sayak myself – something I had been told to avoid. The mining town was apparently 'full of bandits' and competing Mafia groups. More worrying for me were reports of the corrupt Sayak police. Apparently they were known to kidnap people or arrest them on false grounds, drive them out onto a remote part of the steppe, steal their valuables, and leave them for dead. Rumour or not, it sounded like a good place to avoid.

After dark, a sack of grain, some rice and some canned meat were delivered. I settled into camp near the tracks, relieved to be safe and restocked. Just after tethering the horses, however, a special workers' train pulled in and around twenty men piled out. The workers, who had arrived from Sayak for a week of track maintenance, swaggered over to an empty dormitory hut. I was dragged into their smoke-filled den, where men sat on their bunks spitting on the floor between drags on their cigarettes.

One man with straw-like hair, pockmarked skin and an unblinking stare poured me a glass of vodka. 'Give me one of your horses! Or at least sell it to me cheaply! After all, what do you need *three* for?' When I refused, he backed off and replied: 'There are thieves from Sayak coming to steal your horses tonight, so be careful.'

When I left the hut I found Tigon curled up by the door, guarding my boots. He leapt up at me, paws on my chest, whining, desperate to be close to me. I ran my hands along his snout, caressed his head behind the ears, and buried his moist nose in my coat.

It should have been obvious: I needed to stick close to my animals. Instead, I took up an invitation for dinner inside the hut – a decision that would very nearly end my journey.

I was partway through a slop of canned meat and fried potato when Tigon let out a bark and a growl. When I stepped outside there was a great thwack and a muffled thump from the direction of my camp. Running towards my tent, I could make out the silhouetted figure of someone scurrying away from Taskonir. The mystery figure had leapt bareback on Taskonir for a brazen getaway. What he hadn't realised was that Taskonir was tethered on the lower front leg with a twenty-metre line. Taskonir had only made it to the end of the rope before he and his passenger had somersaulted to earth.

The semi-concussed thief was quickly dragged into the hut with the help of the other workers. It was the very same man who had warned me about thieves earlier.

A tall bearded worker took command. 'You know what we do when there is a problem like this?' he announced, slapping me on the shoulder and knocking the air out of my lungs. 'There is just one solution.' The men around him looked on, captivated. 'To drink!'

They went back inside and raised toasts of vodka to anything and everything. Even the would-be thief joined in. Outside, I tied the horses on short ropes and lay in my sleeping bag on the frozen ground among them until dawn. Tigon wound himself up into a tight little ball that reminded me of those little grey slater bugs that I used to play with as a child.

At six am I was up and ready to go. There was just one last issue to resolve: Taskonir's hobbles were missing. I roused some men and told them to wake the thief. As he emerged I mustered the fiercest look that I could manage.

'I need my hobbles!' I said sternly.

With a sigh he walked around to the rear of the hut and came back with them.

As I set off other men came out, rubbing their eyes, to say goodbye. Tigon was already far ahead.

'Have a good journey! We hope you are not offended!' they cheered.

I kept my eyes straight ahead for hours, and didn't slow until the railway was gone from view. All I could think about was retreating to the safety of the land and avoiding humans for as long as I could. I didn't care if it meant drinking salt water for a whole month.

I rode on under a low ceiling of dark clouds. In camp, I tied the horses in close around the tent and curled up on a luxurious bed of horse blankets. The aroma of horse sweat and hair had become familiar – by now I could identify each individual horse in the dark just by smell alone – and it added to the sense of cosiness.

A storm raked over the land through the night, and by morning there was enough snow on the ground for the horses to rehydrate. To the south I could see where the smudgy horizon merged with the broad, silvery waters of Lake Balkhash.

In the afternoon the sun came out and I descended some gullies to the shore. Salty air filled my lungs. Soon,

I pondered, these two vast bodies – the sea-like steppe and the lake itself – would freeze up and fuse as one.

Over the next few days and, as it turned out, weeks, the lake would become my companion. I watched the shore-line flats grow into muscled hills, which in turn became stony ridges. Sometimes the lake's shifting moods seemed to mirror mine. It offered me a lifeline too. Although the water itself was saline, polished stones of ice would wash up on shore that were relatively fresh. The horses would crunch through these like they were giant icy poles, and I would collect them to melt in the evening. I loved the feeling at night when the big, sometimes overwhelming world contracted to the size of my tent, and my close-knit family of animals.

There were some signs of humans during this time – the mud huts of reclusive illegal fishermen and distant silhou-ettes of horsemen once or twice – but the most significant were the graves of nomads who had once lived here. The most obvious graves were tall clay domes. One in particu-lar caught my attention. It was several metres high and had an entry facing south to the sun, just like a yurt. Tigon and I ate our lunch inside, huddled out of the wind.

I closed my eyes. I could almost hear the distant sound of children as they brought the herds back in for the night. When I opened my eyes again, however, there was just the sound of the wind in the grass. It was both sad and comforting: sad because of the destruction of nomad life that had happened in Soviet times, but comforting because it meant I was not alone. I was travelling in the hoofsteps of the many who had gone before me.

It was after pausing by a similar grave days later that I began to find some peace with the thief on the railway. Was it not honourable, if not polite, that he had warned me of the theft? Didn't that mean I had a good horse worth treasuring? As I rode away from the grave, it sank in: horse rustling was an art as old as horsemanship itself, and traditionally he who has the skill to steal horses deserves those horses more than the owner.

What's more, in getting my horse back I had engaged in an ancient custom called *barimta*, which means 'that which is due to me'. It ruled that he who has been stolen from has the right to steal back, and if he is good enough, he can confiscate the offender's entire herd or even his wife until the dispute is resolved.

The thought that the thief had attempted to steal Taskonir in keeping with the spirit of his ancestors made me feel a hint of privilege that I was partaking in the old ways. It was also true that if I wasn't good enough to look after my horses, then the thief probably deserved them more than I did. From here on, I would clearly have to embrace every attempt at stealing my horses as a compliment.

*

110

As the shadow of the horse theft faded, my mind returned to my animals. For much of the day we moved briskly, the horses' hooves clipping the frost off plants. The horses were getting fitter and stronger, and also more alert. We trotted ten to twenty minutes each hour and set a fast walk in between. While food was often scarce, Ogonyok seemed to have a knack for finding grass even when there was none. He had developed a fine skill at eating on the move, stealing mouthfuls with every second step. It wasn't unusual in the mornings to have to lengthen his girth straps.

Tigon on the other hand was beginning to show his tender young age. Each night he would fall asleep long before his head even reached under his tail, and some mornings he seemed to keep his eyes firmly closed, hoping I wouldn't realise that the sun had risen. In the mornings his half serving of porridge was no longer enough for his growing bones. He would make a note of spying on where I went to the toilet, and would make a run for it to eat up my 'scraps'. 'Tigon!!!' I would shout as I came trotting over, only for him to gobble down the remains and go running off, tail between his legs but nose high in triumph. 'Disgusting!!!'

Our intimate little bubble was broken one frosty morning when we came face-to-face with a herd of shaggy camels. Their twin humps wobbled like jelly and their long winter hair swayed like grass in the wind. Up close their eyes appeared ringed by frosted eyelashes, while frozen slobber hung from their lips in long tangled beards of ice. Unfortunately, all three horses – which were from eastern Kazakhstan and therefore had never seen camels – reared up, muscles tensed and nostrils flaring. I was riding Zhamba at the time and could feel his heart pounding through my lower legs. I held on for life as the horses bolted away. Tigon decided that he could save us – only, he began herding the whole group of camels *towards* us instead.

'Tigon!!'

He paused momentarily, ears cocked, before once again rounding them towards me. I held on for what seemed like hours until we managed to canter beyond them and into the hills.

The next morning I was woken at dawn by a whinnying from Ogonyok. I broke out of the tent and stopped in my tracks: Ogonyok and Taskonir stood facing me with their ears back and hind legs flexed. Behind them in the half-light was the ghostly figure of a dark, woolly stallion. He snorted, demanding a confrontation. Beyond him, hidden among the shrubbery, were a hundred beady eyes and ears straight as nails. They were barrel-chested little horses with thick necks, coarse split manes, and brands on their hindquarters.

We all froze until Tigon came to his senses and sprinted over with the most aggressive bark he could muster. Foals, mares, and geldings broke into a gallop. Tigon returned, chest puffed out, ribs heaving up and down with frosted-up whiskers on his brow and a great look of pride.

It had been so long since I had seen another horse that I had nearly forgotten the magic of it. I missed the cry of a herder, the rustle of a flock of sheep, and the movement of horses.

It was time to take a gamble with humans. Besides, I was out of grain. And the next day was my twenty-sixth birthday.

9

Calm Before Storm:
The Starving Steppe

I sat bolt upright and fished blindly for the tent entrance, but all I could find was something hard and flat that resembled a wall. It was only after I had completely woken up that I recalled where I was. The previous evening I had found a nomad's camp, and a man called Kuat had taken me in to his mud-brick hut. At first I'd been unsure about accepting his invitation – was this just a trap? After dinner and a cup of tea, however, I had felt my tired body collapsing in surrender. Without trusting in humans my journey would simply not be possible. Just like Tigon, who seemed to always expect the best from people and animals, I would have to appeal to their better side, no matter who they were.

On my way out to check on the horses I stepped over Tigon, who was asleep guarding my saddle at the hut entrance. He opened one eye briefly before tucking his nose further under his tail and pretending he hadn't seen me.

I would have gone back to bed too, had I not noticed a shadowy figure coming out of the corrals.

Bazibek, a sixty-year-old herder who worked for Kuat, was limping bowleggedly over to a camel. His body looked as rigid and gaunt as an old skinny sheep. For forty years straight he had worked as a herder. I watched as he set about saddling the camel, his motions sure as the rising sun, silent and unrushed. Age had worn away his agility, but everything he did, from fitting the felt blanket to tightening the girth, was done with precision. I had the feeling he was trying not to wake the land. Even when he spoke to me he did so in a husky whisper. How was it that, despite its size and harshness, the land felt so tender at this time of day?

When the flock of sheep had been let out of a pen, Bazibek hauled himself into the saddle, clung on to the front hump, and the camel rose. Directing his sheep with a long pole and whip, Bazibek set off into the distance.

Long after he had gone, the look in his eyes stuck with me. There was a humble, faraway expression. This man knew his place on this earth. He reminded me of something a horseman had told me once: 'When things go all pear shaped around you, you must be the calm in that storm.'

To me Bazibek, whose eyes were looking far beyond the trivial problems of here and now, *was* that calm. He had learnt to work with nature, and to appeal to *its* better side.

What I couldn't yet know on this clear still morning of my twenty-sixth birthday was that Bazibek, and my time here on the shores of Lake Balkhash, would also prove to be the calm *before* the storm.

My aim from here was to follow the lake to the western end, before setting off into the Starving Steppe. Prior to rejoining the wilds, however, there were some surprises in store.

In the evening a Russian-made jeep turned up with police in uniform. Word had clearly spread via the *uzun kulak* or 'long-ear news' of the steppe. My heart sank.

They ordered me over. 'How can we understand your journey? What is your business here? Are you really Australian?'

I nervously reached for my passport. The problem was that I did not actually have any official permit for my journey.

'We don't need papers. Just tell us, are you *really* from Australia?'

'Yes, where kangaroos are from,' I said.

'So it's true! We have come to wish you a happy birthday!' they bellowed.

One of the men went out to the jeep and brought in a bag of barley.

'This is for you, a gift for turning twenty-six. My grandfather taught me that a palmful of this uncrushed grain is enough to keep a horse going when it is tired.'

After the police had gone the herders put on a birthday with all the frills, including a feast of fish from the lake, fresh mutton and horse sausage as well as delicious creams, yoghurts and a cake. Even Bazibek, who had returned from his day herding, combed his dishevelled, unwashed hair and donned his finest old creased dress pants for the occasion.

Over dinner we sat on cushions on the floor around a low table called a *dastarkhan*. The difficulties of the impending winter temporarily dissolved around us.

Tigon decided that it was also a night for him to celebrate. At one point when everyone stepped outside I heard a clattering sound from inside the house. I poked my head back through the door: there Tigon stood, right on the middle of the dastarkhan, head down in the long narrow neck of the cream jug. It was only a fraction of a second before he whipped his head out and turned to me with ears, eyebrows, whiskers and nose all dripping with cream. His frozen look of panic fast became one of action as he leapt from the table, knocking the cream jug to the floor as he went.

'Tigon!' I growled as the jug smashed into pieces and he vanished into the dark.

From Kuat's farm I carried on for two weeks along the shoreline of Lake Balkhash. On land there was still no snow, while the lake was frozen as far as the eye could see.

Cold, dry conditions like this resembled what is known in Mongolian as *harin zud*, or 'black zud', and feared by nomads even more than deep snow cover and ice. Without snow in winter livestock face dehydration, often wiping out millions of animals.

Technically the water in this western end of the lake was fresh enough to drink, but the only way for me to collect it was by tethering the horses to stakes onshore, walking out onto the ice, breaking a hole with my hand axe, and returning with pails. If the snow did not come soon, branching westward away from the lake into the Starving Steppe would be unthinkable. On the other hand, collecting water at the lake was becoming too dangerous, and soon the lake would be frozen solid anyway.

In the aul of Tasaral – my last port of call on the lake – my luck changed. I was greeted and taken in by Shashibek, the son of the local akim. Not only were my horses generously wined and dined, but I witnessed a proposal. The plan was simple: Shashibek's girlfriend was invited to dinner to join me – the Australian 'bait'. Little did she know that Shashibek was about to ask for her hand in marriage and half the aul would in fact be waiting for her, hidden in another room.

The girl was dropped off by car, and just as she was sitting down to eat, the hidden guests suddenly broke their way in and flooded the room. Fistfuls of confectionery were showered on the couple and a white scarf was placed on the bride-to-be's head – a symbol that she had been embraced as part of the family.

Celebrations went long into the night. Meanwhile, out in the cold and the darkness, only my horses, resting in the corrals, would have seen the great curtain of winter darkness hit. By dawn when I got up it was still snowing and the land had been transformed.

It was the stroke of luck I'd been waiting for.

For the first day out of Tasaral the temperature hovered around –25°C. A headwind whipped up clouds of serrating snow, making it almost unbearable to look straight ahead. My ski goggles were forever icing up, and even with thick mittens, my fingers quickly grew numb. Tigon delighted in chasing foxes and hares, but when he stopped his paws swiftly became painfully cold and he would look up at me, eyes narrowed, as if asking why the weather was offending him so badly.

My emotions undulated like the land. When I was moving forward, I felt like I was floating, gunning towards the empty horizon as if in a dream. The snow cover gave me the freedom to travel wherever I wanted. But when I was unsure about how to read the landscape, or a saddle loosened and I needed to stop and refit, I felt the shadow of danger on my heels. In the darkness the following morning while I was preparing the horses, Taskonir took a bite of my hand. The skin between the first and second knuckles came off like a sheath, leaving it raw and bloody. I stared back at Taskonir in bewilderment, struggling not to cry. It was too much.

In the days to come, the cold and dark spiralled, and the journey felt like a game of survival. The inner tent was forever laden with hoarfrost, and ordinarily simple tasks, such as pulling stakes and tent pegs out of the frozen earth, became epic struggles.

It was −28°C the day that I caught my last glimpses of Lake Balkhash. The ice had turned black, strangled in a web of frost. Ahead to the west stretched the Betpak Dala. Renowned as a desert of extremes, it was empty even by Kazakh standards – a reminder of the origin of its namesake, as the Starving Steppe. My aim was to trek 300 kilometres across its southeast corner to a village on the Chu River called Ulanbel.

As I climbed up a snow-encrusted slope to look over the land I could feel the cold and remoteness go up a notch. The wind died, and in the intense stillness, sparkling ice crystals fluttered to the ground like dead butterflies snap-frozen in flight. Ice rings had formed around the horses' nostrils, and clouds of frozen breath blew back onto their necks and flanks, spraying them white. Even my eyelashes gathered frost.

Soon there were no sounds, no trails, and no people. Over the sea of pearly white, I watched the sun creep into the empty sky. I had begun to think that Tigon wanted to see where the sun disappeared to each day. When it rose in the mornings he was desperate to know where it had been and what stories it had to tell. Yet try as he might, the faster and harder he ran the longer the sun seemed to disappear at night, and the further it was from reach.

There was little time for my mind to drift. One slip could mean trouble. My greatest fear was falling off, or having a horse slip over and crush me. In these conditions having a broken leg, and being abandoned by the horses would almost certainly be a death sentence.

I carried on until sunlight had nearly vanished, then raced to make camp.

The cold pressed harder on the earth. My first priority was Tigon, who was whimpering inconsolably. I wrapped him in a spare horse blanket and zipped him inside my canvas duffle bag. Later, when the tent was up and dinner was on the boil, the bag began hopping towards the stove. I opened the bag a little way and dangled a piece of salted pig fat over it. Tigon swiftly snapped up the offering before drawing back inside his cocoon of warmth.

The horses meanwhile stood tired and still like statues, their fur standing on end. They had a look of great knowing, and seemed accepting of this cold. The one exception to their sense of composure was at feeding time. The mere rustle of a grain bag brought whickering from all three as they raced to the end of their tethers, demanding food.

By the time I finished feeding the horses my feet were numb. I leapt inside the tent, where Tigon had been warming my sleeping bag, and took off my boots. To prevent moisture freezing in them, I wore large plastic bags over my outer socks, and a smaller bag between them and my thermal socks. As I took the bags off and shook them out, the pooled sweat instantly turned to ice.

Inside the tent it wasn't much warmer than out. Tigon was covered in frost, his whiskers were tentacles of ice, and his breath rose in clouds of vapour. I tried running my hand down his bony spine: he growled angrily. Although I had come to love Tigon, I had hardly had a chance to show him warmth or affection, and no doubt he had picked up on my lack of love in earlier times. Now, just when I needed it myself, he had learnt to get by without me. How could I have alienated the one little creature who had stuck loyally with me all this time? Before I pulled the drawstring of my sleeping bag tight I doused his paws in vodka to help prevent frostbite and let him snuggle inside my down jacket.

When I woke the next morning my body was tense, and for some reason I couldn't get warm. It was cold – around –40°C as it turned out – but something else was amiss. I realised my sweat had formed frozen clumps in the down feathers of my sleeping bag. I had no way to dry out my bag in these conditions, so I shivered into my jacket and decided to get moving.

I had learnt some methods that helped me to stay calm in situations like this. Mostly it was about focusing on the challenges one step at a time. For example, I would concentrate on getting to lunch, and then camp, and so on. It was better not to look at the bigger picture sometimes.

But this morning I felt increasingly spooked. I discovered that my GPS had frozen, and all the coordinates had been wiped. The tent also seemed particularly fragile, and I hated to think what might happen if a windstorm blew in. Above all though, it was the twenty-third of December, just a couple of days before Christmas. The thought of being alone and freezing on the Starving Steppe on a day when my family was celebrating together was too much.

I panicked. I fished out my maps to see if there was anything remotely closer than Ulanbel. On my large tour map of Kazakhstan there was one dot on the Starving Steppe marked 'Akbakai'. I didn't care who lived there, or what this place was, I just knew that I *had* to get there.

It was a relief to get moving. The sky was clear and the air eerily calm. Just after lunch, when the pale sun was limping towards the horizon, I found myself in the shadows of a narrow gorge. Ogonyok's load had come loose, and I leapt off to reload.

All day I had tried to keep thoughts about wolves at bay, but now they came rushing forward. I'd been told by Kazakh herders that wolves would follow me unseen, possibly for days, before choosing their moment to attack – a moment like this, no doubt. Midwinter was the time when they were at their hungriest. I had long known that wolves could take down fully-grown camels, yaks and horses, but it was the stories I'd heard about attacks on humans that worried me most now. One of the most common wolf stories I had heard in Kazakhstan was of an attack on a woman and her daughter who had been waiting at a bus stop on a lonely road in winter. The woman had saved her daughter by lifting her onto the roof of the bus stop. All that was found of the mother were her valenki, still filled with the lower part of her legs. It was hard to know if this tale was rumour or truth, but out here it was a terrifying thought either way.

I regained some composure once I had climbed out of the gorge, and calmed myself with the thought of a saying that Russians had told me long ago:

'If you never know where you are, then you can never be lost.'

My interpretation was that as long as I had food, water, and I was healthy, then it didn't matter if I couldn't place myself on a map. And vice versa: one could know precisely where one was, but be very unsafe.

I knew all this, yet as the sun began to dip, my heart once again raced. I began to believe that my life depended on getting to Akbakai by Christmas.

The shadows grew longer and longer, until night had fallen. I took several wrong turns up narrow, winding ravines and had to backtrack to the main valley. On I pressed, willing the horses into a trot. My hands became numb, and so again and again I removed my mittens and slid my bare hands into the warm sweaty hair under Taskonir's saddle blanket until life returned to my fingers.

Tigon was exhausted. At one stage when I took a short break to check my map he must have curled up under a grass tussock in the snow, thinking we had stopped for camp. I carried on without realising he had been left behind – that is, until I heard a desperate whimper ring out through the frozen night air. He was sprinting to catch up.

By the time I made camp the temperature had fallen further and the snow glowed an ethereal blue. I struggled to hammer the tent pegs in, and the tent poles broke through the fabric sleeves. My camping stove refused to ignite, and I had to pull it apart and clean it – a task involving bare, and already freezing fingers.

A voice inside my head reminded me that as long as I took care and didn't rush, everything would be okay. Stupid decisions such as these – making camp long after dark and trotting blindly over snowy terrain – could prove disastrous. Yet I couldn't break my obsession with getting to Akbakai. I imagined sitting around a table, bathed with the golden light of a fireplace, telling stories about my travels.

At dawn we were up again and rose to a plateau where the fragile calm was broken by raking winds. A great, hazy, white emptiness flowed down from all sides. There were no features, shadows, or depth to give any scale at all. Usually this emptiness instilled a sense of freedom, but now it brought dread. Even if Akbakai was somewhere out there, my compass bearing only had to be marginally off and I could pass it without knowing.

Just as the sun was gliding into my line of vision I caught sight of something that gave me hope – a tower. The horses were tired, struggling to lift their hooves. I egged them on with the promise of hay and shelter.

At times I was sure Akbakai was just a derelict ghost town; other times I thought I could see a tendril of smoke. I could make out strange buildings, which made me think it might be an abandoned Soviet military base.

When Ogonyok's load came loose after dark, I lost my cool and let out a string of curses. The intoxicating vision of hot tea and company possessed me.

*

As we limped through some twisted scrap metal on the deserted outskirts I began to stir. Wind filled my ears, and Tigon's whimpering rose in pitch. We had made it to Akbakai, but I'd forgotten that no one was waiting for us. No one here, for that matter, even knew we existed.

10

The Land that God Forgot

The only sign of life was the shadowy figure of a man hunched over a pile of firewood. After much pleading, Maksim – who suspected that I was either a lost Russian geologist or an escaped prisoner – reluctantly led me to a half-built mud-brick shack. I tied the horses to one end, then, together with Tigon, climbed into a small adjoining room. Inside, the flickering of a coal stove revealed two old spring beds, mattresses, and cardboard-matted floor. Vitka and Grisha, the Russian labourers living here, were too drunk to speak, but details didn't matter. I was out of the wind, I was warm, and I was not alone.

Christmas morning brought a more sobering reality. Woken by a couple of puppies licking my face, I peeled open my eyes to take in a panorama of dog poo, piles of empty vodka bottles, and a frying pan filled with congealed fat. Vitka and Grisha were dead to the world but alive with the stench of body odour, tobacco and alcohol. They were truck drivers from southern Kazakhstan who had been stranded in Akbakai since losing their licences two years earlier.

Eventually they were stirred by their own snoring. When they learnt who I was, they cried: 'Australian! We understand that today is your Christmas. By all means we will have a celebration tonight. A treat!'

Akbakai was not the community I had hoped for. The streets were littered with frozen clumps of rubbish, and lined with rubble and mangled machinery wreckage. To the west and south heavy trucks laboured through dirty, blackened snow. Akbakai was a gold-mining town with no natural water supplies. Food and water were both precious resources shipped in from far away.

After hours of searching, a local hunting inspector let me climb up his ice-encrusted water tank to fill pails for my horses. He also agreed to sell me hay to last twenty-four hours – but no more than that.

I returned to the mud hut in the evening hungry and stiff. Grisha and Vitka had caught a couple of street pigeons earlier that day and had boiled them up for dinner.

'Everything will be fine! Sit down, lie back, have a

vodka, a cup of tea, we will find you a wife . . . and you can use your horses as a bride-price!' they chanted.

I watched as Grisha and Vitka argued, stumbled, and fought into the early hours. When they passed out I lay awake listening to the wind, unable to sleep. I clung to visions of home and being close to my siblings, mother and father.

I had sought refuge in Akbakai, picturing a family and a barn full of hay, but come the early hours of 26 December, that vision was in tatters. And things were about to get a lot harder.

When I woke to pack, Taskonir was holding his back left leg in the air. An infection had formed an abscess in his hoof – most likely the result of a stone bruise suffered during our rushed ride to Akbakai. It would be many days, or even weeks, before I could expect it to heal. The nearest village, Ulanbel, was another five days across wild steppe. Carrying on was not an option, but there was no feed for the horses here.

The abscess was to be the first of *many* hold-ups and failed attempts at leaving Akbakai. It would, in fact, be three and a half months before I managed to depart.

For two days I scrounged for fodder and water, to little avail. When I approached Maksim, who owned the mud hut where Vitka and Grisha lodged, for help, he retorted angrily, 'What makes you think anyone should help you?

You are better off selling your horses for meat before they are too skinny!'

Like many others, Maksim had come here lured by the promise of work but found himself unemployed and stranded far from his hometown. He lived in a derelict apartment block where he had rigged up a woodstove in a room on the third floor. To support his wife and two children, he had turned the basement of the building into a makeshift workshop, where he made furniture out of scrap wood. Without a network of relatives or friends, it was hard to imagine what fallback he had if this venture failed.

Maksim's scenario would have been unthinkable for nomads in old times. A tradition called *ata-balasy*, which means 'the joining of grandfather's sons into one tribe or family', was the bedrock of nomadic life, and in many communities it is still only by banding together in wide circles of kin that it is possible to support those fallen on hard times. But here in Akbakai, a town built by the Soviets to extract gold, the traditional sense of community did not exist, and the people had been abandoned by the government and left to their own devices.

Three days after Christmas, Taskonir's leg was worse, the wind had picked up to gale force, and clouds were marching in. Come what may, though, I had decided that *anything* was better than staying in Akbakai. After saddling up, I went inside the mud hut to say goodbye to Vitka and Grisha. They were sad to see me go and worried about what would become of me. In the throes of this farewell, my fortunes changed.

Stumbling into our hovel came a short, squat man wearing thick, crooked glasses that magnified his eyes and pinched his red nose. His voice was deep and husky, and as he spoke, his defrosting moustache wiggled.

Curiosity eventually got the better of him. 'Who is he?' he asked, pointing at me.

'We have a guest from Australia,' Grisha related. 'He came here to us by horse . . . from Mongolia.'

The man stepped back, straightened his glasses, then leant forward. 'Come to my home!' he exclaimed. 'Why freeze here? I'll give you a sack of wheat to help you on your way!'

Grisha and Vitka were excited for me. According to them, Baitak, as the man was known, was a 'millionaire' and a 'king'. I would surely be safe in his hands. Their description proved to be a bit of an exaggeration. His house was an underground one-room hut. He didn't own a car, had no washing facilities, and the toilet was a long drop full to the brim with frozen poo and just a tarpaulin to protect one from the elements. His water supplies were trucked in, like everyone else's, and the much talked-about cafe and bar he owned was a coal-heated hut within shouting distance of his house that backed onto a mountain of rubble.

At the time, though, to me everything about Baitak's empire shone. I was presented with a series of fried eggs, and each one I finished was replaced with another. Tigon ate buckets of stale bread and milk, until his belly bulged out to twice its normal size and he sprawled out royally on the floor.

The true meaning of Baitak's wealth became clear over the weeks to come. As one of the most established people in town – he had been in Akbakai since 1976 – he had unique authority and knowledge. Above all, though, I think Baitak's status as a 'king' was a measure of his generous heart. Certainly that is what ultimately saved my life, and those of Tigon and my horses.

After our meal, Baitak inspected Taskonir and shook his head. He knew I was in trouble, but he also knew what to do. He co-owned a kstau six kilometres out of town, where cattle were kept. 'You can ride there and stay until your horse heals and the weather improves. Tell the herder there, Madagol, that he can feed your horses with my hay.'

There were times in my journey when I felt like I was a captain, firmly in command, on a course of my choosing. There were other times, however, when I simply had to let go of the reins and accept that the journey – or, in this case, Baitak – would guide me.

*

To reach the kstau, which was hidden in a valley between two knobby ridges, took two hours, by which time Taskonir was reluctant to move at all. As I arrived I was greeted by Madagol – a gruff, wiry old fellow with tightly coiled greying hair and heavy, calloused hands. He invited me in with a fusillade of curses regarding the weather.

'Wind is the worst thing in Akbakai! When it blows on the third day, you know it will blow for seven, and when it blows on the eighth day, it will blow for fourteen . . . after that it will blow for a month. It's not like that where we come from!'

Madagol and his wife lived in a shabbily constructed hut that was below freezing indoors. Curled up on a bed under a mountain of blankets, Madagol's wife sat looking frail and utterly miserable.

It must have been terribly isolating for them both, especially Madagol's wife. Although the town was not far away, few braved the weather to visit in winter. When the blizzards set in, there were some periods when they were completely cut off.

For me, on the other hand, the isolation appeared to be a godsend. The vet in Australia had suggested by satellite phone that the abscess would heal within a week. All I had to do now was sit tight.

In reality, Madagol's hut proved to be not quite as isolated as I had believed, and it was wishful thinking to assume my journey was back on track. After just my first night with Madagol and his wife a man known as Abdrakhman – a friend of Baitak – came barrelling down in his old Russian four-wheel-drive vehicle and hauled me back to Akbakai, exclaiming, 'My daughter's birthday is tomorrow night. You will be an honoured guest! We are chaining you to our home until the new year!'

As the guest of honour, I was expected to raise a toast to the stream of guests visiting Abdrakhan's home. In the coming days I fell into a whirlwind of feasts, culminating with a New Year's Eve dance in the snow to Kazakh, Russian and Uzbek music, while Chinese firecrackers flew around like rockets, rebounding dangerously off the walls of the house. It was a fleeting opportunity for us all to forget about the realities of Akbakai.

The celebration was brought to an end by the onset of severe frost, and come New Year's morning there was a price to pay. I woke in a cold sweat and by afternoon was lapsing in and out of fever. Abdrakhman was exhausted and bedridden. He decided it was time for me to leave.

I once again found myself taking refuge with Baitak. He took me in without question, and for three days insisted I sleep on the only bed in his home while he, his wife, and their son slept on the floor.

I intended to stay for one night, but the flu took hold and this drew out to two weeks. I spent days lying disoriented while Baitak's wife, Rosa, fussed over me. Far above there was the faint raking of wind. Only on rare excursions into the elements to relieve myself did I become aware that the weather was closing in. A blizzard was gathering, and the town battened down. I could only hope that Tigon, who I had left with Madagol, had found a warm and safe sleeping place.

About a week into my sickness, Baitak too fell ill, and we lay side by side in our sickbeds, waited on by Rosa. We spent hours discussing politics, the contrasting realities of the Western world and Kazakhstan, all things nomad- and horse-related, and of course life in Akbakai.

Although it was hard for Baitak to relate to my life in Australia, he seemed to understand the reason for my journey. Baitak had grown up in the foothills of the Tien Shan Mountains in Southern Kazakhstan. He reminisced about how he and his friends used to catch the collective farm's horses from the herd and gallop bareback until they fell off. Although he no longer rode, he owned a herd of thirty horses that roamed the steppe around Akbakai. This was a source of great pride, and once every two weeks he set off by motorcycle to look for them. Later, when we had recovered from the flu, he pulled out two old saddles from a rusty trunk. 'Not to have a saddle would mean becoming an orphan. Not to own horses would mean death,' he said.

When Baitak and I were finally on the road to recovery, we regularly dined in his cafe. This gave me a valuable opportunity to gather a broader picture of life in Akbakai.

Judging from the clientele, there were two types of locals. The first were pale, beaten-looking men who would arrive to eat and drink vodka after their gruelling work in the mines. Their work was poorly paid and dangerous. Then there were those people who had come seeking riches, often out of desperation.

Baitak described Akbakai residents somewhat differently. 'There are two kinds of thieves in Akbakai: those above ground, and those below.'

I learnt that many of the 'above ground' thieves were workers in the processing plant who stole ore from the production line and sold it to locals to supplement their poor wages. They would pay off their bosses and the security guards to get the material out of the plant. People who didn't work at the plant could also get ore and tailing debris by paying off security guards at night. For this reason there were many unemployed people from faraway regions who had come to try their luck.

The work of thieves 'below the ground' was more treacherous. They would often rappel as far down as 400 metres into disused shafts to mine the ore. Sometimes, it was said, these people fell to their deaths.

Over the course of my stay I came to realise that almost

everybody I met – except Madagol, Vitka and Grisha – was involved in the so-called 'secret business' of stealing ore and tailings and processing it in backyard labs. As the scale of the operation dawned on me, I realised it was not possible to make an honest living in Akbakai and prosper. And for those who did manage to successfully sell on the gold, there were hefty dues to be paid to the local police. One Russian family who were involved in this business could not feed themselves, and were forced to eat dogs to get by. They bred puppies exclusively for this purpose, eating them when they were still young and leaving just one or two to mature from each litter.

The portrait of life in Akbakai painted a bleak picture for Kazakhstan as a whole, but Baitak discouraged me from attempting to understand the system. He wanted me to focus on recovering from the flu and protecting my horses. 'At this time of year the hunger begins, and one horse can provide food for a family for months. Every year, two or three horses will be stolen from my herd. This is normal. However, I am afraid that your horses may be stolen and eaten as well.'

As it turned out, Madagol had run out of hay for my horses and had released them into the steppe. It was the only chance they would have at surviving the winter. In spite of the difficult circumstances, Baitak assured me that the safest place for Tigon was with Madagol. I worried for him, especially now that the horses were no longer there. Apart from the threat of being stolen, would Tigon think I had abandoned him?

Most of my stay in Akbakai was removed from any real experience of traditional steppe life. There were, however, some customs I was lucky to observe.

After we both recovered from the flu, Baitak informed me there was a special occasion I needed to witness. It was *sogym*, the winter slaughter of animals – and not just any sogym, but the most sacred of all, the slaughter of a horse.

On a mild mid-January morning, Abdrakhman, Rosa and others gathered at Madagol's hut armed with knives and axes. The horse in question was an eleven-year-old gelding that had been fattened on a diet of wheat, barley, and hay. 'The fatter the horse, the better the *kazy*,' explained Baitak. Kazy was a prized national Kazakh dish of horse-meat sausage made from the meat and yellowy fat that runs down from the spine along the ribs to the stomach. This meat and fat are cut into strips and stuffed into intestines with a mixture of garlic and salt before being boiled.

Specialists can tell at a glance whether a horse is 'one finger', 'two fingers' or 'three fingers' fat. I had become accustomed to Kazakhs routinely approaching me and prodding the ribs of my horses, specifically quantifying their fat. Ogonyok was always judged two or three fingers, a reminder that travelling with a fat horse through Kazakh-stan was fraught with danger.

After the horse was led out of a corral, things swiftly got underway. The gelding's legs were bound together, and when the horse lost balance and fell, the men hurried to roll it upside down.

Sensing my apprehension, Baitak talked me through it. 'We have different horses for riding, racing, milk and meat. But whatever the case, you won't find any horse dying of old age in Kazakhstan. It is forbidden to let such precious meat go to waste – a single horse can keep a family alive for winter. More than that, to let a horse rot provides no dignity for the horse – it is like abandoning your animal, disowning it. And another thing, a horseman here will never slaughter his own favourite mount – it will be given over to someone else for the task. I could never imagine putting the knife to my own horse.'

I stood back and watched the men heave the horse's head over a chopping block. Madagol cupped his hands in prayer. I focused on the horse.

At first his eyes were wide. His nostrils flared, sending frozen breath shooting into the air. But then he stopped struggling and his eyes panned skyward.

I wanted to look away as Madagol cut back and forward with the knife, but it was all over very quickly. The horse was unmoving; its spirit had gone.

Within a couple of hours the various cuts of meat were being sorted into hessian sacks. We sat around a table dining on *kurdak*, a traditional dish made of fried innards, including heart, liver and kidneys.

Most of the horsemeat would be shared with people less fortunate than Baitak, including Madagol, and Baitak's relations in the city. This was a nomad tradition known as *sybaga*, when the prosperous wing of a family shares the meat and milk from its herds with less successful relatives. Sybaga also requires that the most respected and honoured guests be given the best from the table. In Baitak's case, family status now appeared to have been extended to Tigon, who could be seen outside, head deep in a bucket of blood and scraps. Thankfully, it seemed, rather than just surviving here with Madagol, he'd made himself right at home.

There was no denying I had found horse slaughter very confronting. I'd grown to love my horses and could not imagine putting them to the knife. And yet as I sat chewing on freshly fried liver and watching the swelling happiness in the eyes of Baitak, Madagol and others, I was overcome by the miracle of life on the steppe – that the morsels of grass the land offers can be turned into life-giving fat and muscle. Partaking of the flesh of the horse was a crucial part of the horse worship that had sustained nomads from the beginning of time. These people could appreciate the value of meat more than most of us could even conceive of doing.

The celebration continued for two days, after which I prepared to leave. By this stage I had become so much a part of the family that the prospect of departure saddened me. Even Madagol, who seemed to have his reservations about me, had warmed somewhat. This was partly because I had let on that Australia had about half a million wild horses roaming in the outback. He had been dreaming of mustering a herd and bringing them home to sell for meat.

'That Indian Ocean, is it a shallow or deep lake?' he asked one night.

When the day came for my departure, Baitak was furiously opposed to my decision. His gripe with me was because Ulanbel, my next stop, was apparently renowned for its criminals. He was afraid for my safety.

It was nevertheless a relief to ride out from Akbakai, and once again be together with Tigon and the horses. I made good progress, following little gullies and valleys, picking out features on the horizon and setting new bearings from there. By the time I made camp the mountains surrounding Akbakai were a blip on the horizon. But then came another blow. The seal on my fuel bottle split, and before I could begin cooking, the petrol had all leaked out onto the snow. By morning a blizzard had come in, and the abscess in Taskonir's foot was back with a vengeance.

I packed up and turned back east, knowing it was the end of winter riding.

Madagol was over the moon to receive advance pay to look after my horses, and Baitak was relieved to hear of my new plan. I left Akbakai for a few weeks to restock my supplies and renew my visa, and when I returned I found that winter had taken a heavy toll. The temperature had stayed around −30°C for a month by that stage. During that time Baitak and Madagol had lost track of my horses, and after a week of searching discovered them in a gully, sheltering from the wind. They were alive, but for how long? Not long after this episode, Madagol had fallen off the roof of his animal shelter and snapped his leg in several places. His son had taken over responsibility of the kstau.

Above all, winter had not been kind to Tigon. One night I had been haunted by a dream in which Tigon was looking at me with big sad eyes. He was covered in grease and muck, trapped in a dark place, looking frightened. Upon my arrival, Baitak and Rosa relayed the bad news. While on a visit with Madagol into town, Tigon had vanished for some time, and was feared eaten. One of the mines had gone bankrupt, and some of the hungry, unemployed workers were hunting dogs. While Baitak searched for Tigon, his own pet dog had disappeared without trace. Eventually Baitak had heard a rumour that Tigon was being held by a Russian dog-eater named Petrovich.

'If that Australian's dog doesn't come back, I'll know it was you. Don't you dare eat him!' Baitak had told him. Seven days later Tigon had been found locked away in an old mining shed. He had been badly beaten.

'No one thought he would survive, so I arranged immediately for him to spend several hours in a sauna, then fed him raw eggs and vodka,' Baitak told me. When I was reunited with Tigon he was all skin and bone and barely moving. Even his eyes had lost their flicker.

To think about the ordeal he had been through was almost too much to bear. Worst of all was imagining his lonely cries for help – like from my dream – when I had not been there. And yet good luck, and a good heart (in Baitak), had intervened. Beyond my rage and sadness, I felt grateful. All that mattered now was that Tigon was alive and we were together.

It took another three weeks before Tigon could walk and we could contemplate the journey onwards.

Come the end of March it was hard to believe that I was still stuck in Akbakai. I had been there more than three months, and was beginning to doubt whether I could pull through the rest of Kazakhstan, let alone make it to the Danube.

11
Otamal

By the end of March, as the days began to draw long, there were signs that winter had capitulated. Frost was broken by slush and rain, and snow began to retreat. In its wake the surrounding steppe melted into a swamp. In Akbakai, people were emerging from their homes, pale, gaunt and broken-looking, counting the costs.

I spent several days tweaking my equipment, gathering my animals and preparing them for travel, and during this time the steppe dried out enough to be navigable. With a healthy-looking Tigon, and a little extra weight on my own frame, I figured my window of opportunity had arrived.

On 4 April – the day earmarked for my *fourth* attempt to depart Akbakai – I stumbled out of Baitak's hut into a predawn blizzard. The thermometer read –15°C, and by the time I had watered the horses I was chilled to the bone.

I didn't bother saddling the horses, and instead returned to bed. Baitak saw me come back in. 'So Akbakai is still holding you here? Only that man in the sky knows what is best for you, and he is keeping you in Akbakai for a reason. You have done the right thing.'

Baitak had warned me about this early spring phenomenon, known by nomads as *otamal*. It was a period of sudden cold that usually occurred in mid-March, just as it appeared the weather had turned the corner. Spring, Baitak told me, was the 'season of greatest weakness' for all living things.

For me there was a larger message in all of this, summed up in an oft-repeated saying: 'If you ever have to rush in life, rush slowly.' On the steppe, time was measured by the seasons, the weather, the availability of grass, and, most importantly, the condition of one's animals. To think I could hurry the seasons was as foolish as rushing with horses.

Two days later, the sky had been blown clean and the sun glinted off the frozen streets of Akbakai. After a meal of horsehead, Baitak, Rosa and Abdrakhman escorted me out of town. Baitak's farewell toast was simple: 'I suggest you stay away from young people, and stick close to the elders.'

Bundled up in an old woollen vest that Baitak had

given me, I hauled myself up into the saddle, whistled for Tigon, and hunched forward into the wind. When some time later I took a peek over my shoulder, the steppe was empty.

Ahead of me stretched nearly 150 kilometres of the Starving Steppe before I would reach the aul of Ulanbel. I hoped to find puddles of remaining snowmelt to get through what was now an arid wilderness.

For the first three days we hugged the edge of salt flats, passing in and out of cloud shadows that wobbled and rippled over the land. There were early signs of spring: yellow wrens jumping towards the tent door and V-formations of geese cutting the sky. What captured me most were the shoots of grass emerging beneath tough desert plants. The horses tried furiously to reach the new growth, often scratching their noses on the tough, brittle plants above.

Tigon was beside himself with excitement. The snow was nearly gone, so his paws didn't freeze, yet it wasn't too warm, which meant he could run forever and barely had to let his tongue out to cool down. He galloped about, digging, chasing and sniffing, often running parallel to us on distant ridges, at times returning to give the horses a lick on the face. Taskonir, being the hardened old grump he was, still hadn't warmed to this, and snapped back, warning Tigon with a hoof pounded into the dirt. Tigon, however, had gained strength. He would ignore Taskonir and then, as if proving a point, take a run-up behind us before turning around and, with ears back and nose forward like the nose of a plane, sprint past so fast and so close to all of us that it was like a bullet whooshing by. There were other signs of his growing confidence. At dinnertime as the horses crowded around to pinch food from my pot Tigon got down on his elbows, tail high, and barked and growled at them to steer clear of what he thought was rightly his.

On the fourth day the temperature had risen and the remaining snow had melted. Dust devils hurled across the flats, sometimes hitting us with a cloud of dust and sand. I became stuck in a series of salt bogs and was forced to retreat. The horses were thirsty, and the absence of sturdy ground made the going slow.

Late in the evening I put my compass away and followed an eagle instead. It took me up into red rocky ridges, from where I looked down on never-ending salt flats to the south and at rising steppe to the north.

When I reached the top of the ridge the bird took off again, and led me to some rocky pools of melting snow and a set of old wheel tracks heading west. The bird was now perched on one of two large round piles of rocks and earth – the unmistakable sign of ancient nomad graves.

The following afternoon we reached the outer edge of the Starving Steppe. To the south, the plateau I had been on dropped away to the Chu River. Just beyond its glinting waters lay the aul of Ulanbel, and beyond that, the burning red sands of the Moiynkum Desert.

I dismounted and stood for some time. I couldn't help but feel that I had rediscovered both a sense of freedom and the ancient nomad trail too. And if I could make it this far, then maybe Hungary was indeed possible.

Everyone in Akbakai had warned me that in Ulanbel my horses would be stolen, and I would be 'stripped naked and left with nothing'.

Abdrakhman had shaken his head: 'Timurbek!' he said sternly, using a Kazakh name that was often given to me while I was in Kazakhstan, 'Be careful! You won't find any Baitaks in Ulanbel!'

With this in mind I nervously crossed the Chu River to the southern banks where Ulanbel lay. The bridge did not bode well – halfway across I had to dismount and lead the horses around holes big enough for a car to fall through. No sooner had I safely made it across than a man came rushing from his mud-brick home and stood at a distance, hands on hips:

'*As-salam aleikum*! Sell me your black horse! I like your black horse!'

'No! I need my horse! I will not sell!' I said, clambering back up into the saddle, ready to make my escape.

As the man drew near, Tigon's hackles went up and he sniffed at the man's crotch. The poor man raised his hands in surrender, and I came to my senses.

The man's greeting had been a compliment. Five minutes later, I was in his family home drinking tea.

Temir, as he introduced himself, was adamant that I stay the night. He began to tell me about nomads and how they lived out there in the Moiynkum, and migrated to the Starving Steppe for summer.

'You are in luck, Tim. Word is they are on the move, and will be coming through Ulanbel tomorrow.'

Just after lunch the following day the idleness of the aul was broken by a wildfire of barking. A great cloud of sand and dust billowed in from the southern horizon like a mainsail. Tigon, who had made friends with a rabble army of local dogs, charged off in hysterics.

By the time I made it to the bridge I had been hit by the wafting aroma of livestock. What had only yesterday been a desolate road angling into the aul was now throbbing with a tangle of five hundred sheep and goats, fifty horses, twenty shaggy camels and a few donkeys. Ahead of them, breaking through a wave of dust, grunted a Russian truck full to bursting with belongings, and behind it a motor-cycle with a sidecar brimming with wide-eyed toddlers. At the rear were several men, one of them an old grey-bearded man who wore a purple fox-fur hat and sat astride a grey horse.

Upon reaching the bridge, the leaders in the truck lay down planks and boards to cover the holes. After a brief pause to let the animals drink, the whole caravan then rumbled over to the northern bank. Within half an hour the caravan had come and gone, and the dust had settled as if they had never been.

I paid Temir's son to follow the caravan by motorbike. Tigon came with us, leaving his own plumes of dust and sand.

What had been a silent steppe the previous day now bustled with movement. Toddlers played with baby goats in the back of the truck while a team effort got underway to build a yurt.

First the collapsible walls were put up, then the many roof poles to support the ring at the top of the ceiling. After the felt had been pulled on, a young boy was sent scrambling up to the top to make adjustments. The silver-bearded elder directed with stern but soft commands.

When the yurt was up the women decorated the insides with felt carpets and wall hangings. Outside, sheep pens were set up, and a trench was dug around the yurt. As proof that the pens were necessary, I was shown two horses with bloodied, shredded rumps – the victims of a wolf attack the day before.

By dark, the yurt was furnished, sheep were settling into their pens in a chorus of snorts, farts and snuffles, and freshly slaughtered lamb sizzled on an open fire. Tigon crept closer and sat straight-backed, licking his chops, his paws shifting restlessly.

Men came to earth with sighs of relief and I rested among them. One of the eldest men turned to me and grinned.

'You realise that the Starving Steppe isn't really that hungry? There is good grass out here, and our animals always come back fat. It's just that you have to know when and how.' His eyes were lit up, as if he were describing a feast.

I asked him to go on. He requested a pen and paper, so I handed him my diary and he drew a basic map.

'Every winter we live in the Moiynkum Desert. The soil is sandy and soft, there is little snow, and it is much warmer than other places,' he said, drawing a desert at the bottom of the page.

'Then just before the ticks come to life in the spring we pack up and leave and come north. If we stay too late, the animals suffer from the ticks, and the grass won't have time to recover for the next winter. Our next camp is here, on the northern banks of the Chu River. There are reeds to be eaten on the riverbanks, and grass is beginning to grow. We will stay here until the lambs and kids have strengthened. But this river runs dry in the summer and the pasture gets burned by the sun. In just a few weeks, the grass will be long enough in the Starving Steppe so we can go there.'

At the peak of summer, the family would continue north to uplands that provided cooler weather and winds that kept the mosquitoes away. Once there, they would mingle with other nomad families who had migrated from other regions. Timing the return south was a matter of life or death – too late and they risked getting trapped by blizzards, too early and the winter pastures would not sustain the herds until spring. By the time they reached the Moiynkum Desert for winter they would have completed a round trip of around 600 kilometres.

The man finished his sketch. 'This is my land, and that of my ancestors, the Naiman tribe, and we have camped in the same places for generations,' he said. The completed map was an oval shape running from north to south, bordered by the traditional lands of other tribes who had their own migratory routes. At the northern and southern ends the winter and summer stopping places were shared with their neighbours. It was here that families social-ised with other tribes and clans. Summer was a time of festivity.

I had always imagined Kazakhstan as one great big blank canvas of steppe, and the nomads as living somewhat free-wandering, isolated lives. Now, however, I began to picture a map of traditional grazing lands, stretching from the Caspian Sea to the Altai, the Kyzlkum Desert to Siberia. Each had been home to generations of nomads, who, like this family's ancestors, had developed a unique pattern of life according to the local lie of the land.

There was no official map, of course, because Kazakhs had never relied on fences or maps. Instead they had known their territory through detailed knowledge of ancestry, known as *shezire*.

I was already familiar with one important element of shezire – that before choosing a marriage partner it was necessary to know the details of seven generations of the paternal line, for it was taboo to marry anyone within those lines. This information had been passed on through the centuries via epic poems that wove together a riddle of names, stories of land, and important historical events. In the present day, as I witnessed in many Kazakh homes, it had survived in the form of family tree diagrams.

Also at the core of shezire was knowledge of clan, tribe and *juz* (union of tribes).

This family was part of the Orta Juz. Within the Orta Juz they were Naimans – a tribe descended from the Naimans of Mongolia. First and foremost, though, this man was of the Baganali clan.

'This here is Baganali land. We are the most honest clan. But see that woman over there?' the man said, pointing to a woman turning the frying lamb. 'Don't trust her, because she is Tama!' There was much laughter.

'And when you get into an aul, Timurbek, be sure to

find out which clan lives there. Then when you arrive and they ask who you are, you should tell them that you are one of them. They will take you in like a brother . . . but when you get down to the Karatau Mountains, don't tell them you are a Buzhban, because they are wild people!' There was more laughter.

For me, a foreigner, shezire would prove to be an icebreaker, just as the man advised, but had I been a Kazakh wandering the steppe, it would have been a much more important part of greeting strangers. By asking, 'What clan do you come from?' two Kazakhs can quickly gauge one another's homeland, common ancestors, enemies and relatives. Shezire was much like a passport and a map combined, allowing people to understand who they were, the land to which they belonged, and even whom they could marry.

It must have been nearing midnight by the time Temir's son pointed nervously to his watch. The man with whom I had been speaking tried to persuade me to stay: 'Timurbek! Maybe you could even travel with us into the Starving Steppe. We could find you a Kazakh wife!'

If only I could. But my animals were waiting, and spring beckoned with the promise of smooth and problem-free travel. I climbed onto the back of the motorbike and clung on as we crashed through the darkness.

*

A day's ride west from Ulanbel I made camp by a lake flooded with overflow from the Chu River. As my mash of rice and canned meat boiled, I watched the horses rubbing their sweaty backs in the sand. Taskonir went first, digging with his front hooves before falling to his knees and attempting to roll over. It took him several tries before he managed to get up onto the ridge of his back, where he thrashed about, his unkempt mane mopping up the sand. Once he had gone down, the other two followed. When they had all stood up and shaken off, they, like me, stood gazing to the west. By the water's edge white swans fished about in the water and small birds practised daring acrobatics. Beyond them the silvery glint of water was cast into the land as far as the eye could see.

For the next week or two I would follow the Chu River west as far as possible. Like many rivers in Central Asia, it started off with great promise from high in the Tien Shan Mountains but shrank as it flowed inland, finally disappearing in a series of salt lakes and thirsty flats. Every year in spring, however, fresh snowmelt flushed through its system, bringing a fleeting abundance of life. For the first time on my journey this thin green line suggested the kind of reprieve I had been dreaming of: ready access to water and the prospect of plentiful grazing.

That first night out of Ulanbel I slept in the tent without a warm hat for the first time in six months, and rose in the morning feeling light and clearheaded. By sunrise I was in the saddle, and I knew at once I was in for a good few days. Following a series of horse tracks, we crossed empty flats, then threaded our way between tall desert bushes. There was always water to our right and grazing to our left. By lunch we had covered 20 kilometres; by dinner more than forty.

There was a lightness and freedom to every step, and it reminded me of the original vision of my journey – riding through a land where no thoughts, feelings or the land were fenced in. I gazed admiringly across at Tigon, and our eyes met in happiness. No one had ever told this skinny little pup from the back blocks of eastern Kazakhstan that he would never survive a journey like this, and so there was truly no limit to what he dreamed to become.

The following evening I brought the horses to a slow walk among a carpet of orange and red tulips. Between them crawled hundreds upon hundreds of tortoises. There were so many it was nearly impossible not to tread on them. Tigon was fascinated at first by the plodding tortoises, but soon decided they didn't play fair when they receded into their shells. Later, at our camp, he growled half-heartedly when they crossed by the tent, and watched curiously as they waddled past his nose and onwards into the scrub.

I soon came to understand that tortoises and wild-flowers were not the only life unharnessed by spring. Tigon's ears rose suddenly to attention, and the horses went stiff and tall.

I turned, and locked eyes with a chestnut stallion, his tail raised like a war banner and ears speared forward. At first I watched, captivated, as he snorted, pawed at the earth, and marked his territory with droppings. But then he pranced forward and my mind began to race. Spring was a time of chaos and conflict for horse herds, as maturing mares were kicked out of the family and stallions fought for mating partners. I'd heard stories of competing stallions wielding their hooves like hammers and fighting to the death.

The stallion began circling, his focus bearing down on my horses, who stood defenceless in their hobbles. Tigon leapt to defend them, but the stallion charged anyway. I ran between the stallion and the horses, taking aim with rocks and sticks. When finally a rock landed between the stallion's eyes, he retreated for a minute or two, but then came charging in again.

This routine went on until midnight, at which point I managed to chase him beyond camp. At dawn, he was back again, and just as I became absorbed in cooking porridge he took his opportunity.

When I looked up, a blur of mane, tail, and teeth was bearing down on Ogonyok. Ogonyok turned to run, but the stallion mounted him from behind, dug his teeth in, and dragged them along his spine from head to tail. Ogonyok reached the end of the tether that was tied to his front leg and somersaulted to earth. Almost at the same time, the stallion came crashing over the top, and the metal stake

Mongolia

▲I set sail on my journey with my first three horses – Bor (white), Kheer (bay, left) and Saartai Zerd (chestnut, right). Ahead: a world without boundaries, 10,000 kilometres of steppe to the Danube River.

▼In a land without fences hobbles are crucial for allowing horses to graze without risk of flight.

▶It was scenes of nomad life like this that had inspired me years earlier. All nomads across the steppe once lived in these collapsible, wool felt tents known as *gers* in Mongolian or yurts in English.

▶▶A proud Mongolian horseman near Kharkhorin. I can barely ride, but I am inspired to learn from nomads like him whose ancestors have been riding horses for at least five or six thousand years. The same evening after I met this man my horses were stolen.

▲I was lucky to learn that a 'man on the steppe without friends is as narrow as a palm . . . and a man on the steppe with friends is as big as the steppe'.

▼A *ger* being deconstructed for migration.

▶Riding Rusty with Kheer in tow on the way to Bayankhairkhan. I'm starting to feel a little more confident in the saddle.

▶▶A proud woman leads her caravan down from the Kharkhiraa-Turgen Uul mountains to the plains for autumn camp. Each camel can carry up to 300 kilos.

▲◄For nine months of the year most school-age children from nomadic families live with relatives in towns or in boarding houses at their schools. In summer, however, the steppe is alive with children as they partake in the daily work rituals.

▼Preparing for the long winter is never far from the minds of nomads. The meat cut into strips and hanging to dry is known in Mongolian as *borts*. In this way the meat can be preserved for many months. As I discovered it is also very light and easy to carry – no wonder they say that in old times by using *borts* horseback warriors could carry a sheep in their pocket.

◄◄The endless summer task of churning fermented mares' milk, *airag* (*kumys* in Kazakh).

▲Rusty and I survey Khokh Nuur (Blue Lake) near the 3,000-metre-high pass between Kharkhiraa and Turgen Uul. This photo and many others were taken on a tripod with a twenty-second timer – I had to run and jump on and hope for the best!
▼Dashnyam's oldest daughter, carrying her baby sister.
▼ ▼Dashnyam, a nomad from near the village of Tarialan who guided me across the Kharkhiraa-Turgen Mountains (centre) sits with his wife (right of photo), friend (left), and several of his five children.
▶Dashnyam astride his one and only horse.

▼Kazakhs of Bayan Olgiy Aimag in Western Mongolia still live a traditional nomadic life such as might have been the reality for Kazakh communities from the Altai Mountains to the Caspian Sea.

Kazakhstan

▲From the Altai Mountains in Eastern Kazakhstan the vast Kazakh steppe spreads out to the west as far as the eye can see. Ahead lies nearly 3,000 kilometres of plains and desert to the Caspian Sea.

▲Aset, with his disabled son, Guanz, who is trying out my Australian saddle on Taskonir, Zhana Zhol, Eastern Kazakhstan.

▲▲Tigon's first winter – he was desperate to get his paws off the snow. Days later Aset would give Tigon to me. 'In our country dogs choose their owners. Tigon is yours,' he told me.

▼Taskonir had an aura of seniority, soul and leadership about him. He was always the calm in the storm, and when things became hard I could rely on him to keep the other horses in line.

▼▼A patient yet wary Ogonyok stands as I finish loading my gear. In winter it was a task that usually took around three hours and mostly in the dark.

▶Bakhetbek and his family took Aset and myself in just as a fierce blizzard descended. In line with the traditional Kazakh culture of honouring guests, Tigon was fed even before their own dogs, and my horses were given pride of place in a barn with precious feed supplies.

▲Kazakhs believe that when a guest walks through the front door, luck flies in through the window. The magic of this belief was embodied by my meeting with Bakhetbek.

▲▲As winter descended I rode south to escape deep snow, but here, north of Lake Balkhash, there was no snow at all – and therefore nothing to water the horses with.

▼A lonely Kazakh grave on the north shore of Lake Balkhash – the kind that Aset advised me to sleep in for protection by the 'old men' of the steppe.

▼▼Self-portrait on the Betpak Dala, the Starving Steppe, two days to Christmas. Temperature was dropping below – 30°C.

▶Bazibek and his camel rise to greet the morning sun near the town of Ortaderisin on the northern shores of Lake Balkhash.

◀▲Getting porridge cooking in camp on the Betpak Dala. Tigon is out of sight, curled up in my sleeping bag.

▲The grim goldmining town of Akbakai on the Betpak Dala where I became holed up for the best part of three months.
▶Baitak – the man to whom I owe the life of my horses, Tigon, and the journey itself. Akbakai.
▼The snow has melted, giving me a window to ride out from Akbakai. Ogonyok and I survey the view across the Betpak Dala.

▲Spring has arrived. Children hold some freshly picked tulips next to their woolly camel near Tasty on the river Chu, Kazakhstan. Soon it will be time for the camels to have their spring haircuts.

▼Fresh spring grass breathed colour and life back into the steppe. This morning Taskonir shares my morning oatmeal porridge – not to be outdone by Tigon, of course, who is also fighting for his fair share.

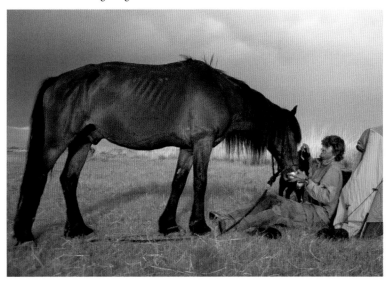

▲It was this family in Zhuantobe who nursed Tigon back to health after his near death run-in with a car. We are about to ride out and find my horses that have been grazing all day in the steppe beyond the village.

▲▲A nomad child wanders casually amid a giant camel herd.

▶Tigon and I often took naps during my night riding routine. This time we have slept past dawn, but here on the banks of the Zhem River there is fortunately some shade to be found.

▼I film Murat Guanshbai's vast herd of camels being herded across the Zhem River, Western Kazakhstan.

© CORDELL SCAIFE

▶In mid-summer in Central Kazakhstan they often have at least forty days in a row of above 40°C. To escape the heat, I rode at night, and relied on finding shelter and water before the sun rose too high. It was the people who came to my rescue with extraordinary hospitality and generosity.

▶Tigon leads the way, and Taskonir and I follow along the banks of the Zhem River, Western Kazakhstan.

© CORDELL SCAIFE

Russia

© IGOR SHPILENOK

▲The 'Golden Temple' in Elista, Kalmykia – the largest Buddhist temple in geographical Europe. The Kalmyks are the descendents of Mongolian nomads who made the great trek from Asia to Europe in the seventeenth century.

▲Ogonyok, my loyal packhorse of the Dzhabe breed. Pictured on the frozen banks of the Volga after crossing out of Kazakhstan. This was only days after I thought the trip was lost when the horses bolted into the night near Astrakhan.

▲▲A male saiga *(Saiga tatarica)* on the Kalmyk steppe. Its horns, which are much sought after in China as a flu remedy, have made it the target of rampant poaching. Saiga are now critically endangered.

▶A Cossack Ataman of the Kuban with his son in traditional dress.

▼Ogonyok, Taskonir and Utebai happily grazing in one of the first fields I had seen on my journey . . . only moments before I am told that they have ruined a winter crop of barley. Stavropol Krai.

▼▼Cossacks of the Kuban Steppe in South Russia, a once proud horseback society, have become cultivators of the hallowed 'chernozem' (black soils). Their generosity of spirit, culture of hospitality and fierce will endures.

Crimea

▲Taskonir, Tigon and I stand on the edge of the Karabi Jayla, Crimea, overlooking the Black Sea. The high plains of the Crimean Mountain range were once a summer haven for nomadic Tatars.

▲▲Seryoga, a Russian from Staryi Krym, spent two weeks leading me through the forest and mountains of Crimea.

▶Seryoga and I eat the last of our remaining food as Tigon politely enquires about the status of his meal.

▼After more than two years on the road it was like a dream to bathe in the Black Sea waters. Here I am swimming with the palomino gelding, Kok.

▼▼Early morning, I lead the horses through the dry interior of the Crimea on my way to mainland Ukraine.

Ukraine

◄A 'Welcome to Ukraine!' Tigon receives a hero's greeting as we reach mainland Ukraine. Tigon had always been anything but a passenger on my journey, and by now he had grown into a fierce leader who guided the way.

◄Tigon expected the best of human beings everywhere we went, and perhaps because he appealed to their better side they almost always showed it to him.

▼One of the last photos of our family taken together with my father. My father Andrew, mother, Anne, seated. My brothers Cameron (left of photo) and Jonathan (right of photo). My sister Natalie sitting. Our family dog Pepper, who died during my early weeks in Kazakhstan.

▼▼A Hutsul man in traditional dress at the church in Berezhnystya on Saint Nikolai day. The felt hats are called *krysani*, and the heavy sheepskin vests are *kyptars*.

◄Yuri Wadislow carefully guides my horses over a snowdrift high on the Chorna Gora ridge of the Carpathians, Western Ukraine. There were many known challenges like this where I had always known things could easily go wrong. And yet the journey with all the unexpected obstacles had equipped me with the confidence and skills to deal with just about anything.

◄◄Tigon poses on a peak in the Carpathians. By this stage of the journey he has probably run more than 15,000 kilometres and it has come to light that he has become a father (at least once).

Hungary

▲Keepers of Hungarian nomadic heritage: Kassai Lajos, demonstrating his prowess as a horseback archer.
▶▶Tamas Petrosko, who rode horses from Bashkiria in Russia to the Danube in honour of his ancestors.

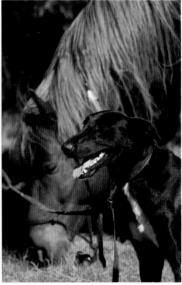

▲Peter Kun, a professor and ranch owner who became an example to me of how to integrate the wisdoms of nomadism into modern life.

▲▲The last morning of my journey was bittersweet. I had started the trip terrified of horses and unable to ride, but now I could not imagine life without my horses. Taskonir (pictured) was a true hero who had carried me most of the way.

▶Tigon is a picture of strength and courage that inspires me each and every day. His heart and spirit had always been so much bigger than his frame. I don't know how to explain to him that this is the final day of our journey.

▼I dismount on the banks of the Danube – the end of the steppe, and the completion of my journey.

that Ogonyok had been tied to torpedoed overhead. It wasn't over yet, though. The stallion reared up and began preparing to charge at Taskonir. Taskonir had no chance, hobbled and tied as he was.

That was when Tigon came to the rescue.

'Tiigoon!' I screamed as he launched into action. Tigon might have been growing fast, but he was no match for an experienced stallion. The stallion turned and gave chase, catching Tigon immediately. I watched helplessly as the stallion bit down on Tigon's back before flinging him a good 10 metres through the air like some kind of rag doll. Tigon landed like a bag of bones, but was up and running almost before he hit the ground.

Only after I had chased the stallion with yet more rocks and sticks did he retreat to the dunes. When the dust had settled, Tigon lay curled up and whimpering in the tent. He didn't seem to be injured, but the same couldn't be said of Ogonyok. As I brushed him down I uncovered two deep, bloodied fang tracks from neck to rump. I cleaned the wounds and resolved to carry rocks in my pocket from now on.

The stallion was not the only danger that seemed to have blossomed overnight. As I packed to leave, I noticed small bugs jumping aboard my boots and crawling up my legs. They were ticks, and on further inspection I found that hundreds of them had burrowed under the skin of the horses to suck their blood. The ticks were now swollen specimens the size of grapes hanging off the horses' chests, the sheaths of their penises, and under the tail around their anuses. It was dangerous work to pluck them off, especially from Ogonyok, who was sensitive at the best of times. In the process, many ticks exploded, and by the time I had finished, dark oozing blood as thick as sap had congealed with moulting horsehair and stuck like glue to my hands.

It was a relief to eventually climb into the saddle and pick up the momentum of the previous day. Yet while the coming days would not be quite as eventful as the past twelve hours, it was clear that my encounters with the stallion and the ticks were part of the many rhythms of spring I would have to learn to take in my stride.

A week's ride west from Ulanbel we approached an aul called Tasty – a cluster of houses on a peninsula of land that jutted out into a bend of the river. It was evening as I drew close, and herders were returning for the night with sheep and cattle from all directions.

I decided to wait it out before unpacking in darkness and making camp, but a herder spotted me with his binoculars and invited me to his home. The following day, while the herder's children took my horses out to graze, I joined him at a gathering of the aul's elders.

I squeezed in on the floor in the cool confines of a mud-brick house with whitewashed walls. Opposite me sat men with faces as old and gnarly as camel-gnawn desert bushes. Most had patchy grey whiskers and wore traditional Kazakh hats. Women wore silky vests and were wrapped up in white head scarves. Like most places I had been in Kazakhstan so far, most understood Russian. But here in the remote Moiynkum Desert where the people were further removed from the historical effects of the Russian Empire and the Soviet Union, Kazakh language was predominant and few could speak Russian fluently.

On the table between us sat a freshly boiled camel's head surrounded by mountains of baursak (the deep-fried dough Mongolians call boortsog) and plates of the national dish, beshbarmak.

'C'mon, Tim, eat!' the old men demanded.

Using the communal knife to cut meat from the cheek of the camel was one thing, but I was yet to master the eating of beshbarmak. The name means 'five fingers', and it is a dish of meat and boiled squares of pastry often cooked with wild onion. The technique of eating it involves scooping up the meat and angling it into the mouth so that the fat doesn't spill. When I tried, the hot fat and meat burned my fingers. As I shovelled the food down, pieces inevitably dropped to the floor, and the elders laughed.

That evening my host, Serik, led me to his one-month-old baby boy, who lay in an old crib sucking on a giant piece of sheep tail fat. As I bent over and smiled, Serik gripped my arm and gently pulled me back. In silence we left the room. Once out in the kitchen he told me, 'We Kazakhs believe that for the first forty days a baby has not been fully born and released by God to us, and must be protected from bad spirits, especially the evil eye of Zyn, which is like the devil. We would not usually show our baby to strangers during this time, only close relatives. We think you will bring good luck to our baby, but you should not look into his eyes.'

I had often wondered why babies I had seen in Kazakhstan and also Mongolia had black dots, usually from charcoal, on their forehead. My host explained, 'We make those dots to draw the attention of onlookers away from the baby's eyes. You would not even know yourself if you had the evil eye – don't be offended.'

Traditionally, Kazakhs used many techniques to keep bad spirits from harming the young. One involved giving the baby an unpleasant name that would make people laugh and therefore distract evil spirits. An amulet called a *tumar* was also worn, traditionally filled with a sample of the baby's own poo, although more commonly the tumar holds a prayer from the Koran nowadays.

From Tasty there remained just 40 kilometres of riding along the Chu River to the town of Zhuantobe. During the two days it took me to get there, I never quite found my rhythm again.

Leaving Tasty was awkward after I discovered that my headlamp and watch were missing – it turned out they had been stolen by Serik's children.

Then, just half a day from the aul, Tigon's life very nearly came to an abrupt end.

It all happened in the blink of an eye. Floodwaters had forced us up onto the edge of the deserted dirt road that ran to Zhuantobe, and it was there that Tigon caught sight of a car for one of the first times in his short life. It began as a dot, hurtling in from the west, and quickly grew into a large approaching missile. Tigon stood in the middle of the road, transfixed, eyes narrowed into the sun, cocking his head to one side, then the other. Only as the car began to bear down on us did I realise that Tigon was not going to move.

'Tigon!!'

I closed my eyes. There was a sickening thump.

When I opened my eyes Tigon lay bleeding and unconscious, tongue out and sprawled. The car was long gone.

I was sure he would not survive, but we were in luck.

I waved down the very next vehicle, a motorbike with a sidecart.

'Is there a vet in the next village?' I asked in panic.

'*I am* the vet from the next village!' he replied, switching the engine off and coming to my aid.

It was at that point that Tigon regained consciousness, rolled over onto his back and demanded a pat on his belly, one eye slightly open.

TIM COPE

Tigon had a broken rib and concussion. The vet arranged for him to be taken to Zhuantobe, where he would be looked after until my arrival.

When I reached the town two days later I was greeted by a throng of barefoot children eager to lead the way to Tigon. I found him lying like a prince in the shade of an outhouse. He had been dining on bowls of fresh milk, meat scraps, and his favourite, eggs.

After two days Tigon was on his feet again, but it was clear that both spring and the respite of the Chu were over.

The heat had arrived, and not far west of Zhuantobe the river came to a finish, spilling into a series of salt lakes and swamps. In what would prove a taste of the conditions in coming months, we covered the next 120 kilometres in two long, hot days. At first I was guided by a local man and his friend on a motorcycle, but halfway across their fuel ran low, and we ran out of water.

The last 60 kilometres to the next aul, which I rode alone, were unbearably thirsty and hot. I pushed the horses across the shadeless steppe and desert until finally the olive-green ridge of the Karatau Mountains emerged from the dusty horizon. Beyond them lay the Syr Darya – one of Kazkh- stan's biggest and most important waterways – which I hoped would be my next lifeline, carrying me deep into central Kazakhstan.

Not long ago I had dreamed of the sun and its life-giving rays. Before long, however, I would be living in fear of it.

12

Ships of the Desert

In the late autumn of 1219, Genghis Khan rode along the freezing banks of the Syr Darya, leading somewhere between 90,000 and 200,000 men and probably at least twice as many horses. In Genghis's sights was the city of Otrar, which lay on the northern banks of the river.

A year earlier, the governor of Otrar, Inalchuk, had enraged the Mongol leader by executing a 450-man merchant caravan from Mongolia. This was more than enough to invite the wrath of Genghis, and he set forth with a carefully planned campaign to conquer all of Central Asia. As a nomad, Genghis was well aware that the success of any campaign depended on timing with the seasons. Travelling in autumn and fighting through winter was a crucial part of his strategy. That way he could avoid the heat of summer, and because there would be dew on the ground there'd be more pasture and less need to find water. As rivers froze over in late autumn and winter, his army could also cross them at will.

When the scorching heat of summer arrived in 1220, Genghis Khan's timing was proved nothing short of genius. Otrar had been destroyed and its governor, Inalchuk, executed by having molten silver poured in his eyes and ears. Following a trek across the Kyzlkum Desert, a section of Genghis's army had also surprised the holy city of Bukhara, where Genghis proclaimed that he had been sent by God to punish the city's rulers for their sins. Samarkand was the next to fall before Genghis and his army retreated to the hills to rest and graze their animals for the summer.

At the age of fifty-seven, Genghis was now the ruler of an empire that stretched from Persia to Peking.

In contrast with Genghis Khan's first major foray into Central Asia, *my* approach to the Syr Darya was not going well. Two days west of the aul of Karatau I woke at midday, slumped against a twisted tree root, and listened to blood throbbing through my ears.

The sun burned through my eyelids and pressed down on my cheeks like an iron. During my snooze the sliver of shade under the poplar tree had moved, and the horses likewise had shifted, their heads propped forward in the shade. Tigon had dug himself into a fresh hole and lay panting with his tongue out on the dirt and his eyes reduced to slits.

I felt lethargic and dizzy, so it took me some time to pull myself away from the tree trunk and reach for the battered plastic soft drink bottle that held my drinking water. Earlier, I'd been lucky to find a well next to an abandoned winter hut and managed to lower my collapsible bucket to the water using tether ropes. As I pulled the bucket up it had broken away from the ropes, but I had managed to lower this drink bottle, and I had watered the horses from my cooking pots.

As this hot, algae-filled water now flushed out my throat, the stench of dry manure rose through my nostrils. The smell would have been a comforting symbol of family and togetherness in the winter and early spring, when there might have been hundreds of cattle, sheep and horses milling about this tree, the only one I'd seen in two days. Now, though, the lingering fragrance of livestock was a sharp reminder that the people had moved away to the safety of summer pastures and I was alone.

The sickly feeling that I was travelling against the grain of the seasons had been building. In recent days the land had been dotted with empty huts with boarded-up windows and abandoned yards. The only people I had seen were a family who had just migrated from the Moiynkum Desert. They had looked at me gravely. 'Soon the flies will be here,' they told me. 'Down on the Syr Darya River, where you are going, they will be even worse. If you leave your horse tied up for half an hour there, it will be dead. And don't forget, here in Central Kazakhstan we never go a summer without forty days in a row above forty degrees!'

Neither flies nor forty degrees had yet come, but it was only April and the temperature was reaching 30°C by nine am. I'd been riding as much as I could in the cool of the early hours and resting through the heat of the day, then plodding on when the sun had backed off. It was terrifying to think that summer was yet to even officially begin.

The goal of this leg of my journey was to navigate about 2000 kilometres through Kazakhstan's arid centre – a vast, sparsely populated region of deserts that lie midway between Mongolia and Hungary – and then west to the Caspian Sea. It was here that Friar Carpini, who had travelled to Mongolia from Europe around 800 years earlier, recorded the most harrowing leg of his journey. He wrote that it was so dry 'many men die from thirst', and that he had 'found many skulls and bones about in heaps over the ground'.

My original plan had been to make this traverse in the winter, when the slightly warmer temperatures and a thin layer of snow would have been an advantage. The hold-ups in Akbakai, however, had left me on course for one of the driest parts of the country at the hottest time of year – a prospect that any nomad, and certainly Genghis Khan, surely would have done all they could to avoid.

Late in the afternoon, when the sun's heat waned, I rode on. I had broken my planned route into three stages, each of which I estimated would take a month. The first and easiest would be to drop south to the Syr Darya River and follow it about 500 kilometres to the point where it spills into the Aral Sea. From there I would break away towards the river Zhem. The final phase would be southwest along this river, which I hoped would see me through the western deserts to within range of the Caspian Sea. If all went according to plan, I would be entering Russia come autumn.

A few days later, when the Syr Darya finally came into sight, it appeared just as it did on my map: an improbable artery lined with banks of leathery green flowing through mustard-yellow desert towards the Aral Sea. It was a fabled river dotted with ancient towns and cities, but equally known for environmental catastrophe. In the 1950s waters from the Syr Darya had been diverted to feed the cotton industry. While irrigated crops in the desert had bloomed, further downstream the Syr Darya had slowed to a dribble. As a result the Aral Sea – into which the river flowed – had shrunk to a puddle, leaving whole fleets of fishing boats and ships stranded in the sands.

For the first week or so the river offered reprieve. I moved with rhythm, watering the horses regularly in irrigation canals. In the early morning the horses moved swiftly, their hooves shuffling quietly through sand. Tigon was enlivened, sniffing, digging, ears up and alert, and taking regular dips in the canals whenever he got too hot. As the sky grew from purple to shades of crimson, I could see the glassy surface of the river, and yurts nestled among sand dunes.

During the day it was hot and suffocating, but there was shade to be found, and evenings were pleasant, particularly in the dusty, sun-baked auls. At dusk young children – already with dark summer tans – played on the sandy streets, and old women sat on benches, chatting in their long, colourful gowns and scarves. Dung-fired stoves came to life, the bittersweet aroma of the smoke mingling with the smell of camels, which, naked and grey-skinned after recently being clipped, wandered freely through the streets. I was offered fermented drinking yoghurt, *airan*, which had a tangy flavour that lingered well into the next day.

But this smooth passage was fleeting. After little more than a week, vegetation gave way to shadeless plains of clay and sand. The canals dried up, auls became rare, and the days longer and hotter. And then, as I had been warned, the flies came.

The first swarm descended on me one stifling morning as I attempted to descend the muddy banks of the river. The sludge was so thick there was a risk of the horses becoming bogged, so I had improvised a new bucket for carrying water to and fro. No sooner had I dismounted, tied the horses and returned with the first pail, than the sound of a thousand little race engines filled my ears. As Tigon dived into the water to escape the hordes – only his ears and nose rising above the water line – the poor horses bucked this way and that, swished their tails and shuddered intensely. Within minutes, each horse had streams of blood running from their spines, down their rumps, ribs and necks. I raced about swatting as many as I could, but as numbers built I abandoned the river and rode out as quickly as possible. The river that brought life into the desert would, from now on, also be a curse.

For the next three weeks – the time it took me to reach the river mouth – I watched the silty brown water grow sluggish and the land fade to pale yellow. There were no crisp edges to the horizon anymore, or even to days, or thoughts. Everything wobbled, frayed and melted in surrender to the heat.

Then, just as I broke away from the Syr Darya, things really started to get tough.

Temperatures were now hitting 40°C daily, and when the sun came up there was simply nowhere to hide. The horses' sweat dried off as quickly as it beaded, and my saddle was hot to touch. But it was poor Tigon with his black coat who was hit the hardest. He would sprint ahead, searching for even the frailest desert plants, where he would dig furiously to find cooler sand and soil. No sooner had he dropped into it, tongue flopping lifelessly onto the ground, than we would catch up and pass him. He would watch us go past with a look of dread, and wait until we were nearly out of sight before making another dash. When there was no shade at all, he would stand there desperately thirsty, his black coat as hot as melting tar, feet burning on the sand, crying. All I could do was fill my hat with water for him to drink from and sprinkle some of the precious supplies over his back. Every now and then we were lucky enough to find a drinking trough, and he would always be the first to leap in – a bone of contention for the horses, who would nip at him until he leapt out and away.

The only way to survive the summer from here on was to ride at night. And so began a routine of saddling up the horses at sunset and riding through those shallow, life-giving hours – the aim being to find water and some kind of shelter before sun-up. It was a routine that would see us through the remainder of summer alive, but which also had its dangers.

A couple of days in, it became clear that getting sleep during the daylight hours would be near impossible. Despite covering the tent with horse blankets and pads for shade, inside it was still so baking hot that it felt as if my blood were cooking in my veins. Sweat pooled in puddles inside the tent beneath me. Keeping an eye on the horses was crucial, and at this particular camp a stallion that had pursued us earlier in the morning remained on the attack. Every time I felt a hint of sleep pulling me under, I found myself having to reach for the nearest stick or rock and go charging off again.

When the sun went down my spirits lifted, but all my body wanted to do was sleep. In the hours that followed it was only the constant task of keeping a lookout for Tigon that kept me awake. He spent his time roaming far and wide, his black coat impossibly hard to spot in the night.

When grey-blue light bled back into the landscape I was half asleep, and only vaguely aware of my surroundings. It was a dangerous state of mind to be in, particularly when I found myself crossing some old dry and empty canals via crude bridges made of ramps with narrow, wheel-width steel.

In my delirious state I tried to cross without doing the safe thing and dismounting first. Halfway across the bridge, I felt Taskonir's lead rope pull out of my hand. As I turned from my perch, Ogonyok – who was tied to Taskonir from behind – reared up, then planted his front hooves wide in an effort to reverse off the bridge. Taskonir was pulled off balance. I heard the scuffle of hooves on steel, then a crunch as he fell off the bridge and between the two ramps. The plastic pack boxes kept him from falling all the way through, but now he was wedged between the ramps, his legs dangling over the drop to the empty canal below! Ogonyok, still tied to Taskonir's pack saddle, was pulled forward by the short lead rope and now teetered on the edge of the bank, threatening to fall on top of Taskonir at any moment.

I rushed back to untie Ogonyok, then cut Taskonir's girth strap and ropes. As half a tonne of horse went tumbling down, I shut my eyes. No sooner had I reopened them, however, than Taskonir darted out of the canal, saved by the soft canal bed. I couldn't believe how foolish I'd been, or how lucky – Taskonir came away with little more than scratching and bruising.

When I left the bridge my little caravan was shaken up, and the temperature was pushing 40°C. It took another two or three hours to reach water and shade in the next aul, by which time the horses were stained with sweat and looking shrivelled. Come nightfall, when it was time to ride again, I had once again barely rested. And there lay the conundrum – it was dangerous to ride sleep-deprived at night, but suicide to move through the heat of the day.

*

By the time I reached what would once have been the shores of the old Aral Sea I had begun to develop some semblance of a routine, but it was here one afternoon that Tigon nearly reached the end of his tether.

We hadn't found shade that morning and had trudged on under the blazing sun in search of refuge. We had been going nearly twenty-four hours, much of it trudging through sandy dunes. With each climb came the hope of an oasis of shade, water, and pasture. But when the dunes finally gave way to plains all that lay in front of us was the endless, thirsty seabed. Fifty years earlier one might have been able to dive into cooling waters, but the shoreline had retreated by 100 kilometres and now the land was better known for its windstorms, which frequently whipped up clouds of salt, sand and toxic dust.

Tigon, as always, had taken the lead to the top of the rise. But even before I reached him, I saw his spirits crumble. His tail dipped between his legs, his ears, normally so tall and proud, flopped down to the sides listlessly, and his eyes looked sad and glazed. There was a hint of defeat.

'C'mon, Tigon,' I said, dismounting. Kneeling, I lay him backwards across me and stroked his long snout and his floppy, worn-looking paws. He closed his eyes, and for a time I did too. His head flopped over my thigh. The feel of his whiskers, and those little bumps where they came out around his chin, felt so familiar in my hands, as did those giant ears. It wasn't that long ago that I'd watched the tips of those ears covered in white frost, and he had growled at me for touching them. Now I stroked them, and I gave his chest a scratch and he didn't move a muscle. If anything, his body went even limper.

Beyond this little bit of comfort there was nothing I could do but get back on the horse. But when we did move on, Tigon refused to budge. He watched us sail away, believing perhaps that he could not go on. I couldn't look any more, so turned my back and kept riding. When I looked again, he was a mere black speck in a landscape that was impossibly huge. But that speck was now moving – he had begun a slow march on our trail.

From that day onwards until reaching the Zhem River the only water to be found was in auls. And so for the next few weeks I sought cover with families through the heat of day and did not camp. Typically, I would stumble into a community feeling spaced out and ask for somewhere to rest. My arrival was usually greeted with fanfare, but I could rarely last more than a cup of tea before passing out. The horses would be set free to find whatever grass was available around the aul. Tigon, meanwhile, would usually lap up an offering of milk and meat scraps before digging himself into a shady hole.

Sometimes I would wake to discover that my saddle or hobbles or ropes had been stolen. I would inform the oldest man or woman in the house, go back to sleep, and miraculously when I woke again everything would be back in its place.

Then, just as everyone was preparing to roll out their mattresses I would re-emerge, saddle up, call for Tigon, and ride on. It was a feeling of acute isolation, moving while the rest of the world slept. I missed my family and friends so much that I would put sunscreen on at night because the smell reminded me of fun times on the coast as a child. But there was a kind of dreamlike quality to this period of my journey that I loved.

As a child I had lived in fear of the dark, and gone running inside every time the wind rustled through the trees. But out here, the darkness was a lifeline, allowing me to fly under the radar and feel safe.

The cover of darkness also brought peace, and calm. With such a wide, trackless land, I was able to navigate by matching my compass bearing with star formations, following them for hours until they blinked out, one by one. I regularly napped in the saddle, and woke to discover that the horses had taken me astray. Other times I dismounted and slept on the earth. Tigon would often end up snoozing hard up against me, and he had begun a routine of pawing me in the face for one of two things: more pats, or because he wanted to keep running.

Sunrise was a sublime time of the day, when it felt as if I were riding the waves across the steppe. I would watch as our shadows gradually emerged on the land. Tigon's ears and head loomed huge, as did his tail and tongue – a more accurate projection of his bold and fearless spirit than the story that his sleek but muscular body told when the shadows had all but gone.

But once the sun was up, the long hours of the doldrums would begin.

It was on an afternoon in late June that I first laid eyes on the River Zhem. It was a shallow band of ale-brown water that carved its way through sandy hills dotted with dust-coated bushes and wormwood. In the distance the river split into multiple channels among the curves and ripples of sand dunes. No matter how tepid, broken or even saline the waters of this river were, they brought unspeakable relief.

No longer relying on auls for water, I could camp along the riverbank to see out the heat of day. During the hottest hours, I would roll out of the tent and lie in the river's shallows together with Tigon. Whenever Tigon was thirsty he would open his jaws wide and take sweeping bites of the water, as if he were a king luxuriating in a feast. The horses also relished the Zhem. They spent hours in the middle of the river, nibbling on fresh green reeds and overhanging bushes.

This section of the journey was made easier for the horses by a special addition to our team – a young Bactrian camel that I named Harvette. Her primary purpose was to carry some of our gear, but she also brought a welcome new cadence to these long hours of riding. She had a stoic rhythm and planted her feet carefully with every step, unlike the moody, short-tempered and sometimes careless horses. She was forever foraging around my kit bags, and it was not uncommon to see her sucking on my sauce bottle or getting into other food. On one occasion she devoured an entire watermelon!

Another change became evident in the early days along the Zhem. For two months I had been so absorbed with the task of surviving summer, there had been little opportunity to get a real feel for the people. Now, however, more accustomed to the rigours of summer travel, I could turn my attention to the people who called this desert home.

I was now in the lands of the Kishi Juz, or the Young Horde, a group of Kazakh tribes renowned both as a hardened warrior people of the desert, and also for holding on to their nomadic traditions.

At sunrise one morning I had ridden onto an elevated plain looking for water when there came a billowing plume of dust and the distinctive rumble of sheep and goats. After some time, the unmistakable figure of a man on the back of a camel came into view. The gap between us rapidly shrank until the man was leaning down from his giant animal with a handshake, imploring me to return with him to his home.

The herder's summer camp was a sight to behold. I was led through a huddle of around two hundred camels. Some sat on their haunches asleep, while babies frolicked on shaky stick-like legs, and two or three bulls sauntered about, their front thighs thick as tree trunks. There was something dinosaur-like about their lumbering power and grace.

In the centre of the huddle lay the camp itself – animal pens, a rusty old wagon, and an underground hut dug into the top of the riverbank. In this region Kazakhs spent summer squirrelled away underground during the day, and the cooler nights sleeping in a yurt or simply on mattresses under the stars. All the work – primarily milking camels – was done at dawn and dusk.

After unsaddling, I was led to a young woman who stood barely as high as the camel's back legs, her own right leg bent up to support a milk bucket on her thigh. While she milked, her infant daughter, who had barely learnt to walk, stumbled about among the camels, unfazed as a couple of particularly gigantic specimens edged closer and gently sniffed at her hair.

When the milking was done, the full pails were whisked away for the production of cream, yoghurt, dried curd and fermented camel milk, known as *shubat*. Two teenage boys who had been lying in wait for the last camel to be freed mounted their horses and roused the herd with shouts and whistles.

As the boys and their horses worked, the camels rose reluctantly to their feet, then moved to the edge of the riverbank. Only when the animals were bunched up did the first camels take the plunge. It began as a trickle – a few camels clambering down to the water – but soon became a torrent. Legs flew, saggy lips wobbled, the earth trembled, the sky filled with dust, and one by one they leapt into the river.

The boys continued after them, whistling and charging, urging on the lazier ones at the rear. I watched as the herd crossed to the far side, where they rapidly shrank to nothing more than faint specks in a land of empty horizons.

Back at camp, the temperature was cranking towards 40°C and what had been a hive of activity was now a picture of desolation. Hot wind gusted from the west, picking up dried dung from the empty pens and tossing it viciously through the air. A couple of dogs lay under the rusty wagon. Nothing moved. Tigon stuck close to my horses, who were standing still in the river below.

I was invited down some clay steps into the underground hut, where the glare and exposure gave way to darkness and intimacy. The family and I sat propped up on cushions gulping down fresh bowls of fatty camel milk in the dark until our host, a man named Murat Guanshbai, lit a candle. The light revealed a room padded with felt mats and wall hangings.

Murat was as exotic as his surrounds. He had a square, open face with a short flat nose, and his almond eyes were protected by bushy, overhanging eyebrows. Unlike most Kazakhs' hair, his was thick and curly, and his jaw was masked with stubble. Murat and his family were Kozha – a tribe known to be descendants of Bedouin nomads from the Middle East who had travelled to Kazakhstan some one thousand years ago.

Today Murat carried on nomadic traditions of his fore-fathers, moving between five different camps each year with a staggering 500 camels and untold numbers of other animals.

I stayed with Murat for two days and drank in every detail, from the sound of the camels moving back under moonlight to the sensation of lying down under the stars and waking under an eternally blue and cloudless sky. There was a completeness, an intertwining of nature, animal and man, that could not be replicated in a home divided by walls and fences.

One day south of Murat's the land became flatter, and the pasture grew thin. The temperature climbed over 50°C and the water became brackish, but still fresh enough to drink. Over the next week there were times when I was so exhausted by the struggle to keep cool during the day that I'd saddle up the horses at night, only to fall asleep before leaving. But the courage of Murat's family to live in this world inspired me to accept things as they were. And besides, a little hold-up here or there didn't matter anymore – the end of this chapter was drawing near.

It was the end of July when I packed up for my last day of riding along the Zhem. I had planned to carry on immediately along the Caspian coast to the Russian border, but the heat had taken a heavy toll on the horses. Back in the early days of summer I had traded away my older horse, Zhamba, to spare him from the ordeal. My replacement horse, a young stallion, had in turn quickly grown thin and weak and so I had traded him for a nuggety little grey horse called Kok. Kok, who had grown up in the deserts of Central Kazakhstan and was fresh from a life of grazing, was faring well, but now it was Taskonir and Ogonyok who I was worried about. Although they had shown incredible endurance, they were beginning to look a little bony, and their hair was pale and dry. I decided to find somewhere to leave the horses for a month of rest while I went to the city to apply for my Russian visa.

The thought of having time away from the punishing routine of night riding made me giddy. And come the cool of September, when I planned to return, summer would be over and my horses would be fat and energised. At least, that was the plan . . .

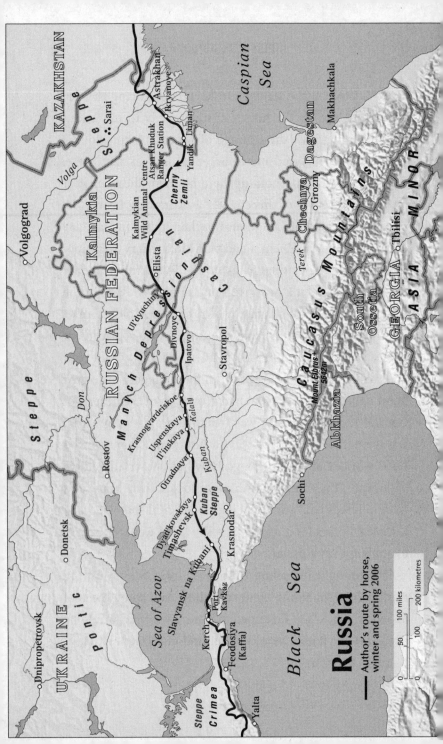

Russia

— Author's route by horse,
winter and spring 2006

KAZAKHSTAN

Caspian Sea

RUSSIAN FEDERATION

Volgograd

Steppe

Astrakhan
Kryanoye
Sarai
Steppe
Atsan Khuduk Ranger Station
Kalmykian Wild Animal Centre
Yandik
Tuman

Kalmykia

Cherny Zemli

Makhachkala

Dagestan

Elista
Urdyuchini

Manych Depression

Caspian Steppe

Chechnya
Grozny

Terek

Volga
Don

Rostov

Divnoye
Ipatovo
Stavropol

Steppe

Pontic

Donetsk

Dnipropetrovsk

UKRAINE

Krasnogvardeiskoe
Uspenskaya
Il'inskaya
Otradnaya

Kalaly

Kuban

Caucasus Mountains
Mount Elbrus
5642m

South Ossetia

GEORGIA
Tbilisi

ASIA MINOR

Abkhazia

Sochi

Kuban Steppe
Dyadkovskaya
Timashevsk
Slavyansk na Kubani
Krasnodar

Sea of Azov

Port Kavkaz
Kerch

Feodosiya (Kaffa)

Steppe
Crimea

Yalta

Black Sea

0   50   100 miles
0   100   200 kilometres

13

Hoofsteps into Europe

For four months my journey had been all about summer in Kazakhstan. The vast sunburned land had taken its toll, but those long nights under the stars had also given me strength and a sense of confidence and calm that I thought was unbreakable. I was well past the halfway mark to the Danube, and about to exit Asia and enter the kinder weather conditions of Europe. I had visions of tracking along the edge of the Caspian Sea in a cool breeze, taking swims on sandy beaches, then effortlessly sailing into Russia and beyond. Surely the toughest part of the journey was behind me. Tigon and I were prepared for everything that lay ahead.

In reality, I would never see the Caspian Sea – as it turns out, the river Zhem dries up before reaching the coast, and the shores are mired with mosquito-infested swamp – and my journey would soon be on the brink of total failure. I was about to escape the hardship of the unforgiving land, only to be caught in a dangerous web of human design.

My first glimpses of this very different world I was entering were on the outskirts of Kulsary, an oil town 100 kilometres shy of the Caspian Sea. I had planned to leave the horses here to graze and recover while I went to apply for my Russian visa.

On approach to the town the open desert gave way to mangled earth that had been bulldozed into a maze of mounds and ridges. Then came twisted, rusty pieces of steel, shattered glass and burned-out cars. Heavy trucks and SUVs hurtled past on the asphalt road at unchecked speed, spraying gravel and leaving us in a wake of dust and fumes.

The brave Taskonir trembled, and Tigon looked on, unsure. This was more hostile, unkind and difficult to survive than any desert we had seen.

Eventually I paid some herdsmen in a nearby aul to look after the animals while I was away. But as it turned out the people there were in desperate times struggling to feed their own animals. When I returned after a month I was in for a shock. Word had it that the grain and hay I had bought had been used to feed the herdsmen's own animals. I found Taskonir tied up at the back of a corral.

He was skinnier than when I had left him and his eyes were dull and lifeless. His coat was sun-bleached and as dry as straw, and he barely had the energy to acknowledge me. How would he survive the journey ahead?

Even worse: the other two horses were missing.

After a tip-off from a neighbour, I found men swinging axes into freshly slaughtered horse carcasses in a nearby gully. The horses weren't mine, but the men knew who I was and waved me on further, where I spotted Kok and Ogonyok being raced at full gallop! They had been entered in a *baiga* – a horse race – that was to be held the next day!

Albek, the herdsman I had paid, was partially forgiven when Tigon came running and leapt up onto my chest with those big white paws. His long tail, as always, didn't so much wag as swing in long, wide roundabouts. After a frenzied pat and embrace he leapt away to run figure-of-eights, before finally coming to rest by my legs on his back with his belly upturned, jaws snapping and paws pedalling in the air.

I left the aul thankful to Albek and his family that my animals were at least alive and intact.

It would only take me a couple of weeks to reach the Ural River and technically cross into Europe. But as it turned out, the issues with the horses' care were just the beginning of my problems. In theory, Russia was only a couple more weeks' ride beyond the Ural River. In practice it would be more than three months before I successfully crossed the border, and even then only by a thread.

Besides being taken in by police who accused me of being a terrorist, and falling ill with food poisoning, the biggest threat to my journey was when Russian border guards stopped me in my tracks:

'You do not have the right papers for your horses, so you cannot pass. You can leave your horses and dog impounded with us, and go alone into Russia . . . or you can go back to Kazakhstan.'

When I tried to return to Kazakhstan, the Kazakh border guards complained that I had illegally exported my animals from their country and therefore could not re-enter. I spent a day grazing in no-man's-land before eventually being allowed in. I then had no choice but to leave the horses and Tigon near the border while I went to a nearby city to get all the necessary papers. But that's when I hit a roadblock.

There were no such things as permits for travelling horses, or dogs for that matter. For two months I barely slept. Every attempt to persuade the authorities failed. My visa would expire soon, which would leave me no choice but to abandon all my animals, Tigon included. What would become of them?

Meanwhile, the beautiful riding weather of September slid into winter. Come December and my twenty-seventh birthday, the first snow already lay on the ground.

In mid-December, on the day before my visa expired, I began saying my goodbyes to the people who had tried to help me. The next task was to find a new home for my animals. I did not have the money to buy new ones in Russia, so it seemed this was the end of my journey.

That's when a miracle unfolded.

The secretary to the local veterinary department came to me with tears in her eyes and whispered: 'I got it.'

She held up a fresh fax from Moscow in her trembling fingers: *This is to certify Australian traveller Tim Cope can transport his three horses by riding them. His one dog can be carried by its own four legs.*

But my troubles were not over just yet. Upon arriving in Russia the first obstacle was to cross the mighty Volga River.

The only bridge lay smack in the middle of Astrakhan – a bustling metropolis of more than half a million people. We wove a dangerous path through a sea of trucks, trams and cars, hordes of pedestrians and lethal, ill-fitting manhole covers. Tigon was the only one of us who didn't seem worried. He strode proudly out the front, chest puffed up, nose in the air and tail high 'like a pistol', as the Russians told me. Crowds parted on the footpath to make way for this strange black dog who had come in from who knows where – perhaps like a fearless Mongol warrior of old.

The horses, on the other hand, were terrified. Upon reaching the far side of the city after dark Ogonyok was so spooked that as soon as I dismounted he bolted, still packed and saddled. Taskonir and Kok bounded off into the darkness after him, leaving me nothing but my thermos, video camera and satellite phone.

Local police and emergency services came to my aid, but after a fruitless all-night search we retired empty-handed to the police station. At six am I was woken by shouting. One of the policemen was leaning over me, his machine gun slung over his shoulder. 'Wake up! You have to get in the car! I have had a dream that I went fishing and caught three fish – a brown, a grey and a red one, the same colour as your horses. I just know we are going to find your horses this time!'

An hour later we came across a long trail of equipment leading to my horses. The policeman, machine gun and all, strode over to Ogonyok and planted a kiss on his nose. It was the one and only time that I would ever see Ogonyok *not* fart anxiously at the approach of a stranger.

Once again, it seemed that while misadventures often began with a sense of terror, they usually ended in a new friendship.

It wasn't until after Christmas as we travelled southwards along the banks of the Volga River that we broke free of the tangle of cities.

Although the Volga was beginning to freeze, the sun was out and grass and water were plentiful. In the evenings we rejoiced in the simplicity of our campsites – the horses rolling on their backs on the thick, frost-nipped grass, Tigon curling up with one eye on the dinner pot, and me looking forward to a long, unbroken night of sleep.

Taskonir's winter coat began growing back, thick and luminous, and he once again became the leader of the group, nipping Ogonyok in the rump whenever he could.

But it was Tigon who made the biggest mark on our milestone crossing into Russia.

There were the usual signs of excitement: running circles around our little troupe of horses, rolling around on his back to scratch himself on the rougher plants and grasses, and delighting in giving any animal that crossed our path a little bit of a scare. He would bound over, pounce in front of them, and with his elbows on the ground and bum and tail in the air, bark at them until they were spooked and went running.

However, one afternoon as I watched him sniff about the reeds next to the water's edge, I witnessed the biggest step forward for my little but growing companion.

After burying his nose in a clump of reeds a few times he paced back and forth and side to side, until suddenly it happened: with his nose lifted high into the wind and his ears back, he cocked his back leg and took a pee. He missed the target of course – it would take months and years to perfect that. Until now, he had only ever squatted on all fours to pee. This new trick of his meant that he had officially moved on to his young adult years.

For the rest of the day, and for every day ahead, Tigon seemed to realise that not only did his world expand with every new smell and every new sight, but he had an ability – an obligation, in fact – to leave his own mark for others. Later that evening when we reached a hilltop overlooking a vista of steppe plains, he looked at me, seeming a little weary and burdened: 'Tim?' he seemed to say, gazing over the thousands of grass tussocks, bushes and other important marker posts of our route . . . 'When are you going to start getting off your horse and helping me?'

Where the Volga began to spread out into a giant coastal delta I turned the horses west. It was inevitable that my journey from here would take me deeper into settled lands. Ahead lay the steppes of southern Russia, Crimea, Ukraine and Hungary – places where nomad cultures still existed, but where migratory life had, for the most part, slipped into the past.

But there was one last outpost of nomad life. Just west of the Volga lay the famed nomad lands of 'Kalmykia'.

The Kalmyks were a people of legend that had burned bright in my mind for years. They were Buddhist Mongolians whose ancestors were the last nomads to make the great trek from Asia into Europe. For centuries they had carried on their traditions here in Russia, migrating with their vast herds on the edge of the Volga delta.

It was said to me that in the thirteenth century the Kalmyks – or more specifically, the Torghut tribe of Kalmyks – were handpicked as the bodyguards of Genghis Khan. But they were now better known as survivors of an unimaginable tragedy. In the winter of 1771 roughly 150,000 Kalmyks and their animals set out on foot and horseback to return to Mongolia. They fell victim to the bitter conditions, and also to their old enemies, the Kazakhs. Wells were poisoned along their route and their caravans terrorised. Barely 50,000 men, women and children survived. As it turned out, my own route from Mongolia had unwittingly followed much of this death march, but in reverse.

It took only a couple of days of riding from the Volga to reach the end of the road, and the beginning of wild, waterless steppe. A local Russian ranger, Anatoliy Khludnev, had agreed to guide me in his Russian jeep through a steppe wilderness known as the 'black lands' and into Kalmykia proper. He would take his gun in case we ran into wolves or thieves.

I packed a week's supply of food and set off. Far from the waters of the Volga now, the air chilled, the sky cleared, and horizons opened. Frozen shallow ponds sparkled like silvery discs embedded in the earth.

Through this picture of sky, earth and grass cut the figure of Tigon – sometimes on the horizon, sometimes close on our tail but always on watch, the roaming ears and eyes of our little caravan. Among his many subtle traits, I had noticed for months now that when he led the way and his ears were up and forward, the tip of his left ear quivered ever so slightly. I could become lost in thought for hours as I watched this wobbly, furry antenna.

When Tigon did take a break, he would be quick to find a tussock of grass, and after walking around in circles, one way and then the other, he would curl up. Unfortunately, when Tigon happened to rest on a particularly desirable piece of grass, Taskonir would make a beeline for him, and with a gentle nip and push with his nose, send Tigon rolling off onto the frozen earth.

For three days I followed Anatoliy along a centuries-old trail. By day Anatoliy told tales about the gruelling journeys of the merchants who had once used this trail. By night, as the temperature plummeted to around –20°C, he froze inside his vehicle and slept little.

We had a late lunch at an abandoned hut and decided to part ways. We had crossed an invisible line into Kalmykia, and besides, Anatoliy was short on fuel.

'See this trail here?' he said, pointing to a vague line of ruts and hollows that was more sketch than road.

'If you follow it and keep your compass between 270 and 290 degrees, then you should come to another hut.'

For the next three hours I rode with urgency, wanting to reach the hut as soon as possible. The sun sank into a smudge of black cloud and the cold drew in like a noose. I called Tigon in close and kept an eye on my compass. When the moon rose, my transition to an older world felt complete. I slowed to a walk, opened the bell on Taskonir's neck, and snuggled deep into my winter coat. After travelling nearly 40 kilometres I was beginning to worry I had missed the hut, but at around eleven pm three dark shapes emerged from the moonlit steppe, one carrying an oil lamp.

I was greeted by an old man reeking of vodka who introduced himself in Russian as the caretaker. I was led inside to a mattress, where my body withered, my vision blurred, and I collapsed into sleep.

When I woke I heard banter and heavy footsteps, and I opened my eyes to a group of four or five men clambering into the hut, dusting the frost off their army fatigue coats. The men's eyes were long and slender, and when they spoke I was astonished to hear the familiar sounds of Mongolian.

I joined the group around a wooden table. They opened a bottle of vodka, poured a shot each, and dipped their ring fingers in the liquid three times, before rubbing a little on their foreheads, sprinkling a bit over me, and throwing the rest in the air.

I imagined for a moment that these men were nomads who had just returned from a nighttime wolf hunt. In reality they were Kalmyk scientists and rangers. One of them, a professor, promised to show me the reason they were here.

The sky was still dark when we left the hut, the residual glint of stars sparkling above. An hour later I was told to crouch down. The faint twitching of a grass tussock betrayed the presence of an animal, and as I focused, a shaggy creature darted away.

By the time the professor had handed me the binoculars the grassland before us had shimmered to life and a flock of these creatures lifted like startled sparrows. The animals possessed goat-sized bodies draped in a thick winter coat and were scuttling along on twig-like legs. They were saiga.

I had heard stories about these enigmatic antelopes of the Eurasian steppe, but the herds of the black lands were the first I had seen on my travels. 'We have around eighteen thousand saiga left on the black lands,' the professor explained. Only twenty years ago there had been almost a million across the steppes of Kazakhstan and Kalmykia, but poaching was rife, and the males' horns were highly valuable on the Chinese medicine market. These days there might be fewer than 60,000 alive.

A short way past my first sighting, we startled another herd, this time much closer to us. No more than 100 metres ahead stood a male saiga. Backlit by the sun, his horns rose with a slight inward curve and a ribbed texture, looking like a set of glowing amber pincers. His head and trunk were so large and heavy-looking it seemed his matchstick legs might give way. It wasn't hard to believe this was a surviving ice-age species that had once lived alongside the mammoth and the sabre-toothed tiger.

When the male and his herd sprinted away, I was left breathless. The professor turned to me:

'Kalmyk steppe without saiga would be like tea without milk – very poor indeed. To protect the saiga we need to preserve our culture, and our heritage.'

In the coming months, I would begin to see that, like these Kalmyks, I would need to learn how to tread this difficult path – trying to hold on to the magic feelings, heart, and knowledge of the steppe while riding into the realities of a fast-changing modern world.

14

Cossack Borderlands

Winter descended on Kalmykia. Soon only the feathery tips of the very tallest tussocks could be seen protruding from the snow. Like the land, the people retreated into the long nights, biding their time. Saiga migrated southwards to warmer lands, and the wolves emerged hungry from their remote lairs. Word had it that there were more wolves this winter on the Kalmyk steppe than anyone could remember.

Rather than push on, I decided to pause for the coldest months. The horses were to be rested and grazed under the watch of Kalmyk herders until the beginning of spring.

It was on a chilly evening in early March that I found myself back in the saddle. I rode with a Kalmyk man named Anir, eyes locked on the horizon.

I rode in stony silence, gritting my teeth. All was not well.

I'd always imagined that spring would herald a new blossoming for my journey. Rejuvenated, and with what was surely my last winter on the steppe behind me, Tigon, the horses and I would press on, bristling with confidence and energy. For this next chapter we needed to travel almost 1000 kilometres to the Azov Sea, and although there were no major mountains or deserts to be tackled, it was a region of particular historic importance. It was here, after all, on the rich grasslands along Russia's southern rim that, in 1222, the Mongols first made their mark on European soil. In what became known as one of the most remarkable military campaigns in history, a small detachment of hardened nomads conquered their way from Central Asia to the Caucasus Mountains before descending onto these steppes and crushing an entire Russian army. In 1224 they rode back east through the deserts of Kazakhstan into Central Asia, where they rejoined the main Mongol forces and delivered their triumphant news to Genghis Khan.

But on my expedition into these historic lands, the unexpected had once again played its hand, and as spring dawned, the news I had to report was anything but triumphant.

At some point in late January, Kok, my hardy grey

packhorse, had stepped on a five-inch rusty nail that lodged deep in his hoof. It had gone unnoticed for many days before being removed. Sheila, the vet in Australia, said the infection had most likely reached the bone, meaning he would probably never recover; if he did, it might take six months.

I treated Kok as best I could for two weeks before making the heartbreaking decision to leave him behind. If he did make a recovery after I had gone, the Kalmyk herders would keep him. I had not asked them what they would do if he did not.

As we had turned our backs and ridden on, Kok had attempted to follow us. After falling to his knees he watched on, whinnying. I couldn't bear to look, and didn't turn around until his desperate cries had all but faded away.

I now had a replacement horse called Utebai – a small, young gelding who was not strong enough to make it to Hungary, but who I hoped would tide me over until I found a more appropriate replacement.

I tried to put aside the echo of Kok's grief and bewilderment, and concentrate on the here and now. But it was proving almost impossible. Even if I did finish the journey, wouldn't it be a failure anyway, without Kok?

Anir took me to a lone tree on a windswept hill. Covered in prayer flags and ribbons, it had been planted on the grave of a lama, perhaps centuries before. Following Anir, I led the horses clockwise around its thick old trunk three times. Tigon followed suit, marking it. 'Bullseye,' he seemed to exclaim. Anir threw vodka into the air.

'Tim,' he said, turning to me after maybe half a day of near silence.

'My grandmother told me that big problems and heart-break in life, is just like the rain. Keep riding forwards and the rain will eventually dry out, and once more you will be in the sun.'

I was starting to understand that happiness was not a just feeling, or something that happened when the stars aligned. It was a decision to weather the hard times, and focus on the positives, even when all hell might be breaking loose.

Later that day we paused once more. Framed between Taskonir's ears, the ridge we'd been following angled southwest, then gave way to empty plains. Forty kilometres ahead lay the Manych Depression, a system of rivers and lakes that marked the end of the wild steppe and the beginning of more fertile land.

Not long before descending, Anir broke the silence once more.

'You might think the hardest part of the journey is behind you, but it is only beginning. Ahead are towns, fields and roads – down there not even a wolf would find cover, and I don't know where you will camp.'

He finished with a Kalmyk blessing:

'May there be a white road ahead for you, and the sun shine on your horses.'

We rode long into the night to cross the Manych. When dawn broke the next morning, Anir had gone.

Somewhere during the night, the steppe had given way to fields, canals and endless lines of poplar trees. I rode along the outskirts of a town where locals were already out tilling their backyard plots. Out in the larger fields a horse and cart rattled its way along a lane, and an old tractor billowing smoke pushed through thick, brown mud and soil.

Until now I had always avoided roads and navigated the land by compass, but it soon became clear that I would need to rethink my approach. In the deep, soft soil of ploughed fields, the horses tired fast, and I became hemmed in by a web of irrigation canals. While trying to jump across one such canal Taskonir fell up to his chest in muddy water and spooked the other horses. As I tried to calm them, Tigon ran off chasing a hare and did not return. An hour of searching led me to a railway track where he lay stuck, his collar snagged on the metal rails.

I thought my luck had changed when I crested a hill the next evening and found myself looking down at a green sea of virgin spring pasture. It was sweet, thick, grass – the kind I could only have dreamed of in the arid steppes of Kazakhstan and Kalmykia. I found a hidden hollow for my camp and the horses ate until their stomachs were as tight as drums.

In the morning, I had only just emerged from the tent when a Russian jeep came barrelling down on us. The driver was on his feet before the engine cut out. 'So, you think you've found some good pasture?'

I nodded. The man angrily explained that I had destroyed his autumn-sown barley – there were apparently hefty fines for such 'vandalism'. I explained that it was one of the first fields I had seen since leaving Mongolia. But the man didn't leave until I had tied the horses to a row of trees on the edge of the field. As he drove off he shot me a venomous look. 'I hope you *do* keep grazing fields. Soon the mouse and rat poison will kill your animals anyway.'

Over the coming days remnants of open grasslands became increasingly rare, and just as Anir had warned, the only grazing to be found was among single-file rows of trees so narrow I could barely fit a tent on them. I could no longer afford to let the horses graze free, and tethering ropes had to be especially short. Afraid that Tigon, who loved catching mice and rats, might be poisoned, he too was permanently tied. I put him on a long leash and let him guide from the front of the caravan.

As I rode I cast my eyes sadly over Taskonir. With his coarse, tangled mane, stormy eyes and untamed spirit, he was a living descendant of wild horses that had only ever known the freedom of open steppe. I felt guilty for bringing him to a land where he did not belong. When animals, like people, are never tied up, then where are they to run? Tied up, and trapped as they were now, they had every reason to escape for their freedom.

A week of riding took me to the 'Kuban', the most fertile and heavily cultivated steppe in southern Russia. I expected conditions to grow more difficult here. Instead, I found the going slightly smoother. I was able to locate pasture along the banks of a series of rivers, and enjoyed the cover of reeds. Most of all, I took heart that I had reached the home of the Kuban Cossacks – the legendary horseback warriors of Russia's frontier.

One evening on the banks of the Kalaly River I had my first introduction to Cossacks. I had found what I had thought to be the ideal place for a rest day – a meadow on the riverbank, hidden from roads and almost entirely encircled by reeds. I had only just unloaded the horses, however, when motorbikes emerged from behind the reeds. My spirits sank as I contemplated a long, sleepless night.

One of the drivers nearly drove into me. Tigon barked and snarled as the driver's mop of curly ginger hair settled, and the engine cut out. The man barked back: 'What the hell are you up to?' He stood with hands on hips, his sights trained on me as I told my story rather pleadingly.

'Did you hear that, boys? Mongolia to Hungary. Bugger me!' he replied.

It turned out that I was apparently guilty of making camp in their private – and illegal – fishing hide-out. A deflated rubber raft was bundled out of a sidecar and pumped up by hand. Meanwhile, a picnic of salami, cucumber, vodka and beer was laid out.

The food and alcohol consumed, my new friends unpacked a pile of fishing nets and set about the main business of the evening. They had only just managed to paddle out from the reeds, though, when the large man received a call.

'Boys! Police! Quick! Let's get out of here!'

The raft was deflated in seconds, and everything was stuffed into sidecars before the bikes were push-started in a scramble of legs. As they tore away they yelled: 'Don't say a word or else! As soon as those cops have gone, we'll be back with more vodka!'

Fifteen minutes later the headlights of a Russian police jeep jittered across the uneven land. Three policemen stepped out stiffly. 'You haven't seen any poachers around here, have you? On motorbikes?'

The jeep had only just taken off when the roar of motorbikes came to life and I was assaulted with backslaps and wild shrieks of thanks. They had managed to collect wood in the meantime, and went about establishing a roaring campfire.

When the nets were set, we bundled up in my horse blankets and lay on the earth roasting salami and pig fat on sticks. Vodka and pure spirits flowed, and by the flickering light the cracked-tooth smiles and tough but boyish faces took on an air of celebration. They shared rude, freewheeling chatter about fishing and fights, using variations of a few obscene words.

I sank into my coat, relishing the feeling of pig fat warming my belly. Tigon sat between us all, one of the gang. It was nice to feel a sense of company and friendship.

Then the large man poked the coals and looked at me. 'You know, us Cossacks, like you, we used to always pack up and leave when we needed. In old times, like for nomads, the steppe gave us all that was necessary to live – horses, wild game and fish.' He cast his eyes over my gear and the horses that were lit up on the edge of my camp. 'I consider that Genghis Khan was a Cossack by definition. Although we did not live in yurts, we adopted the nomad's horses and horsemanship. We have a saying: "Only a bullet can catch a Cossack rider."'

There was a look of sadness in his eyes.

'The Russians turned our land into fields, took away our horses. Brave men became wheat farmers and tractor drivers! Now we're not even allowed to fish without permission.'

In the twentieth century, Cossacks had endured particularly cruel treatment, in part because they happened to live on the most fertile land in Russia. In the 1930s hundreds of thousands of Cossacks were either executed, exiled to Siberia, or sent to forced labour camps. Perhaps just as heartbreaking for these free-living horseback people, private ownership of horses was declared illegal, and their lands were ploughed.

Another of the men spoke up. 'Have you seen the wild dogs yet? You should be carrying a gun – they are even more dangerous than wolves.'

The man didn't seem frightened by the idea of wild dogs, but rather, proud of them. It excited me, too, to think that somewhere in this land there was a wild spirit that carried on even if the wolf was long gone.

I continued along the Kalaly River until it began to curve north, then cut across to another watercourse that flowed west towards the sea. Here I began to travel through *khutors* – villages strung out along the rivers of the Kuban in single rows of timber and mud-brick houses.

Life in the khutors seemed to belong to a bygone era. Babushkas worked the earth, bent permanently at the hip, and old men rowed leaky flat-bottomed fishing boats into sleepy waters. The clop and rattle of a horse and cart sometimes rose and faded along the unsealed streets.

I had hoped I could slip in and out of these settlements inconspicuously, but even the dead would have been woken by the wave of barking dogs and squawking geese that preceded me. Tigon, who was out in front pulling hard on the lead, was alleviating his boredom by scaring every living thing that crossed his path. Sometimes he would be calm right till the last moment, when he would leap up, front legs wide apart, and hackles high. At other times he would simply stop and crouch down, and wait for the curious onlookers to come to him, at which point he would suddenly leap to his feet and bark. It was just for a bit of fun of course, though the poor geese didn't think so.

There was one other skill that Tigon had been honing recently. Along with his practice at 'marking' out his route, he was getting more and more industrious with his scratching afterwards. Typically, after cocking his leg, he would stretch his paws out, and with powerful swipes rip up the earth, sending sand, soil and grass shooting like missiles into the air. Out on the steppe this might have been okay, but when it was hard-won vegetable plants that went flying, local people looked on in horror.

'Tigon!' I would scowl.

Privately, of course, I was proud of what seemed to be an expression of his rebellious spirit.

The longest khutor I travelled through was 15 kilometres but had a population of less than 1000. The kerfuffle of our arrival also gave people time to ready themselves. They greeted me with jars of homemade vodka and preserved cucumbers, peppers, tomatoes, jams, honey, juice, pears, and *sala* (pork fat). The key to getting past was having at least one shot of vodka, although this often became three. On one occasion I was told that if I wanted to become a genuine Cossack, I would have to drink a giant bottle of home-brewed vodka, known as *horilka*, and then 'jump over a fence'.

Within two days I had accumulated so much heavy produce that the offerings had become a serious danger to the packhorses. When I explained this, the gift bearers always glared back indignantly. More than once I was told, 'If I have given it to you, you must take it! You know the saying: "When they give, take. When they kill, run."'

The freshness of spring began to wear off. My body began to ache, and an accumulated lack of sleep took its toll. At the first sign of hunger my mood would crumble. The horses felt heavy themselves, and during breaks they kept their heads down. Even Tigon was exhausted. He had learnt that the most important thing while on the lead was keeping well out of reach of Taskonir, who would take a nip at Tigon's hind legs whenever he caught up, to remind him who was boss. The worst torment was when the front horse happened to step on Tigon's lead at a trot. It nearly strangled poor Tigon, who, pinned down and trampled by the caravan, was spat out the end in somersaults. How he came out of these scrapes without serious injury was beyond me.

Then came the rains. The lanes and tracks turned to sticky black mud – a telling sign that I was riding through *chernozem*, or 'black soil' – the fertile soils that stretch from the Kuban across the southern steppe of the Ukraine.

As mud, however, this precious soil balled up under the horses' hooves until they slipped and fell. I resolved to walk, but within minutes the build-up on my boots turned them into heavy clogs. I walked the better part of three days, descending into a quagmire of filth. The horses were still losing their winter coats, and the shed hair combined with the mud stuck fast to my clothes, my skin and my sleeping bag.

One night, while I was setting up camp in the pouring rain, a local drunk stumbled upon my muddy patch of earth and twisted the knife. 'How dare you camp here on the Kuban, you foreigner! If I tell my friends about it, they will come in the night, take your horses to the meat factory, and drown you in the river for the crayfish to eat!' I swore at him darkly and he stumbled away. But the look in his eye meant that I slept the night in my filthy riding clothes and with my axe by my side.

Out of grain and low on food, the following night I was forced to camp on a narrow strip of grass next to freshly ploughed earth. Despite tying the horses on short tethers, they managed to get out and roll in the earth, and by morning they were all plastered in black grime.

As I sat there with my porridge, which was thick with horsehair, I realised I'd become the picture of a down-and-out, homeless wanderer that many mistakenly associate with the word *nomad*.

Beyond the town of Dyad'kovskaya, the rain came down in sheets. I slipped behind a row of trees and headed down a narrow track into some deserted wheat fields. Protected by the hood of my jacket, I kept my head bowed and considered my circumstances.

I was now only 250 kilometres from the Azov and Black Seas, where I planned to cross into the Crimea in Ukraine. But before leaving Russia I needed to find a replacement for Utebai and get all the papers required to take horses across the border. To do either of these would require a miracle. Horses were a scarcity on the Kuban, and no one would ever agree to trade for a wimp like Utebai. And in my filthy, dishevelled state, I would struggle to convince a shopkeeper to sell me a loaf of bread, let alone a border guard to give me entry into another country.

But when I lifted my eyes, it seemed my prayers had been answered.

The unruly beard of the man before me was what first caught my eye, then his tall velvet hat and long black robes.

He lifted a small broom from a bucket of water, flicking drops from high above his head into the field. Then he turned to me.

'We've come here to bless the wheat fields with holy water! Where are you going?'

He was the priest of Dyad'kovskaya, and it was the role of the Orthodox Church to bless every wheat field of the parish in the spring. As I went on my way, he showered my caravan with holy water.

Just a few minutes later, proof of his friends in higher places materialised. Accustomed to noisy Russian jeeps and Ladas – boxy little cars that had been the workhorse of Soviet times – I'd failed to notice the purr of a new four-wheel-drive Range Rover until it drew up alongside me. Tigon took a sniff, then retreated. As a tinted window slid down silently, a man grinned out at me from the leather interior.

'So, fellow traveller, partisan, Kazakh, Cossack – how can I help you?'

I wiped mud and rain from my eyes and peered down as he stepped out and swaggered up to me. Standing only a little taller than he was wide, he was adorned with flawlessly buffed shoes, a black jacket, sunglasses and a silky tie. There was no doubting it: *this* man was no priest.

'My friend! You do not know me, but soon, I think, we will be friends. I am Nikolai Vladimorivich Luti:

ataman – Cossack leader – of this region, owner of ten thousand hectares of crops, and employer of eight hundred workers.'

I stammered out my story. Luti, as he liked to be called, looked at me thoughtfully. Finally he said, 'Thirty kilometres away at my friend's farm you will have all the services you need. Go there tonight, and tomorrow we will consider your problem. If we can find a new horse for you, we will.'

Over the next six weeks my problems were all solved. I was put up in a hotel for the first night in Luti's hometown, and then given a place to stay at an industrial machinery yard that he owned. While I worked on border permits – with the help of his workers – my horses were cared for by a Gypsy horseman who not only dedicated himself to bringing them back to full weight, but even shampooed their coats and cleaned their manes.

Luti helped me find a replacement packhorse for Utebai. 'Sokol' was a young golden palomino stallion, with an inquisitive nature. Although he was untamed and had never been ridden, I liked him at once. I renamed him 'Kok' in memory of my poor fallen horse in Kalmykia. After several weeks of training – with many close calls with kicking, flying hooves – he was calm enough to accept a packsaddle. On Luti's advice I gave Utebai away as a gift to a local riding school for children.

During my stay Tigon and I regularly visited Luti in

his office. He would sit in an executive chair, smoking imperiously. 'Tim,' he would say at last, pulling a rolled-up $100 bill from his top pocket, 'take some pocket money and go and buy yourself some cigarettes or something!'

When I finally set off, I was fresh, clean and organised, and the horses were positively gleaming. Just two weeks of riding later I approached the border post.

Immigration and veterinary control waved me straight through, and just one obstacle remained: customs. I'd been warned many times that I might be pulled in to pay a bribe for one thing or another. But I was in luck here, too.

Just as I pulled into customs inspection Ogonyok disgorged a gigantic turd. The junior officers laughed, but their superior did not see the humour. 'You are not leaving Russia until you clean that crap up!' he yelled.

'Okay, okay. But I'm not going to shift it with my bare hands. You'll have to find me a shovel,' I replied.

While he sent some officers off in search of a shovel, most of the customs officers came out to see the spectacle. Meanwhile, I went inside to be processed and breezed straight through the unmanned screening post to have my passport stamped. Back outside, nobody had found a shovel, and the boat to Crimea was due to leave. Within minutes I was casting off into the Kerch Strait, leaving behind the cluster of officials still gathered around Ogonyok's parting present.

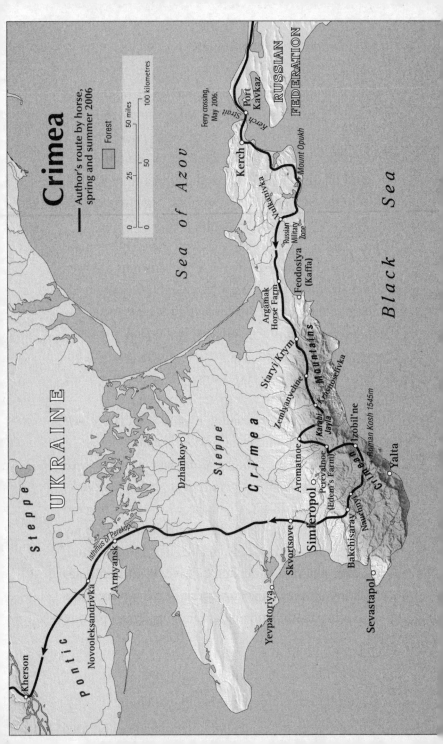

Crimea

— Author's route by horse, spring and summer 2006

☐ Forest

0   25   50 miles
0   50   100 kilometres

RUSSIAN FEDERATION

Port Kavkaz

Ferry crossing, May 2006.

Kerch Strait

Kerch

Mount Opukh

Vulkanivka

Russian Military Zone

Sea of Azov

Feodosiya (Kaffa)

Arganak Horse Farm

Staryi Krym

Zemlyanevtne

Crimean Mountains

Karabi Jayla

Krasnoselivka

Izobil'ne

Roman Kosh 1545m

Yalta

Black Sea

UKRAINE

Kherson

Novooleksandrivka

Armyansk

Isthmus of Perekop

Pontic Steppe

Skvortsove

Yevpatoriya

Dzhankoy

Steppe

Crimea

Aromatnoe

Simferopol

Perevalnoe (Edem's Farm)

Bakchisaray

Nauchny

Sevastopol

15

Crimea: Riding the Double-edged Sword

From the saddle I watched Tigon's tail and ears cut through the tall swaying grass. His body bristled with the muscly physique of a grown and confident adult, yet his teeth were still impeccably white, betraying his youth. Pollen and white flower debris caught in his eyebrows like snow petals. It wasn't long before he reached the top of a rise and stopped, ears bent forward, the sleek shaft of his snout fishing for scents on the breeze.

I, too, was soaking in the view. From a foreground of waist-high grass, red poppies and white chamomile, the steppe dropped away in a sea of green. Directly below, a narrow sandy neck of land cut a straight line between the sea and a series of pinkish salt lakes.

By the time we'd descended to the beach, the wind had eased and the sun was setting the western sky on fire. As I shifted my gaze to the sea, a dark shadow shattered its glassy surface. A school of dolphins rose and dipped effortlessly as they cruised along the shore.

Tigon, still new to salt water, rushed into the lapping waves, lay on his side and took sweeping bites until he coughed it up with a look of surprise. I dismounted, stripped down, and ran in, feeling the water tingle across every cell of my sweaty skin. I even took the horses in, one by one. Once back on the beach, they dropped to their knees and rolled onto their backs on the sand, legs flailing wildly in the air. Tigon copied them, twisting this way and that, jaws wide open in a smile.

By nightfall banks of dark cloud hung heavily over the sea. I pegged the horses out and watched as they buried their heads in the grass, feeding like a pack of hungry lions. Over dinner the sky faded from peach to deep blue, then black. I lay out in the grass with Tigon's sleepy head slumped on my chest.

I meant to write in my diary, but I woke at midnight with rain falling on my face. I'd managed to pen one line: *We're in horse heaven.*

In the morning I woke to a sky flooded with stormy grey. Tigon lay next to me, wound up in a ball with his nose hidden under his bushy tail. It was a technique he had long mastered when the morning weather wasn't kind – pretending to be asleep in the hope that the sunrise might go unnoticed and we would therefore have a sleep-in. On this occasion I was more than happy to join him and relish the time to think, write and reflect.

It had only been two weeks since I had sailed away from Russia, but already I felt that a new chapter had begun.

In the port city of Kerch, as we'd navigated from the ferry port out of the town, we had passed a mother and child. The child, no more than four or five years old, had been fixated on his ice cream – that is, until Tigon loped up alongside. The ice cream was, of course, conveniently at head height for Tigon, who with one graceful movement happily accepted the boy's offering. The world, it seemed, was Tigon's ice cream.

The legendary Crimea was a peninsula of rocky, forested mountains, endless sandy beaches, and grasslands. Nowadays part of Ukraine, it had been the jewel in the crown of nomadic empires for thousands of years – and judging by the abundance of grass, I could understand why.

When the Mongols reached here almost 800 years ago, the sense of revelry and celebration must have been particularly special. It was their first foray into Europe, and they had trounced all enemies that stood in their way. I couldn't quite relate to their war victory celebrations – which included slowly crushing the enemy's royal leaders to death beneath the platform on which they had their celebratory feast – but I did feel that the challenges Tigon and I had overcome to get this far gave us a feeling that we were unstoppable.

When I set off from Mongolia almost two years earlier I had been worried about unknown strangers that lay ahead on our path, but all I could imagine now were the many friends that I was yet to meet. And where once I might have had the illusion that I was Tigon's master, it was now clear that he was fearlessly guiding me across the steppe.

Yet before we launched eagerly forward, I wanted to reflect too.

With my eyes closed and my hand stretched out from my sleeping bag, I found Tigon. He withdrew his head from under his tail and stretched out with a sigh. I took my hand across his damp, cool nose and along his long, narrow snout. I felt the sleep in the corners of his eyes, and his soft eyelids. How many scents had that nose inhaled? How many sights had these eyes seen since those early days in Kazakhstan?

I reached his ears, my hands rising to the tips, then stroking down to that nook behind on his skull for a scratch. Tigon pushed into my hand, and extended his neck and front legs. Those ears had long been a kind of antennae, a weather vane for me and for him. When the tips were frosted over, I'd known to take shelter and rug up, and in the summer when they were piping hot to touch, it was essential to seek shade. At first, Tigon's ears had been enormous, and unwieldy, so much bigger than his head, but now his body had grown to match both his ears and his giant spirit.

I let my fingers slip down around his neck, arriving at his chest. I'd watched that chest grow from a skinny finger-wide gap between his matchstick legs to a proud, wiry ball of muscle, pulsating with a heart that had taken his body wherever his eyes could see. It was a heart full of courage and love, a heart that had found its way into mine, and through the doors of hundreds of homes. And now down the legs to those paws – paws that hung limp and humble, but had carried him across sand, snow, rock and water. Paws and legs that, perhaps unknown to him, had even carried my spirit when I was tired, down and scared.

As I took my hand to the centre of his spiny back, an unexpected reflection filled my heart and rippled out, tears spilling from my eyes.

I recalled those early times, when Tigon was but a runty puppy, all eyes and ears, with nothing more than his will and spirit to see him forwards. I had told Aset that I didn't want Tigon – how would I look after him? How would I pay for his food?

And yet this masked the truth.

I had known deep inside that when Tigon chose me, he was willing to take the risk that I might abandon him, that I might not even love him. What's more, he knew that there was no turning back – there was no way for him to get home.

What really scared me in those early days wasn't the responsibility of looking after him. It was the fear of being a disappointment. What if I didn't turn out to be as good a person, an owner, as he thought I was? Would Tigon regret his decision to choose me? Could I really promise to be his lifelong friend?

I couldn't remember the first time it happened, but we were in a village somewhere. I had been feeling down, and Tigon came running to me. I crouched down, reached out and began to stroke him, from the head, across his neck, and all the way down to his tail. With each stroke Tigon's chest pushed out prouder, and he raised his eyes and chin, his whiskers all aquiver. He craned his neck and looked around at the other people and dogs in the village. That look was unmistakable – pride. He wanted the whole world to see that I was his best friend. Tigon believed in me. And since that day, I had begun, little by little, to believe more in myself.

But as I lay there now feeling every contour, every grain of Tigon's hair and body, head to tail, I thought about someone else.

My dad.

I hadn't seen my him for so long, and now I craved his company, not because I needed him, but because I wanted him to see that I was happy, and that because of his belief and love for me, I had come this far. Most of all, I wanted him to be proud. Back home we hadn't always seen eye to eye. He had been particularly uncomfortable and frustrated with me when I decided to abandon my law degree at university to pursue adventure. And yet he had still supported me, and day by day, week by week, I had sensed from afar that we had grown closer than ever before. In recent times we had even discussed the possibility of him coming to join me for a leg of the trip. My father, I felt, among other things, was beginning to see me as a man. And the more I stroked Tigon now, the stronger, and prouder, I felt to be his son.

When the sun re-emerged, the horses began to restlessly swish their tails. Tigon likewise sprang to life, pawing at the tent door. Pause and reflection had been replaced by the promise and potential of what lay over the next horizon.

It's hard to piece together how exactly things unfolded in Crimea. We were strong, proud and bursting with energy in a land with soaring views. Without the problems of border crossings, fences and lack of grass, I found time to be more introspective, and to recognise that I was growing up.

But things were about to get more dangerous and more exciting than I could ever have imagined. There were violent troubles brewing in Crimea, and that confidence would soon get us into trouble. But it was also an exciting time because, among other things, it would prove to be a summer of romance. Of course, it all seemed to happen at once.

On the face of it, the main challenge of travelling through Crimea was traversing its mountains – a range famed for its dense forests, rock pinnacles, and high alpine plateaus. These high, cool grassy abodes had forever drawn nomads and their animals during summer. Sadly the last great nomad power here, the Crimean Tatars, had lost their nomadic way of life during Russian colonisation two centuries before. The twentieth century had brought even greater grief. In May 1944, the Tatars were rounded up and deported en masse to places like Uzbekistan, and had been barred from returning until 1989. These days Tatars were returning to Crimea and struggling to revive their culture.

My plan had been to reach the high grazing pastures before summer heat set in, then to sail across Crimea's steppe interior to mainland Ukraine. The unforeseen, though, was about to occur.

It was at a horse farm near the foothills of the mountains – where I had gone to seek a horseback mountain guide – that both disaster and fortune struck. Tigon managed to get into a fight with a farm dog, and was violently kicked by someone trying to separate the two. A veterinarian assessed that Tigon had serious internal bleeding and bruised kidneys. I spent all night holding him in my arms, watching him dip in and out of consciousness, sure I might lose him at any moment.

That same night, a very different story was unfolding at the other end of the farm: Taskonir was falling in love. According to the farm's owner, it was love at first sight between one of her mares and Taskonir. In all her years she had seen nothing like it.

Tigon would recover, but it would be two days before he began to eat again, and three weeks before we could contemplate riding on. By that time the green of the steppe had waned to yellow, the days were unbearably hot, and mosquitoes were descending like fog at night.

The upside of this delay was that Taskonir's romance could blossom. He and the Crimean mare were inseparable, often seen with their necks slung over one another. It was hard to believe that this proud, gallant horse with stormy eyes and shiny dappled coat had been all bone and sunken spirits little more than six months earlier.

Eventually the time came for us to leave. The day before my departure, I watched with anticipation as our guide, Seryoga, arrived driving a horse and cart. Seryoga was a forest worker with detailed knowledge of the mountains, and without him the mountain crossing would be impossible. From a distance his heavyset frame, weathered face and tawny, sun-bleached hair cut a handsome figure. As he pulled in with a series of whistles and commands, my eyes were drawn to his disfigured upper lip.

'This is my trophy from an accident a few years ago, when I was even younger and even more stupid!' he said, pointing apologetically to his toothless upper mouth. 'I was drunk and I fell off my horse at a full gallop on the pavement!'

We began our journey by riding eight hours straight in the heat. Seryoga was bareback on his bony old mare, Zera, and wore nothing but a pair of cavalry jodhpurs and a rope tied around his waist. His lean, muscled torso was red with sunburn, and he smoked tobacco rolled in pieces of newspaper, stubbing them out one by one on the soles of his cheap running shoes.

Late in the day we reached Seryoga's home in the forested foothills. 'Give me two days here, Tim,' he asked me. 'I have some things to sort out, then I will be able to come with you.' Two days soon became three, then a week. Seryoga was nowhere to be seen. According to his parents he was off working, but also getting himself into trouble. On day nine, when I had all but given up hope, Seryoga reappeared. He was hungover, and there were open wounds on his hands and wrists. Apparently he was a farrier for hire, and accepted danger money to work on wild horses that no one else would touch. His bravado and disregard for danger were what made him the only one willing and able to get me through the mountains, but they also meant he was on a constant crash course for trouble.

The next few weeks in the mountains turned out to be less of a challenge and more of a respite from the troubles that lay behind us. It was also a time to recharge and prepare for the events that lay ahead.

That's not to say that the mountain crossing wasn't a great adventure, too. By our first evening in the forested slopes we were lost, and spent most of our time traversing overgrown forest paths, unsure of where we were. In the end we ran out of food, surviving on wild herbs, tea, and bits and pieces of dried curd, peanuts, and meat that I fished out from the bottom of my boxes. We also woke one morning to discover that Ogonyok and Kok had run away, requiring an all-day search to find them. But none of that really bothered us. Seryoga was more concerned that we had also run out of cigarettes and vodka. Meanwhile, I found myself captivated by my surroundings. It was the first time I had been in a real forest since Mongolia, and the first time Tigon had ever laid eyes on one. I loved to listen to the wind rustle in the leaves, the sweet smell in the air. For Tigon it was an even greater treasure trove of sights, smells, and sounds. One moment he would be at the bottom of a gorge, tail up and fossicking through ferns, the next he'd be chasing a deer down from impossibly high slopes through the trees. At every turn there was another stream or small lagoon for him to bathe in.

A couple of weeks into our travels we finally rose beyond the forest and onto a sunlit mountain plateau. Cliffs fell away through a veil of sea mist, 1000 metres to the Black Sea. Tigon, in his typically unafraid style, ambled his way right to the very edge and gazed down.

Seryoga didn't share our enthusiasm.

'If we have run out of cigarettes and vodka, and we have almost no food, there is nothing for me to do but sleep!' he said. After setting up the tent, he crawled in, covered himself with a horse blanket, and collapsed.

I carried on with Seryoga until we had descended to the nearest village, then carried on alone. After a week my mountainous journey was coming to a close, but my Crimean adventure was only just beginning.

The end goal of the mountain crossing was the town of Bakchisaray – the ancient capital of the so-called Tatar Khanate where, following the collapse of the Mongol Empire, blood descendants of Genghis Khan had ruled for centuries. Their empire had been renowned as one of the most powerful in Eastern Europe, but was also known for its slave trading, particularly in Russia. The Crimean Tatars were skilled in riding up through Russia's southern borders to capture ordinary Russians who would then be traded through the ports on the Black Sea coast. In 1571, during one raid alone, Tatars managed to burn Moscow to the ground and take up to 150,000 people into captivity.

The tables had long since turned on the Tatars, with Russia firmly in charge of the Crimea for more than two centuries, and many Tatars still living in exile. But, as I would soon learn, Russians had a long memory, and this made for dangerous tension as Tatars returned to reclaim their spiritual and cultural home.

Bakchisaray lay at the bottom of a deep mountain gorge. Tigon's ears pricked up as we sank deeper. He lifted his head and craned his neck to the limestone cliffs that began to block the sky on both sides. Where the gorge seemed to have run its course, the cliffs converged and the track shrank to a narrow cobbled alleyway between old stone houses. Then, unexpectedly, it hooked sharply to the left, and Bakchisaray came into view. A riot of minarets mingled majestically with the bustle of cars and pedestrians in the summer evening.

My first task was to find a man called Volodya – a local who had heard about me on the grapevine and offered to host me during my stay. But as I rode into the crowds, someone else caught my eye. A young woman stood to my left holding a bag of paintbrushes, an easel tucked under her arm. The sun lit up her deep blue eyes and rippled through her hair. She began to approach me, and I froze. My mind raced, I was breathless. She asked me something about my horses, but I could not think of what to say.

Just then there came a voice from further on:

'Tim! Timokha! Over here!' It was Volodya. When I turned again the girl had gone.

Volodya, a short, stocky man who was half Russian and half Tatar, had ridden into town on his bicycle to greet me. He now pedalled in a blur ahead of me, furiously impatient to show me the riches of his hometown. One of the first stops was the so-called *Hansaray* – the Khan's Palace.

I was still lost in thoughts of the woman when Volodya took me across a moat bridge and through the palace's grand wooden gates. I continued under an archway into a courtyard, and as Tigon took the opportunity to bathe in a fountain, I lifted my gaze to the high wall of the palace. Towering minarets inscribed in Arabic cast lean shadows across a courtyard of rose gardens, fountains, lawns and shady trees.

As the palace's guards test-rode my horses, I stopped in disbelief. There she was, standing by a rose garden in the back of the courtyard, her easel set up between us. This time I wasn't going to let her disappear. As I approached she looked my way and put her brush down. 'About time you noticed me! You just walked into my painting!'

Anya, as she was known, was a Ukrainian art student from Kiev who had been given special permission to stay in the palace after hours to paint. I offered her a ride on Taskonir and for the next half an hour nervously led her around the courtyard. Before I left, we agreed to meet again.

At Volodya's house that night a rabbit was slaughtered in my honour, and we celebrated with cheap Russian vodka. My spirits were high: I had fallen in love with Anya, and after the last few hard days of riding, the rabbit was a veritable banquet.

Come morning, my feelings for Anya hadn't changed, but the reality around me began to sink in. Volodya had been born in exile in Uzbekistan and had only returned to Crimea in recent years. Like so many other Tatars, he had struggled to find work and build a life for himself and his family. He lived in the barren lands on the outskirts of town in a hovel he had built out of mud, reeds, scrap wood, glass bottles and a few token bricks. Inside, there was just the one room with an old Russian couch that doubled as a bed for him, his wife, and their two children. The tension between Russians and Tatars was at boiling point in the town, and this put Volodya – whose mother was Tatar but his father Russian – in a particularly tenuous position.

After breakfast Volodya took me to the centre of town, where trouble had been in the making for some time. Stretched out across the road was a picket line of Tatar demonstrators and a makeshift barricade hung with a banner: 'Close the market that is built on our bones!' Lurking in the shade of trees, in cars, and in buses on both sides of the picket line were dozens of heavily equipped riot police, their shields and truncheons at the ready.

Russians had built a food market on a sacred site for Tatars where their venerated Khans and spiritual leaders had been buried. There were eleven mausoleums in total that dated back to the seventh century, which had been internationally recognised for their historical importance. The Tatars had been demanding for years that the market be removed. The only response had been recent attempts to enlarge it.

The showdown that now loomed reflected a broader issue. Although the injustices that the Tatars had endured under Stalin had officially been recognised, many Russians still believed Stalin's accusations, especially that the Tatars had collaborated with the Nazis during World War II.

Many Tatars who had been deported to Central Asia had not lived long enough to see their homeland again. Those lucky few who had fulfilled their lifelong dream to return were met with cruel hostility. I met one Tatar man whose elderly mother had just one wish on her return to Crimea – to be able to drink water from the well at the home where she had been born. The Russian family currently living in it had refused to let her past the front gate.

These stories were deeply troubling for me. I felt an allegiance to Tatars, who symbolised the nomadic cultures that I had grown to love. And yet I had so many Russian friends, and a deep love of Russian culture. This was not the world that Tigon and I normally inhabited, where the good in people was clear no matter who they were.

I spent the rest of the day with Anya, exploring ancient ruins in the cliffs above the Khan's palace. We lay for hours in the shade, marvelling at how magical it was that we had met. When dark came we sat out on the edge of a cliff watching the stars blink on. It felt as if we had been transported to another world.

The following day, sadly, it was time for Anya to depart. I accompanied her to the station and kissed her goodbye. We promised to remain in contact, and to meet up again as soon as possible, but neither of us knew when that might be.

I left the station in a sombre mood, but when I arrived at the market I was promptly pulled out of my funk. The riot police were now stretched across the road between the picket line and the market, and were brandishing their shields. The Tatars, it seemed, were ready to take things into their own hands.

Unlike the previous day I was now aware of glares from both the riot police and the Tatars. Whose side was I on, after all?

I had only just begun mingling with the Tatar protesters when there came a high-pitched whistling from the picket line. Apparently a Russian had come to challenge the protesters. A whole crowd of men leapt to their feet and rushed forward. I dashed after them, but had only taken a few steps before I felt a great force from behind. Within a fraction of a second I was yanked backwards by my backpack and thrown onto the ground.

I lay face up, writhing for breath, watching helplessly as a man above drew his fist back and screamed, 'Hey! Go back! Move out, Russian!'

The mob quickly grew around me, but just as they closed in there came a woman's voice. 'No, no! Leave him! He is one of ours. He is the Australian traveller!' The men helped me up, apologised, and invited me to join them. I declined. From now on I was going to have to be careful.

Tension was thick in the air – the Tatars were clearly readying for battle. Rumour had it a legion of Russian thugs from the nearby city of Sevastopol were on their way, and that others were coming from as far as Russia. In anticipation, Tatars were not only twitchy and nervous, but were beginning to collect wire, wood and whatever else they could find to fortify their picket line.

It was shaping up to be a tense night at the market, but life was not so peaceful back at Volodya's either. As I approached his home I passed one of Volodya's best friends, Eldar. He was stumbling off, swearing, his hands clutching his jaw. Inside the hut, Volodya lay on the couch, speckles of blood down his shirt, a cigarette butt floating in the vodka glass next to his head. Volodya's ten-year-old son rushed to me in excitement. 'Dad's head flew off! First Eldar went down, then Papa, but they didn't share with us the reason for the fight!'

When Volodya rose, battered and bruised, he went to buy beer and credit for his prepaid mobile phone. He then began calling strangers and speaking nonsense until the credit dried up.

The signs were ominous at Volodya's home, but this was nothing compared to the situation at the market the following afternoon.

Rumours about legions of Russians coming in to crush the market protest had proven true. The roads and shops had been shut down, and hundreds of police and soldiers were being bussed in. I could see men of all ages pacing about wielding sticks and planks of wood. The Tatar protesters were now surrounded by hundreds of riot police, upturned cars and wire.

By the time I returned to Volodya's, smoke had begun to rise from the market, accompanied by occasional gunfire. Volodya's wife was in hysterics, tears streaming down her cheeks.

Bakchisaray was on the verge of war.

In the morning I woke early and gathered my things. It was time to get back out on the steppe.

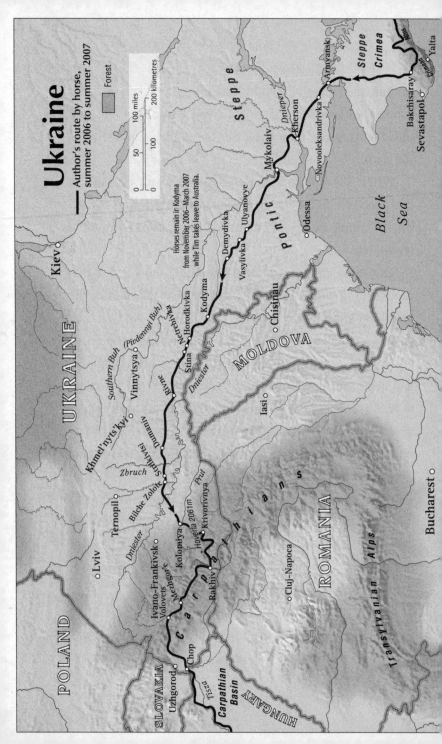

Ukraine

— Author's route by horse, summer 2006 to summer 2007

Forest

Horses remain in Kodyma from November 2006–March 2007 while Tim takes leave to Australia.

POLAND

SLOVAKIA

Uzhgorod
Chop

Carpathian Basin

HUNGARY

Tisza

UKRAINE

Kiev

Lviv

Ternopil

Khmel'nyts'kyi

Vinnytsya

Southern Buh

(Pivdennyi Buh)

Zbruch

Dniester

Bilche Zolote

Sudkivtsi

Dunayiv

Rivne

Netrebivka

Stina

Horodkivka

Kodyma

Demydivka

Vasylivka

Ulyanoye

Mykolaiv

Ivano-Frankivsk
Volovets
Mezhgore
Kolomyia
Hoverla 2061m
Rakhiv
Krivorivnya

Prut

Carpathians

MOLDOVA

Iasi

Chisinau

ROMANIA

Cluj-Napoca

Transylvanian Alps

Bucharest

Odessa

Kherson

Novooleksandrivka

Armyansk

Dnieper

Pontic

Steppe

Steppe

Crimea

Bakchisaray

Sevastopol

Simferopol

Yalta

Black Sea

0   50   100   100 miles
0   100   200 kilometres

16

Crossroads

I headed north through low rolling steppe lands, avoiding towns and villages as best I could. The sun was fierce, so I settled into a rhythm of riding by night, making camp by midday, and sleeping in the open under horse blankets.

In little more than a week I had reached the far north of Crimea, where I woke late one night, half asleep, and gazed up at the dim profile of the horses. Taskonir stood over me, his ears bent forward, back leg cocked, and Kok's head resting on his wither. Tigon was curled up, breathing heavily, his bony spine hard up against my thigh. Time passed unmarked until a fart broke through camp. Ogonyok, who had evidently woken himself up with the noise, put his head down to munch on the sun-dried grass. Tigon let out muffled barks in his sleep, and Taskonir's bottom lip quivered for some time, until once again all was still.

It occurred to me that without my animals I would have lost my sanity long ago. Only from the solitude of the steppe, reconnected with them, did I feel ready for new horizons.

After almost three months in Crimea, I would soon reach the Ukrainian mainland. My final summer on the steppe was coming to a close. In fact, Hungary lay less than 1000 kilometres away, and with the worst of the winters and thirsty deserts now far behind us, this last leg promised to be a piece of cake. For the first time since leaving Mongolia I began thinking about reaching the end. If all went smoothly, I would cross the Carpathian Mountains and reach the Danube by early spring.

What I could not have foreseen was that in Ukraine my journey would be waylaid by the biggest challenge of all. In fact, another summer would pass before I could set my eyes on the finish.

But at that moment, as far as I knew, I was gathering momentum to reach the finish line. Gazing up at the stars, I rolled under the sweaty smell of the horse blankets and surrendered to sleep.

At 3:30 am the alarm clock sprung rudely to life and we were off within an hour, moving through the predawn darkness, the familiar dull ache throbbing up from my feet in the stirrups to my hips and bum.

When the black of the sky dissolved, it seemed the sun was rising just for us. Golden light spilled over the open steppe and Tigon was off, a black speck bounding through the yellow grass. I loved the way his tail and ears remained sky high. When I dismounted to pee, the three horses did the same, and when Tigon homed back in he joined us. I gazed across proudly at our team peeing in synchronicity – a sublime moment that only we could appreciate.

The soft rays of sunlight were deceptive. By seven am hot gusts thrashed at the grass and my eyes narrowed to slits. By lunchtime I had retired to the patchy shade of a lonely tree.

It took another day of riding through dry, hot conditions before we reached the narrow isthmus that connects the peninsula of Crimea to the mainland. The territory beyond was a land blessed with an abundance of fertile soil, rivers, and forests. I'd surely never have to worry about finding grass, grain or water ever again.

As we reached the mainland I felt the first whisper of autumn. A cool breeze from the west rustled through the grass, turning my sweat cold. The horses stopped to gaze in its direction, and Tigon lifted his nose. The sun had done its summer's work and was moving on to new pastures. In its place thick, cottony clouds were filling the sky.

My own transition into autumn was not so smooth. On my first day on the mainland a horse and cart spooked the horses into a wild bolt, and I was forced to run 10 kilometres to catch them. Ogonyok cut his leg badly on a broken glass bottle, and was very nearly hit by traffic while crossing a bridge. And that evening Taskonir managed to run off with a full 50-kilo grain bag in his teeth, open the buckles and spread its entire contents on the ground – it wasn't for nothing that I had resorted to sleeping with my grain bags in recent times.

In the city of Mykolaiv my horses were confiscated by customs and veterinary officials, who said my permits were inadequate. After another round of vaccinations, being issued with Ukrainian animal passports, and buying a bottle of vodka for the head of veterinary control, the horses were released. It would be a month, however, before I got back in the saddle. Unexpectedly, I had been selected as the *Australian Geographic* Adventurer of the Year, and as part of the award they were flying me to Sydney for the ceremony. The opportunity to see my family after two and a half years was too much to pass up, despite the delays it would cause.

Leaving the horses at an equestrian centre I spent some days with Anya in Kiev, then, still dressed in my tattered riding boots and single change of shirt and trousers, found myself in front of a packed audience at the Maritime

Museum in Sydney, Australia. A week passed in a whirl-wind of media interviews, visits to sponsors, and two days at home, culminating with a luxurious dinner with Mum, Dad and my great-uncle John Kearney. Over oysters and champagne we celebrated the award as if it were ours together. Afterwards Dad gave a short speech about what I had done, and in his swelling pride and approval I realised that, just as I had hoped, he had begun to see me as a man.

After staying together in a hotel on Sydney's Darling Harbour, I hugged Mum and Dad and watched their taxi drive off. It was the last time I would ever see my father.

By the time I had returned to Ukraine the air was crisp, the autumn leaves were alight with yellows and reds, and the horses had begun to grow their woolly winter coats. For the third year in a row I donned my winter clothing and prepared to set off.

Anya had come to see me off, and when the day came to leave, she walked alongside my caravan to a small forest on the outskirts, where we kissed goodbye. We knew we might never see each other again, and by the time we parted, both our faces were wet with salty tears.

I aimed to traverse southwest Ukraine before crossing the Carpathian Mountains and descending into Hungary. For the first few days I charged across cultivated flats. The horses bristled with energy, and I sat high in the saddle, feeling Taskonir's powerful chest absorb the shudders of pounding hooves. Tigon likewise galloped about, revelling in that unique autumn sun. Once, Tigon overstepped the mark with his exuberance and decided to take on a giant wild boar. I could clearly see Tigon stretched out in full flight as he chased it into the forest. No sooner had I screamed out 'Tigoooon!!!!!' than from that very same forest, who should appear but Tigon – this time moving even faster, his eyes as big as saucers. On his heels was a whole family of angry pigs.

Gathering momentum, we departed from all signs of main roads, and the flats grew into raised plains. Apart from the odd buckled car and horse and cart, thin trails of smoke rising from villages in the valleys were the only signs of life.

The late autumn chill had lifted the energy of the horses, and each day we seemed to be gaining speed and strength. The local people, however, faced with the onset of the cold, were retreating to the comfort of their homes. It struck me as no surprise that this was precisely the time of year that nomad armies traditionally chose to launch attacks. In Ukraine and Russia, Mongols wiped entire towns off the map in the colder months, when unsuspecting villagers had retired for relative hibernation and the Mongol horses were at their peak.

The downside of this early period of winter for me, I realised, was that there were fewer people to greet me, and those who did seemed more wary, and less inclined to accommodate me. When I enquired whether anyone was willing to put me up for the night, the typical response was, 'Sorry, I can't help you because I do not have space to shelter three horses.'

As the days wore on, the horses tired, and I began to feel vulnerable. On one evening in particular things took a sinister turn. I was in a remote field, where I had pulled up next to a broken-down truck. Suddenly, a hulking man emerged from under the hood. I noticed his powerful hands first, with their grease-stained, calloused fingers, each as thick as a sausage. Then came his face, wide and round as a dinner plate.

He shook my hand absentmindedly as his cheeks, brows, and mouth began to bunch up in a way that didn't feel friendly. I started asking him for directions, but he cut me off.

'Give me at least one of your horses!'

'No,' I replied. 'These horses are going with me to Hungary!'

His eyes grew hard. 'Sure!' he grunted. 'I know that you have stolen these horses, and so I will take them from you!'

There was a stand-off until he moved towards Ogonyok, behind me. Before he could reach the horse, I pulled on

Ogonyok's lead rope, kicked my boots into Taskonir's side, and pulled away. I didn't turn around until the man and his broken-down truck had been swallowed up by the land.

When I descended to the village of Vasylivka the following evening the shadow of danger was still on my heels. I had run out of grain and food, and the horses were exhausted. Some villagers offered the horses a drink on the outskirts, but no one was willing to put me up. I was told to go into the hills to the abandoned settlement of Mala Dvoryanka. 'There is one man who still lives up there, and he can point you in the direction of water and grass,' an old man told me.

After another hour's ride we were drawn to the lonely glow of a house. The sound of the door swinging open filled me with relief, but then two snarling dogs leapt out. Tigon launched into attack, a blinding torch flicked on, and above the raucous barking and snarling came swearing. I could just make out the silhouette of a man and then, right in my face, came the pointy end of a rifle.

'Calm down, please! I came for advice on where to graze my horses and somewhere to camp!' I said angrily.

'Turn around, thief! Get out of here! I will shoot your dog just like that!' he screamed in a mix of Russian and Ukrainian.

I replied in Russian, 'Okay! Okay! I'm leaving!'

After calling Tigon back I rode away and felt my way up a gully until we were safely hidden. My fear and anger subsided only after I had set up camp and the last of my pasta had settled into my stomach.

The morning sun revealed a promising sight for hungry horses: thick, unruly pasture. Plus, there was indeed a well nearby. Despite the risk of meeting the old man again I decided to stay put for a rest day.

While the horses grazed I had just enough battery power to start my computer, connect the satellite phone and post an update to my blog. Before I could manage it, however, an email arrived in my inbox. It was from my father, addressed to me and my siblings, and was in a tone I had rarely heard from him. He expressed his feelings about his early retirement that he had recently taken. *As you know*, he said, *I took a step into the unknown last year . . . I struggle each day to try and determine what I should be attempting to reach forward for . . . and it is a major readjustment not having as a goal the care and maintenance of our children.*

For most of his career Dad had worked in outdoor education at university. As children we got to go out with university students on skiing, bushwalking and sea-kayaking trips. But in the past ten or fifteen years the job had taken Dad into more office work – hence his decision to retire early.

Dad's letter went on: *you are all in the prime of your life with many years of energetic activity to go, but once partnered and with children it would be fun to be near you.* The email finished, *I wish you well and look forward to sharing your ambitions, joys and sorrows and the sound of your voices in our house.*

Love, Andrew

The battery died and my screen went blank. My mind began to twist through images of my childhood, as well as a kaleidoscope of familiar smells, sounds and feelings.

I wanted to tell Dad how brave I thought he was for making the decision to resign. I was lifted from my thoughts by the sound of someone clearing their throat. Tigon woke with a growl, and I unzipped the tent to meet the gaze of a startled cow herder.

'Do you have any cigarettes?' the man asked.

I was the first foreigner that Kolya had ever spoken to, and soon I had packed up and was following him home.

As I pulled in, Kolya invited my horses into a barn. My horses, however, pulled back in fright and refused to enter.

'Your poor horses!' Kolya exclaimed. 'They have been out in the elements for so long they have forgotten what a stable is!'

I gave him a wry look. 'The problem is that my horses have almost never been in a stable!'

Kolya shook his head and grinned, then took a longer look at my horses.

It was difficult to explain to him that his stables would have appeared more prison than refuge to my horses. Many times on my journey, people had pitied me for living out in the elements, but after so long on this journey, I found it hard to imagine living in a town or village, let alone a four-walled dwelling.

That night I proudly tied the horses up outside and Kolya gave them generous piles of hay. In the morning, however, I found myself relishing the feel of my warm clean skin and the fresh sheets. The smell of fried pork, buckwheat and eggs wafted into my room, while outside, the first snow of the season had blanketed the earth. Perhaps there was something to this 'house' thing after all!

With some reluctance I saddled up and rode out over the frozen waves of mud in the streets of Vasylivka. Beyond the village I carried on through high open plains broken by the occasional gully. Bitten by frost, the land had lost its autumn gleam, and by evening it was so cold I was forced to get off and walk to bring life back to my toes.

As had become the pattern, trouble was forever lurking. In the town of Obzhyle I was met by drunken men driving a horse and cart. 'Where the hell! From where the hell?' they hollered when they saw me. There was something rough and aggressive about them, and so I rode out of town fast, aiming to camp in the hills nearby. But as dark fell a car pulled up and a man in police uniform stepped out demanding documents. I told him angrily that I didn't have time, for it was getting late, but a second man emerged and took Taskonir by the reins. 'Hand over your passport. *Now!*'

By the time they concluded I was legal, it was too dark to get out of town and find camp. I told them that since they had held me up, they were responsible for finding me a place to stay. It was a mistake.

I was sent home with a drunk man, who after half a bottle of vodka outlined his plan to steal my horses. I broke out of his hut in the middle of the night and slept on the frozen earth among the horses, who were tied up outside.

I enjoyed two days' respite in the town of Kodyma, but when I rode out the winter ahead was looking ominous. The Carpathian Mountains now seemed cruelly distant, and I wasn't sure how I could sustain my pace through the winter. I tried calling Dad via satellite, but time after time, the call went to voicemail. There was only one solution: it was time to grit it out and get this journey done.

Two days out from Kodyma I rode towards the sun as it set. I passed a herd of cattle returning for the night, and noticed a horse and cart clopping along a track in the distance. Ahead of us, the land planed off into a gully, and

I reasoned that if I hurried, I could make it there to camp before dark.

Before speeding up, I reached into my backpack and pulled out the satellite phone. For some time now it had been beeping – I had accidentally left it on. As I went to switch it off, I noticed a new message. It was from my brother Jon: *Tim! Call home please!*

I leapt from the saddle and knelt in the grass. Clutching the handset, I dialled home. When our family friend Peter Nicholson answered, it was obvious something was wrong. As the handset was carried to Mum, I could hear other familiar voices.

Mum was in the bathroom when she picked up. 'Tim?' Her voice crackled down the line, shaking. There was a long pause. I held my breath.

'It's Dad,' she started, her voice strong, but in an instant it wavered and she began to cry. 'He was in a car accident . . . I'm so sorry, Tim . . . he is dead . . . I can't bring him back.'

It's not hard to remember the moments after I hung up that evening, on 16 November 2006, but they are hard to describe.

Sitting there at the feet of my horses, the journey that I'd been on for two and a half years evaporated as if it had never been. I couldn't breathe, and my back muscles heaved. I nearly vomited two or three times, and cried.

But also there was a numbness, and a sense of normality. I was still in the Ukraine, and I needed to camp, find grass and unsaddle. I split into two distinct parts from that moment – the practical me, and the grieving passenger.

Among the thoughts competing for space was the certainty that I had to be alone, away from anyone who had not known my father. Somehow I knew that if I was quick about making camp, out on the steppe under the stars I had a fleeting chance of connecting with Dad before he was gone.

I worked fast to set up the tent in a gully. Tigon whined for his food, and the horses tried to bolt. For a fleeting moment it felt as though the two parts of me joined to get the job done. But then the horses were tied, the food was cooked and eaten, and I crumpled onto my canvas bag. I gazed up at the sky, and suddenly it was so big and so lonely. Where could he be? Did he know how to find me?

I wanted to know when Dad had died. I took into account what Mum had told me, and weighed up the time differences: he had been alive when I woke up, but had died by lunch. My lungs seized at the thought.

How many times had I called? I could imagine his phone lighting up, my name coming through. Maybe when I made that last call he had still been alive.

I was tired, yet resisted the urge to sleep. To sleep would have been to abandon him. And yet the practical me guided me until I couldn't keep my eyes open.

When I awoke again, there was ice on the tent, and outside a sea of mist was gushing in, devouring us. It must have been about four am. I picked up the phone again. This time I got Jon. We just cried. Then I talked to my sister, Natalie. The first thing she asked was, 'Did you reply to his email?'

'No, I didn't,' I replied.

'I didn't, either.'

There was only one thing to do: go back. Back to the spot where I had eaten lunch after he died, back to where I'd camped the previous day, when he was still alive. Back home, where I could return to the life I'd had as his son.

I packed faster than I had ever managed.

We trotted through the village under the cover of heavy mist, and before the sun could rise over a world without Dad we were lost in the folds of the land. I pushed the horses harder, into a canter. Mist began to swirl, then above me a circle of clear sky turned peach. I craned my neck and twisted around, but urged the horses on.

Dad, I'm coming!

I was catching up with him. But then Ogonyok pulled at the lead rope, I slowed, and the mist began to rise.

I lost Dad for some time. Then, as we entered a tract of forest, he seemed to return. I slowed to a walk, breathing in the tang of rotting leaves that littered the ground. Dad walked to my left in his shorts and hiking boots, carrying one of his weathered old daypacks. We stopped momentarily as he leant over and lifted a plant from under a tree. Cradling it in his palm, he brought it over and held it up. I was back in the Australian bush, one of the many times when he'd turned to me and said, 'Tim, isn't life amazing?' Back then I hadn't understood what he meant, though I could see from the look in his eyes that he was right. Now he looked up at me in the saddle, his eyes alight. We rode on together.

So many times by phone and email we had talked about him joining me on this adventure. Since resigning from work he had taken an interest in the histories and cultures of the countries I travelled through, and read many books on the subject. But neither of us had committed to the idea. I had missed the opportunity, and as the edge of the forest drew near I began to sob.

The farm director in Kodyma agreed to take in my animals while I headed back to Australia. Just forty-eight hours later I walked out through Australian customs. Then they were there: Mum with her pale face and wet blue eyes, Jon behind her, nervously grinding his teeth. I was the eldest child, and Jon was my junior by two years, although as he leant over and hugged my skinny frame he felt like my elder.

Natalie and Cameron were there, too, but it wasn't until we made the two-hour drive home that it felt like we were all finally reunited. Natalie had some good news: although neither she, Jon, nor I had answered Dad's email, Cameron had.

It wasn't long before I learnt the sad details of Dad's passing. On the previous Thursday, the day of Dad's accident, Mum hadn't been expecting him home. He had spent the week helping out at a surf lifesaving camp at Sandy Point – a small beachside town a little more than an hour's drive from home, where we had always holidayed as a family in the summer. He had promised to be back on Friday morning.

Sometime early Thursday evening there had been a knock at the front door. This was odd – anyone who had been to our home knew that the back door was the proper entrance.

It was the police. At about 4.30 pm that day there had been a head-on collision on a stretch of the South Gippsland Highway – the road we always travelled from home to Sandy Point. A man carrying Dad's identification had died instantly at the scene.

In the afternoon I slipped away and had a nap in my old bedroom. I was badly jet-lagged, and woke feeling groggy and disoriented. I stumbled down the hallway into the living room. Surely if I sat there long enough, something would break the silence – perhaps Dad would talk to me, or walk through the door.

As I closed my eyes I heard the screen door open. In my mind I heard his work bags land on the floor and his shoes come off, but when I opened my eyes and looked up it was Mum. She had come running to hold me.

The house was filled with guests, and we spent much of our time organising the funeral. Finally, we had chosen a coffin and Dad had been returned from the coroner. On the eve of the funeral I lay awake, hearing the odd creak of a bed and the rustle of possums on the roof.

I was still struggling to adapt to Australian time, but more than that I craved the calm of night, which held me close to Dad.

The darkness moved slowly until a *cack cack* from a magpie finally sounded, then the warbling of a hatchling. Pale light cracked through the cypress trees, and a thrush hopped by the window.

I couldn't lie there any longer.

From the back corner of the wooded yard I gazed out over the paddocks towards the emerald hills of the Strzelecki range. A fox and her cubs appeared, moving stealthily across the dew-laden grass.

To the east I fixed my eyes on large eucalypts that stood silhouetted against the blanket fog. Dad loved these ancient trees, so much so that they were somehow inseparable from him. How could they still be here, continuing to exist as if everything remained as it had always been?

The funeral passed, then the wake, then the memorial service at his university, and gradually the visitors and letters of sympathy slowed to a trickle.

Since receiving the news about Dad, there had only been room to deal with grief, but as time wore on the journey re-emerged. I received emails saying that Tigon was well, but missing me. The horses, however, had been hastily left at the farm, where they were tied up in a barn with dairy cows. I wasn't sure if the men there had managed to remove their horseshoes, or how often they saw daylight. Fodder was scarce, and it was a big thing to ask strangers to feed three extra horses.

I had to make a decision. If I left it much longer, I might not have horses to return to. But I was the eldest of four children and it didn't feel right to abandon everyone so soon. I knew that Dad would have wanted me to continue, however, and I simply couldn't abandon my animals.

So in March, four months after arriving in Australia, I was back at Melbourne Airport, feeling as if I had left my horses too long but was leaving too soon.

17

Road to Recovery

On a brisk, early spring morning in Kodyma, Ukraine, a small crowd of farm workers gathered to see me off. Among them were the many generous people who had looked after my animals while I was gone. For the four and a half months that I had been in Australia the farm's owner had not charged me a cent. I shook his hand and presented him with an Australian Akubra hat and oilskin coat. In return he raised three toasts of vodka for a safe and successful journey to Hungary.

It was at that point, compass around my neck, that I hauled myself up onto Taskonir, shouldered my backpack and, with Tigon out the front pulling hard on his lead, set off once more.

At first I rode slowly and carefully beyond the town, struck by the rather drab surroundings. Although winter had ended, the land was yet to spring back into life. Grass lay flattened and bleached of colour, furrowed fields were thawing into mud, and trees were mostly bare. The land seemed at its lowest of spirits – which was also the way I felt. It wasn't a pleasant time of year to re-start my journey, but it wouldn't have felt right to return to the bloom of spring or the gaiety of summer either.

If my condition mirrored that of the land, then the condition of the horses was a worrying sign of where my journey was at. I had arrived in Ukraine to find Kok, Taskonir and Ogonyok in a cow barn where they had been tied up for the better part of four and a half months. Their muscles had withered away, their hooves had grown out, and their winter coats were matted with muck. When I saw them, I realised that reaching Hungary would not be a simple matter. Though I had already travelled around 8000 kilometres, the momentum had vanished, and I was still more than 1000 kilometres from the Danube River. These next few weeks would be a journey of spiritual and physical recovery.

There was one last important moment before I could truly get moving. Not far beyond Kodyma I turned onto a muddy trail and pulled the horses into a familiar meadow. Winter had preserved the ghostly footprint of my tent from the previous year. I dismounted and lay on the earth. It was the last place where I had slept and woken while Dad was alive. Beyond this point lay horizons to which I had never been, and which, without Dad, seemed more fraught with danger than ever.

Before remounting I noticed the yellow of a solitary dandelion that had blossomed. With it firmly pressed into my pocket, I moved on.

That night a spring snowstorm swooped, and raged on into the next day. I decided to stay put, and spent the day listening to the snow rap against the tent, and the rise and fall of Tigon's chest. I had sorely missed the sound of Tigon's breathing. His breath brought a comfort that was hard to describe. It was as if Tigon's presence turned the hostile world into a warm and friendly home. For hours I gently caressed his body, from his toes to his ears. Every time I stopped, even for a nanosecond, he would paw me and let out a kind of impatient growl. He was long overdue for my attention, and he was letting me know it.

The storm had given us just enough time to gather some energy, and come the following morning, anticipation of the new day had built. Tigon lay next to me, with one ear cocked and an eye half open, biding his time until I moved. When I rose, he leapt feverishly to his feet, and together we jammed our heads through the tent entrance. The sun was nudging its way into a solid blue sky and sending golden fragments of light splintering through the snow-covered grass.

After packing up I rode quietly through empty meadows before cresting a hill overlooking the village of Horod-kovka. The onion-shaped cupolas of an Orthodox church rose gracefully above a huddle of timber homes, like a priest towering over his flock.

As I rode down the hill we met a funeral procession going in the opposite direction. Leading the march was an elderly man carrying a heavy wooden cross. His face was a landscape of shadowy ruts draining tears from glassy blue eyes. Beyond him and a crowd of mourners rumbled an old truck with an open coffin in the back. The person who had died – presumably the man's wife – was an elderly woman, her pale, uncovered face lightly warmed by the sun. Two children sat in the back, holding her in place as the truck wobbled its way up the road to the grave.

As I turned to move on, the land ahead seemed touched by beauty and sorrow. It felt as if we, too, were passing through the gates into another dimension.

From Horodkovka I tracked west, rising to high plains and dipping into deep river valleys. Passing through a string of villages helped draw me away from sad thoughts. Most were nestled on the steep valley sides and on river-banks, tucked away from the cold wind. I seldom stopped, registering only the greetings as I went.

In Dakhtaliya an old man yelled, 'Hey, sell me your horses.'

In the next village, Netrebivka: 'Hey, Gypsy, where are you going?'

On the cobbled, windy streets of Hnatkiv: 'What's this caravan?'

In Stina, a lady pointed in horror at my packhorses: 'Hey, stop! You have lost your passengers! They must have fallen off!'

It took a couple of weeks before I began to feel the stirrings of life returning – both inside me, and in the land around. I smiled for the first time in months one clear morning when I opened the tent door to see the horses making the most of their rediscovered freedom.

Ogonyok was irrepressible – erupting in fly kicks, shaking his neck, and teasing the others into play fights. Kok was more than happy to join in, rearing on his hind legs and softly biting at Ogonyok's neck.

When the sun rose a little higher and the air turned warm and friendly, Taskonir dropped to the ground with a sigh, then stretched out on his side and closed his eyes. Kok joined him, lying opposite, followed by Ogonyok. Together they lay there, breathing in the promise of spring. The snow and rain had washed away all traces of their ordeal in the barn, and their bodies rippled and shone with vitality.

Tigon took the opportunity to get up close and sniff around the horses. Then he wriggled around on his back, paws punching at the air, chewing lazily on grass. When he was done with that he sprinted circles around camp and cocked his leg on everything in sight. Eventually he lay upside down, playing dead – legs in a tangle, tongue hanging slack, back legs wide apart, proudly displaying his jewels to the sky.

My animals weren't the only ones who had rediscovered their vigour. Not long after setting off that day, a wiry little man pulled up in his car and surveyed me with astonishment. 'What's this? It's my dream! I've always wanted to travel like a free Cossack!' he exclaimed, grabbing my hand with both of his and shaking like a madman. 'You are coming to my village! To Rovnoye! Follow me!'

In the evening I sat at a long wooden table jammed with burly farmers. 'Pork fat is life! Sport is your grave!' they chuckled, slapping their bellies and pouring vodka. 'Eat and drink! This isn't Russia, where they drink a lot and eat little. We *eat* a lot and *drink* a lot!'

My time in the village was marked by a visit to the local primary school. The principal – a fiery lady with red permed hair – ordered the children out into the front yard. There, as she shook my hand and kissed me on the cheek, Tigon proceeded to stick his snout under her dress, then flicked his nose up, lifting the dress up for all to see. Everyone erupted in laughter, then descended on Tigon. While numerous pairs of hands reached out to stroke him, he sat like a prince, then surrendered to a lying position, spreading his back legs in an effort to direct scratches to his belly.

When things had settled down I was ushered into a classroom, where the students divided their attention between this funny Australian and the dog.

'How many kilometres a day do you travel?' they asked, before someone else piped up: 'What do you eat?' 'Do you have a girlfriend?' 'When do you wash?' 'Is Tigon a father?'

Their questions were simple and the right ones to ask, unlike adults, who were full of astonishment that I hadn't been killed along the way. Before setting off, I had never worried about death, bureaucracy, conflict, drunkards, or robbers. I had come here to have an adventure, and live the kind of dream that most forget when they grow up.

I left the school feeling light and happy in a way that I could barely remember. And yet, the most uplifting of encounters on this road to recovery was yet to come.

A week later I willed the horses into the village of Dumaniv in search of food supplies. I had only just dismounted when yet another invite came my way: 'Don't even think about it! Sleep here! You will eat what we eat! Sleep where we sleep! We won't offer more, we won't offer less,' said a man before I even had a chance to introduce myself.

My host, Valeri, led me home and doled out hay and grain. By nightfall I had scrubbed myself clean and sat reborn at the dinner table. Across from me sat Valeri and his father, Volodomor. But it was his grandmother, Ferona, who really fascinated me.

She sat at the table practically jumping out of her skin. 'I might be ninety-three, but I can still thread the eye of a needle, no sweat! And every day I go barefoot to the hills with my goats!'

Her body was miniature and shrunken, but her eyes held the sparkle of youth. She opened a Bible. 'I only learnt to read at the age of eighty-three! My son taught me so that I could read the Bible before I die.' With a giant magnifying glass trembling in her hand, she read aloud. I listened intently, astonished to have met a woman who had survived every violent event of Ukraine's past century. By the time she turned thirty, Ferona had witnessed a revolution, and the horrors of World War II.

Like most survivors of her generation, however, Ferona told me the event that had most affected her was what was known in Ukraine as Holodomor – a tragic famine that many historians still consider the genocide of the Ukrainian people at the hands of Soviet leader Josef Stalin. Mass starvation had begun in the Ukraine during the winter of 1931–32 after poor weather conditions caused the failure of crops. Rather than helping, Soviet authorities continued to demand unrealistic quotas of grain production from farms. When these quotas could not be met, rural Ukrainians were accused of thieving the harvests. While the meagre supplies of grain were locked in storage and shipped away, authorities punished anyone found with bread, wheat, or any other grain that was in their home.

Ferona told her story almost as if it were yesterday: 'To keep us alive my father hid a bag of wheat in between the stones in the wall of our house. One day the authorities found it, and Papa was sent away to a labour camp in Russia. We never heard from him again. I survived on grass and the old leaves of sugar beets,' she said.

As tragic as the first winter had been, it paled in comparison to what followed. By the middle of the winter of 1932–33, people were dropping dead in the fields, on the roads, in their homes. Even then, Ferona explained, the authorities 'came to ask for taxes on everything – the trees in our yard, our animals, all our possessions'. When her family could pay no more, they were evicted and locked in jail. The authorities stole everything remaining in their house.

The government, it seemed, tried to ensure that people could *not* survive. Food aid from outside the country was blocked at the border, and when villagers resorted to eating cats and dogs, quotas for dog and cat skins were suddenly invented. When people began eating wild birds, rodents and fish, Stalin proclaimed that all living things were owned by the state. By the summer of 1933, an estimated seven million Ukrainians had starved to death.

In the morning Ferona took me down to the velvety grass by the riverbank with her four goats. She had promised to sing for me, and after tethering her little crew she put her hands together in prayer and wet her lips.

I was born in Ukraine
I lived here a long, long time
Now they are sending me away
What is happening to me?
They will send me out of Ukraine
They will send me away
Oh, oi oi oi
I am leaving small children behind
And adults go away with me
My small children are not ill
Other people will feed them
And I will be in Siberia
Remembering my children.

From her crumpled, shrunken body came a deep, gravelly voice. It wavered a little at first, but soon strengthened.

And who's going to feed him
When he'll be on his deathbed?
And who's going to feed him?
How is he going to live?

She brought her hands to her face and tears ran over her fragile eyelids and down the worn, eroded gullies of her cheeks.

Avoiding villages, I camped in hidden valleys and cut through fields and forests. At night I sat by the campfire, feeling the cool air on my back and the glow of coals on my face. I listened to the horses grazing and watched the moon rise into clear, starry skies.

I walked a knife-edge of emotions. While Ferona would probably pass away peacefully, Dad, who had lived in one of the safest countries on earth, had met a violent end. Was it destiny? Luck? Or was life just random? How was it that Ferona seemed to have the happiness of a child even though she had seen the very worst of humankind?

One stormy evening several days west of Dumaniv, in the town of Bilche Zoloti, I was pulled out of my introspection. Long after darkness had descended I was clopping along the main street when someone came running into my path wearing a suit and tie. He had a chubby face, a stomach to match, and the stocky, square frame of a bulldog.

'Off you get! We're just about to start dinner!' he instructed in a raspy voice. Introductions had to wait as he seized me by the collar, asked someone to watch my horses, and ushered me inside a bar for a celebratory glass of beer.

I later learnt that his name was Yaroslav, and he was the mayor of the town.

That night I was put up in the local sanatorium – a kind of wellbeing resort. I had barely opened my eyes when Yaroslav burst into the room in a frilly apron holding out a tray of steaming hot eggs, sausages, salad, bread and tea.

'Here you are, traveller! Courtesy of Bilche Zolote's first-class hotel!'

While I appreciated Yaroslav's help, I realised in hind-sight that he viewed my arrival as an opportunity to make a name for himself.

On my first day in Bilche Zolote, my first stop was to Yaroslav's office. He was scheming to hold a national press conference in the town based on my arrival, and handed me a press release that he had just written up. It was titled 'Great World-Famous Australian Traveller Arrives in Bilche Zolote'.

After a flurry of phone calls and faxing, the first of many tours of Bilche Zolote got underway. I found myself in the back of a traditional horse wagon squeezed between two girls dressed in traditional outfits. Yaroslav commanded the girls to sing. The horse cart driver swore monotonously the whole time.

It was on the third evening that things began to spiral out of control. I was invited for dinner with the principal of the high school, and Yaroslav was adamant the horses remain grazing on the soccer oval after dark. 'Don't worry! Nothing can happen in this town, it is mine! I will order the caretaker to guard the horses while we are gone!' But when we returned, the caretaker was passed out, snoring, and Ogonyok and Kok were gone.

Yaroslav's terror was clear as it dawned on him that his grand plans were fast unravelling. Half of the country's media were due at a press conference in the morning!

Yaroslav, the principal, and her husband took off in three different directions. The security guard was less concerned: 'What's the point of looking? The horses will be at a meat factory by morning. You will never find them,' he said.

I raced around blindly on Taskonir trying to pick up the scent, but after two hours all seemed lost . . . until a local was seen leading two horses out of town. I later learnt this person was an orphan who was currently on parole; being caught would have meant a long jail sentence. The sheriff managed to find him and convince him to return the horses, or so we came to believe. At about one am a mysterious figure came running through the street with my horses before letting them go and vanishing into the night.

Come the press conference I was itching to regain control of my journey. After I finished giving interviews, there was one last event – the school concert. The poor principal, who had only been told about the plan the day before, scrambled to get the kids in traditional dress. Yaroslav addressed the crowd with an exuberant speech, then leapt onto an unsuspecting Taskonir and paraded for the TV cameras.

In the afternoon I dug out my gear and attempted to ride off. It wasn't going to be that easy, though. I was serenaded by the local choir and offered vodka and food, and by the time I got going it was almost dark. I made it as far as a lake and thought I was in the clear – until three am, when I was woken by shouting. I wearily unzipped the tent, and there in the pouring rain, with his leather jacket and 'I Love Ukraine' T-shirt soaked through, was Yaroslav.

'I was so worried they would steal your horses! I came to protect you!' He had walked 10 kilometres to reach me, and dangled a pint-sized fish in my face. 'Come and see the rest of my catch and I will make us fish soup! Only, I'm wet – can I borrow a coat?'

I gave him my rain jacket and went back to sleep, but was soon woken by a bloodcurdling noise. Yaroslav lay on the ground, covered in mud, curled up with his pet dog. They had their noses pointed skyward and were howling a duet.

'Listen, Tim! This Bilche Zolote dog can sing! Where is your video camera?'

With what little strength I had left I rode out, and even when the howling faded I didn't look back.

*

A week from Bilche Zolote I pulled into camp on the banks of the river Prut near the city of Kolomiya. The last few days had seemed more like a recovery from Yaroslav than from Dad's passing, but either way the horses, Tigon and I were rejuvenated. I felt ready to commit myself to the task at hand. As I sat with Tigon and gazed to the western horizon, there, silhouetted beneath dark stormy clouds, was our first glimpse of the Carpathian Mountains.

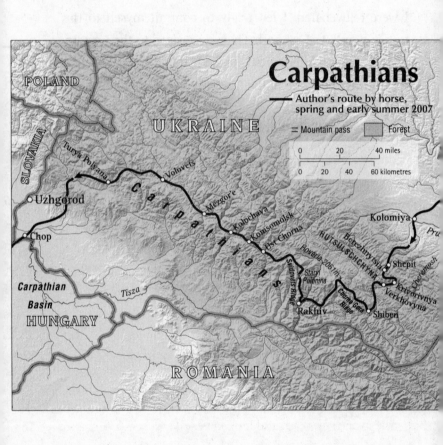

Carpathians

— Author's route by horse, spring and early summer 2007

⊨ Mountain pass   ▢ Forest

0   20   40 miles
0 20 40   60 kilometres

POLAND

SLOVAKIA

UKRAINE

Turya Polyana

Uzhgorod

Chop

Volovets

Mezgore

Carpathians

Kolochava

Komsomolsk

Ust Chorna

Tisza

Carpathian
Basin

HUNGARY

Svidovets Ridge

Starý
Polonina

Rakhiv

Poverla 2061 m

HUTSULSHCHYNA

Kolomiya

Berezhnytsia

Shepit

Pru

Cheremosh

Kryvorivnya

Verkhovyna

Chorna Gora
Ridge

Shiben

ROMANIA

18

Nomad Outlaws:
Crossing the Carpathians

Beyond the village of Sheshory the mountains closed in and the sky shrank to a strip. In the late afternoon dark grey clouds advanced, flooding the valley and blotting out the sun. Thunder cracked, and a heavy rain tore down.

In the evening the sun made a short reappearance, shining light on a babushka who hobbled along the roadside, dripping wet and carrying a sack of hand-cut grass. She looked up at me with a frown:

'Are you off to the *polonina*?' She put her hand on her heart, shook her head, and looked very concerned. 'You are brave! May God be with you!'

I didn't know what the word polonina meant, but I was beginning to think I needed all the well wishes I could get.

The next morning, I reached the end of the upper valley, where the road gave way to a wall of ridges and peaks. Either I could take a three-day detour via a main road, or I could try my luck at finding a path over the top.

I dismounted and set off up a slope that soon became so steep I could almost lean on it. With each step my panicked lungs sucked for air. The horses heaved and moaned, hooves slipping as rocks were dislodged and went clattering down. Even Tigon seemed to be finding the going hard, his tongue hanging out near the ground like some kind of long, limp sea kelp.

Higher up, the slope turned into mud, and after tumbling over many times I reached a grassy ledge and collapsed. As my heart rate slowed I lifted my sights, and the difficulties faded. To the east, back the way we had come, row upon row of forested ridges lined up like ocean swells. My eyes floated effortlessly over the same crests and troughs through which we had struggled in recent days.

I reached up to Tigon and scratched his chest. As I did he swung his eyes in the other direction, up the steep slope ahead of us. Speckles of his saliva dropped onto my face, and I rolled over on my stomach to share the view.

Above us, mist blanketed dense alpine forest. Every now and then treetops tore a hole through it, offering glimpses of endless craggy peaks. These were only the very beginnings of the second-longest mountain range in Europe.

For Europeans, the snowy passes and forests of the Carpathians had always been a natural line of defence, offering protection against attacks from the east. For the Mongols, however, and for me, these treacherous peaks represented the last of *many* geographical hurdles on the long road to the Danube.

By the time the Mongol army reached these mountains in the winter of 1241 they were an extremely experienced team of soldiers who felt very much at home in such terrain.

As a measure of the speed and skill of the Mongols, only four days after Hungary's leader at the time, King Bela IV, learnt that the Mongols had attacked the Carpathian passes, news that they had fallen reached the capital. Once over the mountains, the Mongols flew across the steppes of Hungary, covering 65 kilometres a day.

Nowadays, the Carpathians are crisscrossed by asphalt highways that connect Ukraine with Europe. But riding along such roads, I could not hope to appreciate what it might have been like for the hardy nomads of the past. My plan, therefore, was to avoid roads and travel through the highest and most rugged section of the Ukrainian Carpathians. Besides, out there in the wild reaches of the mountains there existed something much more likely to capture the spirit of the nomads.

Back in Crimea I had been told about a nomadic people in the Carpathians who still rode the descendants of Mongol horses. The 'Hutsuls', as they were known, apparently resided in the most inaccessible valleys and alpine plains, where they lived a horseback life herding sheep and cattle. Their land, orbiting around the tallest peak of the Ukrainian Carpathians, Hoverla, was known as Hutsulshchyna.

Some believe the name *Hutsul* comes from the old Slavic term *kochul*, which means 'nomad', and that they may be a Turkic people who fled to the mountains during the Mongol invasion of Russia. Others believe the name comes from the Romanian word *hotul*, meaning 'outlaw'.

I was to meet the Hutsuls sooner than I thought, and in the end, I would decide that both meanings were fitting.

There came a shout from somewhere above in the forest, then the thud of an axe on wood. My horses stood to attention, their ears pointed forward like pistols, and I pulled myself up in a hurry. Four stocky men and their horses materialised, towing freshly cut logs.

'Good morning, men! Can you show me the way over to Berezhnytsia?' I called, referring to a hamlet on the far side of the ridge.

They took their time to respond, running their eyes over my equipment and peering under my horses, checking their status.

It wasn't long before the youngest of the men unharnessed his horse, leapt on bareback, and led the way. We entered the forest via a track so narrow and crowded with branches that it was more like a tunnel. The fir trees became ever denser, the sunlight withered, and Ogonyok struggled to squeeze between the moss-laden trunks.

At the top of the ridge we came to a wind-raked saddle, then dropped beneath the cloud on the other side. Across the valley timber homes appeared painted onto a vertical canvas of green. The jingle of bells floated across to us from a flock of sheep making their way up towards an alpine meadow.

Sometimes rosy first impressions are deceptive. Not so here. Elevated far above the problems of the modern world, Berezhnytsia, the first of many such communities in the land of Hutsulshchyna, would mostly remain true to this fairytale vision.

The young horseman led me down and straight through the front gate of the first house we came across. 'They will certainly take you in for the night – that's the Hutsul way!' he said, then galloped back up the slope.

True to the horseman's pledge, a portly woman, followed by her sheepish husband and elderly father, soon emerged and ushered me in. Even before they introduced themselves they had invited me to stay for a week. 'First things first, though,' Maliya said, hands on her generous hips. 'You need a bath.'

Berezhnytsia was not so much a village as a community of around eighty homes dotted about the high slopes at the head of this remote valley. My host's cottage was reached via steep, ankle-breaking paths. Maliya described how her grandfather had chosen the place for their home: 'First when he came up here he watched carefully for the places where the cows liked to lie down. Once he found this place, he spent a night sleeping on the earth. According to Hutsul belief, if one dreams about cattle, then it is a sign the site is blessed.'

I would have loved to stay with Maliya, but word about my journey had already spread. Down in the valley below a man called Ivan was apparently awaiting my arrival.

It took the best part of a day to descend to the Hutsul village of Krivorivnya, but barely a minute to find my new host. Standing seven feet tall and built like an ox, Ivan came striding up the street looking so much larger than life that the mountains shrank around him. I was transfixed by his long, flowing dark hair and bushy beard, which was matched by a black robe dragging at his heels.

'Ribaruk, Ivan, priest of Krivorivnya, welcome!' he bellowed as I surrendered my hand to his bear-like grip.

Ivan and I got along from that moment. Mountaineering and travel had been his passions in his younger days. It was while climbing in the high Pamir Mountains of Tajikistan that he had resolved to become a priest. 'I reached a peak around 6000 metres high and realised that I didn't want to go down. Below it was full of problems that humans had created, and I just wanted to keep climbing up to the sky,' he told me.

One of Ivan's jobs as priest was to bless all the houses in the village and the outlying mountain communities – about six hundred of them – as well as the rivers, streams, and wells in the mountains around Krivorivnya. This involved a two-week trekking expedition every winter.

The first job on Ivan's list took us to an old timber church in Berezhnytsia for a ceremony in honour of Saint Nikolai.

As we arrived young and old were streaming down the slopes. Elderly men steeled themselves down narrow paths on walking staffs, and babushkas straddled wooden fences. Some teenage boys rode horses down slopes so steep they nearly rested the back of their head on the horse's rump as they went.

The men wore stiff bowler hats, known as *krysani*, and heavy, sheepskin vests, called *kyptars*. Some hats were covered by hundreds if not thousands of buttons, sequins and metal studs, and topped off with feathers. The women wore handcrafted jewellery ranging from gold and silver coin necklaces to glass beads fitted tightly around the throat. There were tears of joy as this rush of colour came together and people hugged, kissed and shook hands.

The hundreds of people who had come to celebrate could not fit inside the church, so there was a slow shuffling queue moving in through one door and out another. Inside, Ivan and two other priests sang a series of prayer and song.

It must have been two or three hours by the time Ivan led the congregation outside and stood before a wooden barrel of holy water. He held up a cross to the sky and went into deep whispers of prayer. As his prayers came to an end the crowd rushed to drink from the barrel.

Our celebrations were rounded off by a visit to an 84-year-old hatmaker called Vasil, who had been making traditional clothing from the age of sixteen. He invited me to a dark, hidden room in the attic. When he turned on a torch I realised that the hard wooden shape pushing against my thigh was a coffin.

'This is older than you are, boy!' he said, grinning. 'Made of light wood, too, so that when they carry me out of here, they don't drop me! Every real Hutsul must make his own coffin by the time he is forty.' He lifted the lid. There, laid out, was a traditional costume including boots, trousers, and a hat. Vasil shuffled around and brought out a metal headstone plate engraved with his name and birth date. A blank space was set aside for the day of his death. 'Hutsuls don't fear death. But we must prepare to meet God, and for that it is expected you will be dressed in your best outfit.'

Sadly, my time with Ivan came to a close. Ahead of me lay the most challenging, and I hoped exciting part of my Carpathian crossing – the legendary Chorna Gora. Meaning 'Black Mountains', the Chorna Gora were a wall of peaks in the heart of Hutsulshchyna, including Ukraine's highest mountain, Hoverla, at just over 2000 metres. It was a place of legend celebrated through songs and stories.

Hutsul shepherds had been making annual migrations to the high alpine meadows – the so-called polonina – of the Chorna Gora for centuries, and most of the older folk in Krivorivnya had worked summers up there as shepherds in their youth. They offered stern warnings. 'Every year shepherds are killed by lightning on the polonina! You could be caught in a snowstorm! Eaten by wolves! Or, God forbid, lost in the forest – there are such big, dense forests that you can easily get lost for days.'

Our send-off from Krivorivnya was marked by a traditional ceremony. Ivan led on foot as a drumroll, violins and a long horn known as a *trembita* heralded our approach. As I urged the nervous horses closer, a group of pretty girls in traditional dress stepped forward with wreaths of crepe-paper flowers to tie to the horses' halters. When the horses shied away, the girls found a more appreciative recipient: Tigon. As all three wreaths were tied around his collar, he sat with his chin raised high.

Ivan had insisted we take someone to help us find our way across the highest peaks. A mountaineer, Yuri, and a man called Grigori from the mountain rescue squad had agreed to come. For the final part of the ceremony, Yuri, Grigori and I lined up to be blessed. Ivan came to us one by one, said a prayer, and doused us with holy water. He blessed the horses, too, and said a prayer for Tigon. 'This is especially for you, Tigon, so that in the sun, your black coat will not be too hot,' he said.

It took a long day's ride along the Cheremosh River valley to reach the village of Sheben, at the feet of the Chorna Gora. A thunderstorm smacked into the mountains, followed by heavy rain. The river had broken its banks and torn apart several timber bridges. If the conditions were so turbulent down here, what it was like up high?

In the morning we heaved our way up a forest path. We were not the only people making for the polonina. Not far into the trek a squall of curses and neighing rang out through the forest. I soon came across two Hutsul horses harnessed to a heavily laden cart. The cart had become stuck in the mud and sat at right angles to the track. The cart drivers were drunk and beating the horses with straps and chains. They wanted to borrow my horses to help pull the cart up, and when I refused, they turned their abuse on me.

A man with a balding head and fiery eyes flew at Kok and Ogonyok with his fist: 'Come here or I will cut you down!'

The men were attempting to reach a station on the polonina known as Vesnyak, where they planned to live over summer. Cattle and sheep from Sheben had already been driven up ahead.

Leaving the men to their curses, we followed Tigon's leading charge and reached the alpine meadows that afternoon. After overnighting in a cluster of knotted pines we began the climb in earnest.

Not far above camp we reached the top of the main ridge. The mist was so thick it felt like we were burrowing our way through the mountains, but when it thinned out I caught glimpses of the abyss that fell away on both sides. We paused by memorials to two young boys who had died the previous summer during a lightning storm – the first of many such markers we would see in the coming weeks.

When evening came we had been moving for almost ten hours, and we were all feeling a little frayed. Grigori and Yuri had begun to bicker.

After pitching camp, I climbed a peak just in time to see the mist fall away, revealing our first full view of the Chorna Gora ridge. Like the twisted torso of a serpent, it stretched ahead, joining a series of peaks. Above it all towered the distant dome of Hoverla.

In the morning we were back on the ridge. Tigon spent most of the time scouring the slopes, appearing from time to time poised over great precipices of ice and rock. More than once he disappeared, and I was sure, as I had been so many times before, that he was gone forever.

Just after lunch the ridge narrowed to a razorback where one slip on steep rock or snow would send the entire caravan tumbling.

I led the way with Taskonir, watching as he nervously inched his way forward. His hooves scraped and slipped across the broad faces of the rocks. The last 10 metres were the most delicate, as we navigated our way down a ledge to a small flat rock. Taskonir studied the way ahead, then came down in a controlled slide, coming safely to rest at my feet.

Ogonyok was less elegant. He stood on the point of a rock with his front legs together, teetering over the edge, then scraped and slipped his way down, miraculously landing on all fours at the bottom. Kok followed in similar fashion.

The next operation was to get the horses up over the ridge to the far side, where it was rocky but free of snow. This took a couple of hours, and Yuri became impatient, shouting, 'Those Mongols certainly didn't come over this way, did they?'

Yuri and Grigori's bickering became worse as we continued. In the end Yuri strode out ahead, refusing to listen to Grigori, and made his way straight up to the summit of a peak. An hour later we were staring down a face of steep, jagged rocks. Grigori had had enough. 'I am going home! I warned you, Yuri! My body can't take any wasted effort!'

By the time we retreated, the sky had turned dark and the heavens opened. Although Grigori and I shrank into our raincoats, Yuri came to life: 'We will not get through now! We will have to cut our way through these bushes! People have become lost and died here!'

The rain went on for two or three hours. I gave up waiting for it to stop and erected my tent. Tigon followed me inside and we went to bed too exhausted to cook a proper meal.

Come morning, the tension between Yuri and Grigori had gone, and it became clear that the struggle of the journey across the Chorna Gora was also over. We found an easy path around the ridge, and later passed below the mist-shrouded summit of Hoverla.

At the first opportunity Grigori headed down a shortcut to the nearest village. The following day Yuri hitched a ride into the nearest town, and had gone by the time I arrived.

One last challenge lay ahead of me before the mountains promised to drop away to the gentler slopes on the edge of the Hungarian plain: the crossing of a ridge known as Svidovets.

After restocking with supplies I began climbing once more. The summer heat was cranking up and it was a relief to return to the polonina, where the air was thinner and cooler.

On the second day we reached the Svidovets ridge, where rocky slopes gave way to green open meadows. Up here wiry men with the same jerky, bandy gait of their sheep sometimes stood in our way, resting on twisted old walking staffs. Their giant leathery hands looked too hardened to have any feeling.

On the evening of the second day we struck camp at a summer station known as Staryi Polonina. We had planned to continue at first light, but by dinner Tigon was looking seriously ill. Curled up on a horse blanket, he refused to stand or eat. His condition had been getting worse for a couple of days. I suspected it was due to some raw pig lungs I had fed him. For the next couple of days I rested Tigon and set the horses free to graze.

The break was an opportunity to learn about the life of the polonina we had heard so much about.

Staryi Polonina was separated into two parts: one for cow herding and another for sheep. I came to know the latter best. It was primarily run by two lanky seventeen-year-old boys, Bugdan and Vasil. Apart from guarding and grazing sheep, their job was to milk all four hundred animals three times a day – twice in daylight hours, and once at four am. They carried the milk to a cooking hut where it was boiled and churned, the curds and whey separated, and cheese hung up to drain.

The boys had been coming to the polonina as long as they could remember. Vasil, the most striking, had long narrow limbs and wore black jeans that fell straight as timber planks down his bony legs. His childlike body seemed out of place with the aged look of his face. He smoked regularly, and once I noticed him fiddling with a cigarette while he was milking

TIM & TIGON

a sheep. He twitched it up and down until it fell into the pail of milk. He dipped his hand in, put the cigarette back in his mouth, winked at me, and continued.

After the evening milking session, I joined the boys for a meal of porridge and sour cream, washed down with homemade wine. Their camp featured an old dead tree, the branches of which had been turned into a rack for hanging utensils. Pots, pans, sifters, stirrers, ladles and many other items shone a ghostly silver against the sky.

When the stars came out, Vasil pointed across the valley to a distant polonina where a fire lit up the night. 'Over there they have bears. That's why they need to keep the fire burning,' he said in a deep husky voice.

'And what about here?' I asked.

'Here? Wolves are a regular audience!' he chuckled. 'But we aren't afraid of wolves and bears. And this work is a holiday compared to winter, when we work with horses hauling logs through the forest.'

As the blanket of cool air dropped and the slopes turned black, Vasil and Bugdan fired up stoves in cubicle-like huts where they barely had enough room to lie down. The sheep settled, and as all fell quiet the huts seemed to shrink until they were nothing more than specks, as lonely as the stars.

I woke at one am and listened from the comfort of my sleeping bag as dogs barked, my horses whinnied and the sheep rose to flee. Come morning I learnt that wolves had emerged from the forest edge. The boys had been up all night.

The responsibility carried by Bugdan and Vasil left a deep impression on me. I couldn't help reflecting that the traditions of an entire people also weighed on these boys' narrow shoulders. In Ukraine, the people of the Carpathians were renowned as poor, and for every Hutsul boy like Bugdan and Vasil, there were probably ten who had left to try their luck in the cities.

With Tigon back to health I set off again, and a day and a half later reached the highest point of the Svidovets. On the way a hailstorm hit us and the mist closed in, stealing away the view. I dismounted and led the horses along a narrow ridge, watching as the rain came in waves.

Late in the afternoon the wind dropped and the mist began to sink. Just as the sun angled down into our eyes there came an apparition – fifty horses rising through the mist and coming to a standstill right before us. After some time a horse stepped nervously forward with its head up and nostrils flaring. It seemed to be readying to strike, but then nibbled gently on Ogonyok's mane instead. Pressing on, the herd followed in a symphony of whinnies, snorts and the rhythmic beat of hooves. Their coarse, split manes, large heads and thick short necks were all signs of their Mongolian origins. Tigon strode out as if he were the proud leader, and when the herd lost interest and stole away at a gallop, he pretended he had bravely chased them away, shooting an aggressive bark in their direction.

We walked on until the sky turned pink, then called it a day. I sat in a small meadow admiring the horses as they rolled about the luscious green. Tigon came sprinting when he heard the ritual bang of my cooking pot, and we shared, as always, a slice of pig fat before putting on dinner to cook. All day I had been overwhelmed by the sense of freedom. Up here, away from roads and fences, it occurred to me that because my horses were free, they had nowhere to run. We had everything we needed – fresh air, water, open space, and an abundance of grass. In these circumstances it didn't make sense to tie a dog up or fence a horse in.

I filmed the sun as it slid below the horizon. The mist had pooled deep below, and it was clear we had nearly reached the end of the ridge. Ahead of us it twisted and fell into a deep river valley.

If I'd seen terrain like this three years earlier, I might have been too terrified to even begin my journey. As a scared, novice horseman, all I would have seen was the potential for disaster. I had always known that the Carpathians were one of the obstacles that kept me from reaching Hungary – or worse. But now that I had reached these mountains, I realised that the journey along the way, with all its unexpected challenges, had equipped me with the knowledge and skills I needed. I decided that in the future I would not worry about those things that I thought might bring me down. It was obvious that the journey itself would prepare me.

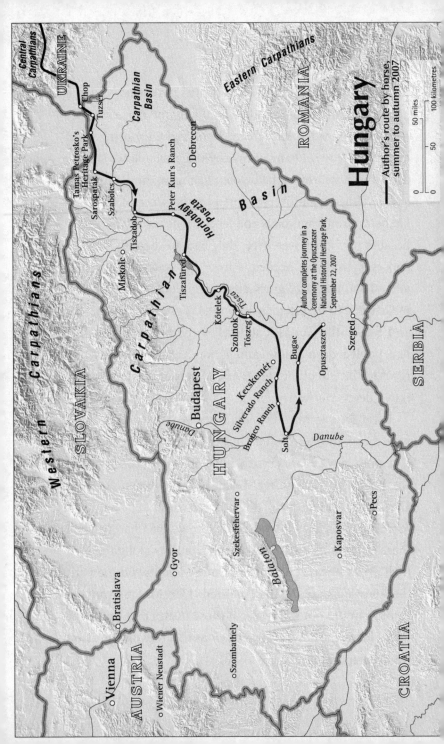

Hungary

— Author's route by horse,
summer to autumn 2007

Central Carpathians

UKRAINE

Eastern Carpathians

Chop
Tuzsér

Tamás Petrosko's
Heritage Park

Sárospatak
Szabolcs

Szabolcs

Tiszadob

Tiszafüred

Carpathian Basin

ROMANIA

Peter Kun's Ranch

Debrecen

Hortobágy puszta

Basin

Miskolc

Carpathian

Kötelek

Tisza

Szolnok

Tószeg

Bugac

Author completes journey in a
ceremony at the Opusztaszer
National Historical Heritage Park,
September 22, 2007

Kecskemét

Opusztaszer

Szeged

Silverado Ranch

Bronco Ranch

Solt

SERBIA

SLOVAKIA

Budapest

Danube

HUNGARY

Danube

Western Carpathians

Győr

Szekesfehervar

Balaton

Kaposvar

Pecs

Vienna

AUSTRIA

Wiener Neustadt

Bratislava

Szombathely

CROATIA

50 miles

100 kilometres

50

0

0

19

End of the World

In the winter of early 1241 the Mongol army were a long way from home. Having recently conquered Russia, they had crossed the Carpathian Mountains and were poised to invade central and Eastern Europe. Although Genghis Khan himself had died more than ten years earlier, his empire, under the leadership of one of his sons, Ogodei, would soon stretch from the Pacific Ocean to the Alps in Austria, from the tropics to the Arctic, making it the largest continuous land empire that the world has ever seen.

Poland was first to experience the Mongol wrath. Galloping in, the Mongols rained arrows from afar and used smoke, false retreats and other tricks to disorient their enemy. The European knights' armour offered some protection, but proved heavy and cumbersome when faced with the speed and agility of the Mongols. Before long the Mongols had defeated a thirty-thousand-strong army. As evidence of the defeat, nine large sacks of ears were infamously collected and sent to the Mongol war general, Subodei.

In the scheme of things, the Polish invasion was just a distraction. Foremost in their sights was Hungary – it was the best place from which to push further into Europe, and there were open grasslands that could easily support the grazing of their horses.

The Mongols were not the first nomad empire to attempt to conquer this land. Even the Hungarians were the descendants of nomads known as Magyars, who had travelled by horse from somewhere on the steppe in Asia and founded the nation of Hungary in 896. But former nomads or not, the Mongols saw no reason to spare the Hungarians.

The Mongolians encircled the Hungarian army and used catapults to send burning tar down on the soldiers. They then created a gap in their encirclement, encouraging the soldiers to escape and triggering a mass retreat. The Mongols closed in on these soldiers and cut them down. The killing is believed to have gone on for two days, during which time around sixty-five thousand Hungarian soldiers were put to death. In the weeks and months that followed, it is believed that half of Hungary's population was wiped out.

The following winter, the Mongols crossed the frozen Danube River and carried on into Austria. Nothing, it seemed, could hold the Mongols back from moving deep into Western Europe. And yet, there was. In March 1242 the Mongols got word that Ogodei had died. They began to withdraw east for the election of a new leader, reaching their homeland in 1243. Although the Mongol Empire would hold together for another century, the Mongols would never return to Hungary, nor realise their goal of dominating central and Western Europe.

My own plans were not of the conquest variety, and certainly I had no desire to collect ears as trophies. But what led me to Hungary was the same thing that had drawn nomads since the dawn of time: the westernmost stretches of the Great Eurasian Steppe. The wide-open Hungarian *puszta*, as steppe is known in Hungarian, suited a nomadic life similar to that of Mongolia. Beyond the Danube to the west, however, open plains succumbed to fences, crops, mountains and forests, and a much wetter climate. This region had long favoured settled society and was no place for a nomad. Hungary therefore signalled the end of the Eurasian Steppe, the end of the world for horseback nomads . . . and, of course, the end of my journey.

Given the devastation wreaked on Hungary by Mongols, someone like me, arriving in the spirit of those nomads, might not expect a particularly warm reception. But the atmosphere on the Hungarian-Ukrainian border was anything but unwelcoming.

Inside the veterinary control building on the Hungarian side of the border, János Lóska was excited. János had ridden all his life, was a horse breeder and had once been part of the national horse eventing team. For months I had been corresponding with him by email, and he had pledged to do all he could to help get my horses across the border.

Standing over the veterinarians as they inspected my animals, János now urged them on with a look of determination. When the last of the documents was stamped, and Tigon had been scanned for his newly installed microchip (he was now officially a citizen of Ukraine), János grabbed my sweaty arm with an iron grip and whispered in hushed English: 'Nothing can stop us now! Nothing!'

We celebrated with hugs, handshakes and whoops of delight, and I rode the horses to the nearby town of Tuzsér, where they were taken in by a family. János then drove Tigon and me to his home. I clung to Tigon in the back seat, determined to fight off sleep so I wouldn't miss a single waking moment. At one stage we stopped for fuel, and I stumbled into the convenience store and picked up a hot dog. The bright lights, white walls and floor, and plastic-sealed 'food on the go' were a novelty and, in that moment, an unexpected measure of how far I had come.

In the morning János spread out a map of Hungary to plot my route. Tigon, typically, planted his paws on the middle of it, demanding a pat. János suggested that I was to travel southwest across the great plain of Hungary, known as Hortobágy, then roughly along the meandering banks of the Tisza River to the centre of the country before turning west to the Danube. 'I have ridden every corner of this country by horse, and I can ensure that you will never have to ride on a road if you follow my directions,' he said proudly.

János's vision was of my caravan being escorted and hosted by Hungarian horsemen and women along a network of tracks and trails and, where possible, cross-country. He had friends ready to take me in and guide me through, and planned to ride with me whenever he could.

János was particularly excited about the place he had chosen for my finale: 'There is only one choice, if you really want to make it the Hungarian way, and that is Opusztaszer. There I will really be able to make you a hero!' he exclaimed.

The first of my hosts in Hungary was a man very familiar with Opusztaszer. I met Tamas Petrosko half a day's ride from Tuzsér. In his sixties, Tamas had slightly sunken shoulders and a hard, toughened frame rounded out by a belly. He rode towards me in a saddle draped with a sheepskin which, much to Tigon's wonderment, had the tail of the sheep still attached.

'You come the Magyar way! I also ride this route!' he said in a patchwork of English and Russian, leaning over from his horse to give me a hug.

In 1997 Tamas had been part of a small group of Hungarians who carried out a 4200-kilometre journey in honour of the great migration of his ancestors. They had ridden from Siberia, through Russia and Ukraine before crossing through the Carpathians onto the Hungarian plain. The end of their journey had been celebrated with a ceremony in Opusztaszer, which, according to Tamas, was the 'spiritual centre' of the country. It was in this nondescript town 90 kilometres east of the Danube that the Magyars' leader, Arpád, had officially founded the modern nation.

I spent several days with Tamas on a sweeping property that featured yurts, a Mongolian ovoo, and a shaman's hut marked at the entrance by the skulls of a horse and a cow. Out in the field flocks of long-haired Hungarian sheep and a herd of horned Hungarian cattle grazed. It was Tamas's dream to inspire young Hungarians to celebrate the spirit of their ancestors.

Unfortunately, my time with Tamas was marked by much more than learning about Hungarian nomad culture, when, one fateful night, Tigon vanished.

It was not uncommon for Tigon to disappear after dark, but when he hadn't returned by morning I knew something was wrong. By day two without Tigon I was beside myself. I rode through the nearby villages asking if anyone had seen a 'tall black dog with a white chest', but was met with shrugs. My blood turned cold. Life without Tigon? And that is when I received the phone call from János . . .

'Have you lost your dog?' he asked. I held my breath.

'. . . the family who you stayed with three days ago in Tuzser think they saw him in their backyard!'

Unbelievably, Tigon had managed to travel more than 40 kilometres back to Tuzser, and had even swum across the mighty Tizsa River. The only clue as to what had happened lay in a piece of wire that was still tightly bound around his neck. Tamas suspected that someone had stolen Tigon and tied him up by this wire, but that Tigon had somehow escaped and gone to the only place he could remember. Luckily Tigon was not a cat – he needed more than nine lives.

Fortunately, over the coming weeks in Hungary there would be no more dog stealing – or horse stealing for that matter – and in a land without mountains or scorching deserts, meeting people like Tamas became the focus of my journey.

Joining me from Tamas's farm, for instance, was István Vismeg, a tall, burly high school physical education teacher with unkempt, shoulder-length black hair and a mischievous look in his eyes. In a wild two-day ride through backstreets, along forest trails, and across fields I learnt how proud he was of his nomad roots.

'This is life!' he would bellow, even as we cantered through the pouring rain. 'I'm Hungarian and I'm not gonna live in chains!'

István took me to the historic town of Szabolcs and handed me over to my next host, a short, rotund man named Geyser. A self-proclaimed shaman, Geyser greeted me with a ceremony complete with drums and chanting in the centre of a thousand-year-old earthen fortress. I camped there and celebrated into the night with Geyser and István.

When I rode out from Szabolcs and waved goodbye to Geyser, I was still only four days' ride into my Hungarian journey. Ahead lay a further five weeks of encounters with people too numerous to recount here. The entourage – arranged by János – included everyone from wealthy businessmen to academics, stud farm owners and simple farmers. There was even a meeting with Kassai Lajos – a Hungarian of great renown who had resurrected the art of horseback archery and turned it into an international sport. Watching him galloping and shooting off an arrow every two seconds, hitting the target every time, one could only imagine the intimidating sight of a group of Mongols, or Magyars for that matter, charging into Europe.

Among these people, however, one man in particular, Peter Kun, stood out.

The morning before meeting Peter, János led me out under the glare of the sun onto a vast golden plain. We had reached the Hortobágy – the last great remnant of wild grasslands in Hungary. Squinting hard, I could make out cattle and sheep inching across the horizon, cutting in and out of focus in the heat mirage. The Hortobágy was home to the Csikós people – the only remaining mounted herdsmen of Hungary. They were renowned as skilled horsemen who, among many tricks, can make their horses lie down on command – a tactic the Mongol army was famed to have used in order to remain unseen.

Just as we idled up to a well and Tigon returned to his old trick of bathing in the drinking trough, Peter Kun came cantering in. Sitting straight-backed astride an Arab horse, his long hair neatly tied in a ponytail, the thirty-five-year-old cast his gaze to my horses, then to Tigon.

'Your dog is *tazi*! And your horses are *dzhabe*!'

I nodded in disbelief. Not a soul had recognised the Kazakh breeds of my animals since I had left their homeland more than eighteen months earlier.

It was not a lucky guess. Peter had been fascinated by everything nomadic since he was a child. As a university student he had excelled in ancient Turkic history, learnt to speak Mongolian and Kazakh, and at the age of seventeen spent a year living in Mongolia. Peter had now chosen to follow what he called a 'true Hungarian life'. He had bought cattle, sheep and horses and moved to a traditional Hungarian homestead on the Hortobágy, and now split his time between lecturing at a university and tending his herds.

With no paths, roads, or fences, we rode five abreast – János, his son Marti, Peter, myself and Ogonyok, who had decided to join us at the front. As we galloped, János veered over next to me and shouted: 'The day there are fences in Hungary is the day that this is not my country. I will leave.'

An hour or two brought us to Peter's ranch. It was a huddle of horse and sheep yards, with a barn and house like an island in the middle. A Kazakh yurt stood out the front. I spotted what appeared to be a pile of old matted sheepskins lying in the shade of its northern wall, but they soon rose and transformed into the figures of two indignant-looking dogs the size of small bears. Tigon got a fright, and scurried in behind Taskonir. The dogs before us were a breed known as komondor, and their trademark long white dreadlocked coat was so thick, it was rumoured that even wolves were unable to penetrate to the flesh.

After János and his son had loaded their horses into a waiting trailer and departed, Peter brought me a piece of rope, slung it over my forearm, and began to tie a knot. I knew in advance what his special demonstration was going to be. On the very first night of my journey, now more than three years ago, the Mongolian herder Damba had spent an hour teaching me a knot that he assured me I *had* to know. It was a knot that could be tied with lightning speed, always held fast, and could be quickly and easily untied. It was a knot I had used for everything from tethering horses to tying improvised reins and fastening pack loads.

During my first winter on the steppe I had begun to realise the importance of this knot. In Kazakhstan, herders had looked on with astonishment. Where had I learnt it? It was, after all, a 'Kazakh knot'. In Kalmykia, more than a year later, I encountered the same reaction from a Kalmyk craftsman, who termed it a 'Kalmyk knot'. Now, just as I predicted, Peter tied the very same knot and claimed it for his own people: 'You know, we say that if you don't know this knot, then you are not a horseman . . . In western Hungary, beyond the Danube and the Great Eurasian Steppe, no one knows this knot. We call it the Hungarian knot.'

After a meal of mutton I lay down to rest in Peter's yurt. Outside, the wind gently pushed against the felt walls. A horse somewhere cleared its nose, and a bleating sheep stirred. Through a narrow gap in the felt of the ceiling, glimmers of moonlight filtered down, illuminating a wolf skin, horsewhip and bow that hung from the wall. Next to me, his head resting on an old stirrup, Tigon was fast asleep and in a dream, paws twitching.

There were many connections that I had learnt of between the modern-day nations and cultures of the steppe, yet I had never dreamed that among them would be something I had carried with me from day one.

I joined Peter at sunrise as he saw off his herd of long-haired Hungarian sheep and grey cattle. Then we opened the gates of the horse yard and watched as Peter's herd thundered off, leaving a cloud of dust suspended in the morning light.

By nine am everything had settled, and the sun brought such stifling heat it had quashed the spirits of even the most exuberant young horses.

'It's too hot to step outside,' said Peter mischievously. 'In fact, it is so hot the only reason to step outside today is to see the *takhi*.'

Peter had arranged a visit to a rare reserve where herds of Przewalskii horses (known in Mongolian as takhi) live – the only surviving wild horse of Eurasia. Access to the takhi reserve was usually restricted to scientists, but Peter had used his connections to get permission.

After following hoofprints for half an hour or so, the crest of a slight rise fell away to a series of reedy waterholes and marshes. There, mingling by the water, were around sixty or seventy takhi, with zebra-striped legs, short manes, and dun-coloured coats.

Peter pointed to a commotion on the far side of the waterhole. A stallion had set upon a younger competitor, who now galloped off. The younger horse darted right and left before plunging headlong into the water. The pursuing stallion crashed in behind, nipping at its quarry. On our side of the waterhole the pursuit continued. The stallions shot past a mare who was leading her foals along the water's edge and careered out into the steppe. My attention returned to the waterhole. The water's surface was shattered by a frenzy of hooves as the herd pulsated through the water, then out onto hard ground.

The takhi's barrel-like chests and thick necks were a feature of my own horses, Taskonir and Ogonyok, symbolising the endurance and hardiness that had carried me safely to Hungary. The speed of the stallions was a reminder of the horses' ability to take flight and reach as much as 70 kph in seconds. There had certainly been many a time when, scared by the tiniest thing, I had seen my horses do just that. Even the way the takhi opportunistically took bites at reeds on the move was reminiscent of the greedy Ogonyok. At heart, horses were nomadic, and their ability to travel long distances enabled them to roam far and wide for feed and water, eating on the move.

I stayed at Peter's place for several more days. When finally I saddled up to leave, he plucked hair from each of my horses, gifted me with a Mongolian sweat stick, and told me: 'I am so happy to have met you, and I hope we have strong connections in the future. In your mind, your head, you think and act like a nomad even though you are from Australia.'

I rode on with my sails filled.

For seven days my caravan travelled south along the Tisza River, covering as much as 50 kilometres from one host to the next. Tigon was a rod of muscle and could sustain long sprints at over 40 kph. A quick dip in any number of oases along the way – river, trough, drain, or puddle – and it was as if he had been recharged. At night the horses were spoiled with hay and grain, and in the mornings they routinely broke into frolic.

In the evenings, I took Taskonir out without a saddle or even a halter. It had taken me a year to feel confident enough to gallop, and another year before we reached the kind of fattening grass where I was tempted to try it. Here, though, the issues of water, grass and distance had fallen behind us. Holding on to Taskonir's mane, with my bare toes tucked into the fur on his belly, I took him for long, exhilarating gallops. As he leant forward and the earth began to rush beneath us, I was overcome by the uncanny sensation that time was slowing down. I sat straight and still, legs wrapped around Taskonir's chest, my rear not lifting an inch from his spine. These same animals that I had been terrified of at the beginning, I could no longer imagine living without.

The momentum of the ride from Peter's farm carried me to the village of Tószeg. From there, I was escorted west for two days by a party of horsemen whom János had described as 'cowboys'. He wasn't exaggerating. They turned up with their lassos, long leather chaps, spurs, bulging belt buckles and broad cowboy hats. Leading them was a man they aptly called 'Sheriff'. En route, we stayed in a horse-friendly hotel. While the horses overnighted in stables, I slept with Tigon in the luxury of my own chandelier-hung room. Impressed with Tigon's exploits, the hotel's owner decided that Tigon, in fact, could have his own bed. Tigon leapt up onto it immediately as if he had deserved it all along, and spread out on his side, his head on the pillow.

It was only as I rode on unescorted from Sheriff's ranch that it hit me: I was just two days' ride from the Danube.

I had dreamed about this time, when I was nearing the end. Mostly I imagined the day my horses would no longer have the burden of carrying me. After all they had done, I wanted to offer them a land where there would never be a shortage of grass. Many times it had seemed that my dream to give my horses a deserving retirement would remain just that, and some horses hadn't made it at all. I was still haunted by Kok, whom I had left behind with an infected hoof more than a year ago in Kalmykia. I hadn't had the nerve to find out his fate. Somehow, though, I'd brought the rest of my team through. Ogonyok and Taskonir had been with me for almost three years, but suddenly it felt all too soon, too quick.

After a gentle ride west from Sheriff's farm through undulating sand hills and forest, I wanted to camp in the open steppe to take stock, but it wasn't to be. My last night before the Danube was spent at a Western-style stud farm, the Bronco Ranch. My arrival happened to coincide with a gathering of Western horsemen, so instead of pulling into camp, I rode in among a throng of four-wheel-drive vehicles and loudspeakers blasting country and western music.

After unloading my gear I took Taskonir and Tigon on a ride into the forest, where I found a small, sandy meadow and lay with Taskonir's rope lax in one hand, and Tigon's paw in the other. I tried to focus on the sunset and let the steppe soothe me, as it had done so many times before, but the constant hum of distant motorcycles, cars and music was unending.

A legend about the makings of Hungary gripped me. At the end of the Magyars' epic voyage from the East, it is said that they offered a white horse to the existing rulers of the land in return for a bundle of grass and a jug of Danubian water. Water and grass were the essential ingredients of life, and the land here offered both in vast quantities. But there was something about this legend that I was only now beginning to understand. The quest for better pasture had lured nomads to this land, which was not actually suited to a pure nomadic existence. By buying into a world of grass and water, the Magyars were trading away their white horse, their nomad way of life. Like nomads who had come before them, their saddles would be replaced with wagons, ploughs and scythes, their vast herds with cultivated fields, and their yurts with permanent homes. After all, in a land of such riches, there was no reason to keep moving.

I thought about this for some time – about what it meant for Hungary's unique past, and what it spelled for my future.

The journey had changed me. I'd fulfilled my dream of riding from Mongolia to Europe, learning to see the world through nomads' eyes. Yet if nomadism didn't belong in Europe beyond the Danube, or indeed at home in Australia, what would become of me? I worried that people back home might not be able to relate to who I had become. Would they even believe my story? I had learnt that I loved being in places where the smallest of things meant the world. How would I cope in a world that had everything, but meant little?

From Bronco to the village of Solt on the Danube was a mere 25 kilometres. It was to be my last day of westward travel, and my last alone.

The steppe came in dribs and drabs. When open spaces appeared I went into a trot, but then a ditch, a road, or a cornfield would stop us. In the evening I passed through Solt, disturbing a few dogs, a cyclist and a pedestrian. From there it was a hop, skip and jump before we dropped down to lush green flats and arrived at the river. Before me lay a wide swathe of silty brown water stretching to the far bank. Beyond that lay the beginning of fences, walls, roads and cities. From the south, a tourist ferry was chugging up against the current. I resisted the pull of Taskonir's head at first, but then let the reins go and watched as all the horses drank. Even Tigon carefully walked in and lapped it up.

That night I camped for just the second time in Hungary. Deep into the early hours of morning I recalled every day of travel since I had set off three and a half years earlier. I could remember almost every step of the way. Rather than being a journey, it had become my life. And yet there was no escaping the reality that it was already fading. The hoofmarks of my horses in Kazakhstan would be long gone by now, the grass my horses had eaten regrown. Some of the people I had met had even passed away. Never again would the horses feel the packsaddle on their backs. Never again would Tigon know the freedom of running day in and day out.

Just as I had felt when I was leaving my life in Australia, I knew that a part of me was dying.

*

The rather anonymous stretch of Danube near Solt offered a personal finish, and symbolised the edge of the steppe, but now it was time to celebrate with others.

The day after reaching Solt and the Danube, I packed my things and made my way to Budapest's international airport. There, stumbling out through immigration, was my brother Jon. During my journey there were times when he had wanted to join me but didn't. Following Dad's death, he had been determined to come for at least the finish.

For the four days it took to ride from the Danube southeast to Opusztaszer, he travelled with me. On the first day, he went by foot, running this way and that, snapping photos and taking in all the details. It was only his second time outside Australia, and his first in Europe. At dusk he approached me with a smile. 'Look, there are so many frogs! I have one!' He opened his hands to reveal a squirming, mud-coated little specimen. Standing there at my side, with his daypack on and face full of wonder, he was the spitting image of Dad – or at least the vision I'd had of my father walking by my side the day after he had died.

For the second day of riding János came to lead us on an epic 50-kilometre trail. We carried on well after darkness, and just as we approached an equine-friendly hotel for the night, there came a familiar voice.

'Tigon! It's really you!'

Ahead of us, Tigon was the first of our troupe to greet my mother. Also waiting there was Graeme Cook, a longtime family friend and neighbour who had been the first person to put me on a horse, four years earlier. My childhood mate Mark Wallace was there, too, with his partner, Nadia.

The next two days were something of a dream. To ride with family and friends by my side, with my caravan of horses still intact, gave me a feeling of togetherness that I knew would never be repeated.

My last camp was a mere 10 kilometres from the finish line. What I had hoped would be a night of reflection became one of drama. Earlier in the evening Tigon had rolled in something dead. I had visions of reaching the finishing line and hearing not just clapping and cheering, but groans as Tigon greeted the adoring crowd with the stench of death. Long into the night I attempted to wash him clean with shampoo and water from my bottle, but he escaped my grip and shook himself off, covering everything else of mine with the smell of death. It was as if he were reminding me that there had never been a day on this trip when everything went smoothly – and there would probably never be one in life going forwards, either. I could have prepared for this journey for forty years and still not been ready – I had to accept and embrace that things were going to go wrong, and in the end, it was those challenges that I remembered most fondly.

For the finale at the national heritage park in Opusztaszer the following day, the Kazakh and Mongolian embassies had sent representations, along with the deputy ambassador from the Australian mission in Budapest. Then there were also many others – some were friends from Europe, but mostly they were Hungarians who had hosted me along the way.

As the remaining distance of my journey dwindled, I felt carried forward on a wave of emotion. The last few steps were made through a guard of honour formed by Hungarian horsemen in traditional regalia.

When the formal side of the ceremony was over, the celebration moved to a yurt camp nearby, where the smell of goulash, the splash of pálinka, and the neighing of horses mingled till morning. Tigon was in his element – pats from every corner, followed by juicy pieces of steak.

At one stage, Attila, the owner of the yurt camp, pulled me aside with a gleam in his eye. 'Tim Cook,' he began, and continued before I could correct him, 'first night of travel you sleep in yurt tent. Last night of travel you sleep in Hungary, yurt tent.' He looked down at Tigon, then at me, almost ready to cry, but shook his head slowly. 'Beautiful, it's beautiful.'

Epilogue

The twenty-second of September, 2007, the day I rode into the national heritage park at Opusztaszer in Hungary was one of the most fulfilling of my life. More than three years after setting off from Mongolia I had achieved my dream to ride across the Eurasian steppe. Looking back, the measure of the trip was the many friends I had made along the way. I truly felt as wide and 'big as the steppe'.

That same day, however, marked the beginning of fare-welling the people, animals and places that had become my life on the steppe.

I had thought long and hard about what I would do with the horses after I had finished. Eventually I decided to give them to an orphanage in the small village of Tiszadob. I had stayed at the orphanage en route, and the director, Aranka Illes, explained that they had long been trying to set up a riding program for the orphans. At the end ceremony I handed over the horses to Aranka and several children who had travelled to greet me. The next morning the horses were loaded into horse trailers and driven off. I was left with a lonely set of saddles.

It had never been a possibility to bring the horses back home to Australia, so I had always expected that I would have to say goodbye. I had, however, had hopes of bringing Tigon home with me, so it was somewhat devastating to discover that getting him into Australia from Hungary would cost around $10,000 – a nearly impossible sum of money at the best of times, but particularly at that point because I was broke. Additionally, Tigon would need to become a citizen of the European Union before being eligible to apply for a permit to enter Australia's strict quarantine, and that would require him to stay in Hungary for a minimum of another six months. János took Tigon home, generously offering to keep him at his horse farm.

Six weeks after finishing my journey I put my bags down at my mother's country house in Gippsland, Australia. I woke in the morning to the familiar warble of a magpie, the smell of Mum's cooking, and the knowledge that I didn't need to worry about finding a place to sleep for the next night, or indeed for many nights to come. I had been told by a Kazakh that 'mountains never meet . . . but people do'. It was an expression that might have been cryptic and meaningless to me in the past, but which now helped me appreciate just how precious it was to be around loved ones. This was especially so when I recalled some of the harder, lonelier times out on the steppe, and the loss of my father.

And yet it was also true that in Australia I felt another kind of loneliness. It seemed that in this very different reality no one could truly relate to my experiences. I dearly missed Tigon and the horses, and I found it hard to know how my experiences were relevant. The journey began to feel like some kind of dream from which I had woken. Re-adapting to life in Australia, particularly without my animals, would be much more difficult than the challenges of being a novice horseman on the steppe.

One of several pivotal moments for me was one evening when my mother, Anne, a primary school teacher, invited me to speak at her school's Year 6 graduation. As I re-told my story, I watched the eyes of the sixth graders begin to glow and fill with wonder: the same wonder that had led me to take a risk and start the journey in the first place, and which I had seen in Tigon's eyes each and every day. The adventure, the people, the stories made sense to these young minds in a way that didn't need translating, or explaining.

It helped remind me that part of my dream had always been to share my story with others – specifically to make a documentary film, and to write a book. I have loved writing for as long as I can remember and have always wanted to be a writer, and more so I wanted to inspire young people to walk a different path in life, to explore unfamiliar cultures, follow the call of adventure, and to make decisions from the heart with passion and curiosity. To bridge the gap between my life as a nomad on the steppe and my life here in Australia, the solution was obvious: I needed to get back on my horse, figuratively at least, digest all my experiences and turn them into something meaningful for others.

I began working on the film first. Together with editor and friend Michael Balson, and my youngest brother Cameron, I started sifting through the 140 hours of video that I had taken over the course of the journey. It was a long shot, but my aim was to convince a broadcaster to fund a three-hour film series for television broadcast.

Then I set about writing. I soon discovered that despite the vastly different world I was now living in, my experiences came back to me with skin-tingling vividness. The subtlest of things would take me back: running my hands along the contours of my saddle, catching a whiff of wood smoke, feeling the breeze wash over the hills near my mother's home, glimpsing a horse in a paddock, or hearing the sound of a distant dog barking. There were endless triggers that worked like keys to unlock a world that only I could see. With each and every sentence I wrote down I was able to make sense of what I had learnt.

As I worked slowly through the journey I re-established contact with many of the friends I had made across the steppe. Among them were Aset, who had given me Tigon, and Baitak and Rosa from Akbakai. Then, in the middle of 2008, I took up an opportunity to guide a trekking journey in Mongolia where I was able to meet some of the very people who had sold me my first horses. Meeting these people gave me the sense that my journey had not only been every bit as real as I imagined, but that the stories and connections would remain alive for much longer than it had taken me to ride across the steppe.

I kept in close contact with János Loska about Tigon, of course. There were many stories of mischief to be recounted, such as when Tigon followed a passing horseman for a day and took all the farm dogs with him. János lamented that he had had to send a taxi to pick them all up. Tigon became a father at János's farm, and one of the offspring was given to the Tiszadob orphanage, where he was named Tigi.

More than a year passed. But then one day I received a letter in the mail. It was from Australian Quarantine – a permit for Tigon to enter Australia had been granted!

With the help of Mike Wood – an owner at that time of a Mountain Designs shop that had been a sponsor – I was able to arrange a special fundraising presentation to pay for his trip home. The response was overwhelming, and with a sold-out theatre of people who had come to listen to my story, $8,000 was raised in just one night.

Tigon was taxied from Budapest to the Vienna airport, then flown to Dubai (where he spent a night in a $500 air-conditioned hotel room) and loaded onto a flight to Melbourne. When I arrived at quarantine Tigon showed no hesitation. He came bounding out of his enclosure to meet me, his paws reaching up onto my chest. I reached my hands over and around his snout to that little notch at the back of his ears, and soon my nose rested on his. The embrace was cut short when he noticed the marrow-bone that I had brought along as a gift. He spent the next half hour exclusively fixated on gnawing the bone clean.

I will never forget our first walk together on Australian soil. With each and every paw forward he paused, ears high, head cocked to the side. Everything was new: the laugh of a kookaburra, the shrill cry of a king parrot and the distinct smell of gum trees. What I would have given to be inside his mind just for a moment – a mind that was once again rapidly expanding with a map of smells, sights, sounds and people. With Tigon I felt reunited not only with him and my journey, but with my inner self.

I knew that together with Tigon every day beckoned with adventure.

In the years that followed, Tigon and I were by each other's side through all of life's events – big and small. He was there, for example, when I received news that ARTE channel in Germany and France had granted funding for a three-hour documentary series. ABC in Australia soon followed with their support of a version of the series, and before I knew it, *On the Trail of Genghis Khan* (*Auf den Spuren der Nomaden* in German) was a reality! The series has since been broadcast in several countries and languages.

For four years, while I wrote my first book about the trip (for adults), Tigon was there, page by page, chapter by chapter. Sometimes he was snoozing on the couch in front of the wood heater while I typed away, his muffled barks in his dreams rising above the crackle of the fire. I listened to a lot of instrumental and classical music while I wrote, and some of these became his favourites to which he howled and howled in a kind of dog karaoke performance. When I stayed too long in front of the screen he always reminded me of priorities – a 'walk' being number one, followed closely by eating a kilo of fresh meat, and lots of pats and cuddles (not necessarily in that order).

For almost six years we lived in a small cottage near Mount Beauty in the mountains of north-eastern Victoria where there were many adventures to be had. Our routine was a three-hour daily walk up the local 'Mount Emu' – most of which for him was off the track, and often in the dark. As always, Tigon moved effortlessly between the wilds and the comforts of domestic life. He was just as at home mingling with dingoes under a full moon, or chasing giant deer through the ferny understorey of misty alpine forests, as he was curled up on the middle of my bed, munching down on roast meat offered to him from a VIP table at a fancy conference dinner event, or accepting multi-pats from adoring schoolchildren.

It wouldn't be adventure without close calls, of course. More than once he decided to tango with a giant male kangaroo – one of whom lured him into a dam in the middle of the night. On another occasion while travelling to Byron Bay in northern New South Wales, Tigon leapt into a flooded rainforest river, only to be sucked through a narrow pipe under the road. I thought he was gone until a minute later he bobbed up in the rapids downstream. After swimming to the side he coughed up some water, took a pee and kept walking. There was a dreadful injury he sustained near home, too, when a deer came down with its antlers, gouging his armpit. It was an accident that brought Tigon within a hairsbreadth of death. I was there stroking him when he opened his eyes after surgery, and for many days and nights to come. Even as Tigon grew older, his spirit of adventure, and his love of freedom, remained irrepressible.

Every day when I returned to my writing I was inspired by his new stories and reminded of old ones.

In 2009 I fell in love with a young Mongolian woman, Khorloo, during a trip to Mongolia, and Tigon was there at home the day she moved in. He was there for all of our adventures together. He certainly found another confidante and close friend (and pat-giver) in Khorloo. He was also there when she moved away, and there were just the two of us once more.

In more recent times I came to appreciate the way that our rhythms, and even breaths, moved in sync. It was reassuring to wake up and hear him breathing somewhere in my home, and to have his paw brushing at my face if I happened to sleep in. Neither of us were happier than when we were on the move and exploring a new land. To watch Tigon run was uplifting on even the greyest of days – his every movement seemed to be an expression of joy.

Tigon's journey into adulthood continued apace in Australia. During the same week in September 2013 that my first book about this journey was published, I was lucky to witness the birth of his first Australian children. After an arranged marriage with my mother's dog, Misty – a Saluki – Tigon had become the father of nine puppies. This was to be the first of three litters – the following litters had seven and eight respectively. His children are now living in almost every state and territory. There are rumoured to be several not so 'legitimate' children roaming about, too, but that's another story you can ask me about another time.

I cannot write about our companionship without mentioning that Tigon was there for me, even when I wasn't there myself. Following my first return trip to Mongolia in 2008, I began annually taking groups trekking in the Altai of Mongolia during the northern summer. I also returned to Hungary twice to see the horses, where they are still alive and well today. During these travels Tigon stayed in his other primary home – my mum's place in Gippsland, Victoria. In my mum Tigon found a loving host, and in her garden he found endless plants, bushes and nooks to explore – and, much to my mum's horror, to *dig*. My mum kept one of Tigon's puppies – Bauvga, meaning 'bear' in Mongolian – and so for Tigon staying at Mum's inevitably meant epic adventures with his protégé. We will never know the full story of most of these, but we generally know the ending – for example, after one such escapade the two of them arrived home covered in muck from head to toe, so tired that after being washed and wrapped in towels they both slept like the dead for nearly forty-eight hours!

During the journey Tigon had learnt to trust me, and this trust only deepened in Australia. Every time I began packing my bags his ears and tail would flop, and yet he also seemed to know that no matter how long I was absent, I would surely be back – whether that was at the end of a plane trip when I opened up his crate at cargo, or when, after a month or two in Mongolia, I pulled back into the driveway. Every reunion was as exciting and emotional as the last. He would run in circles, lie in his bed upside down for a belly scratch, and paw me to continue when I stopped stroking him.

In the last two years I have been able to work towards my other long-held dream – to write a book about this journey dedicated to young people.

Tigon has been here within hand's reach through all the pages, infusing me with a renewed sense of wonder. That is to say, through *almost* all the pages.

It was on 31 August 2018, the last day of winter, that I received a message via satellite from Mum. I was away on a trip in remote Mongolia, not too far from his homeland of Kazakhstan.

At some point on that cold windy night when the driving rain had kept most humans and animals indoors, Tigon had run out into the darkness to seek adventure. He had not returned. We will never know what spoke to him, or what drew him out that night, but we do know that 20 kilometres from home, he had one adventure too many. At the age of fourteen, Tigon passed away.

The last few months have been hard, not only for me, but for Mum, my siblings, and so many people who loved and adored Tigon. Tigon was my sanctuary, and my hero.

I can only trust that he knows I was there for him with virtual pats from Mongolia when I heard the news, and when I turned back up the driveway at Mum's house in tears to caress his beautiful body one last time. And that I was there with him days later when I carried his spirit to the top of our beloved Mount Emu.

I'm walking alone now for what feels like the first time I can remember. It is hard to express how much I miss Tigon. And yet in my grief, I have turned again to writing, and I have realised that this book is no longer a story about Tigon – it is an ode to him. And it is for all of you, so that you may carry some of his spirit in your hearts.

As for my future, I still have dreams of adventure. One day I would like to travel from India to Europe on the trail of the Roma people – also known as Gypsies. I'd like to travel by bike, foot, yacht and canoe from Australia to Siberia along the migratory route of sandpiper birds. And I would love to spend a year living with nomads in the remote Altai of Mongolia. But for the time being I am most looking forward to the publication of this book, and exploring my own backyard in Australia by taking this story to as many schools as I can.

Tim Cope
4 April, 2019

Tigon and I, reunited in Melbourne.

Tigon with his arranged partner and some of his pups.

Acknowledgements

What began as a plan to ride horses for eighteen months from Mongolia to Hungary has shaped my life for more than decade. There have been three stages – the preparation, the journey, and then digesting the experience. The last of these has been by far the longest, and has involved, among other things, film-making and writing. At every one of these stages help, support and encouragement from others has allowed me to go forwards.

Some of the people to whom I owe my gratitude are still close friends, and some sadly did not live to see the end of this project.

In the early stages I owe many thanks to my parents – Anne, and the late Andrew Cope – and my then girlfriend,

Kathrin Nienhaus, who travelled together with me for two months of riding during the early stages of the journey in Mongolia. My great-uncle, the late John Kearney, offered crucial moral and financial assistance.

The horse world is confounding for the uninitiated, and there were individuals who helped guide me into it. CuChullaine O'Reilly of the Long Riders Guild offered generous wisdom, a sympathetic ear, and encouragement that equipped me with the knowledge to travel by horse and the inspiration to carry on with what I learnt far beyond the Danube.

In Australia, Cath and Steve Baird of Bogong Horse-back Adventures gave me my first taste of horseriding – a packhorse trip in the Victorian Alps. In Western Australia, Brent, Sam and Sascha Watson of Horses and Horsemen provided training, then advice throughout my journey. They introduced me to equine vet Sheila Greenwell, who donated a veterinary kit, and throughout the journey offered life-saving vet services by correspondence.

Then there are those who helped me in the countries I travelled. Old friends Tseren Enebish of Mongolia and her husband Rik Idema, Tseren's elderly mother, and her cousin, Bayara Mishig hosted and guided me through the difficult early stages in Ulaanbaatar. Gansukh Baatarsuren, a young enthusiast of Mongolian history and horseman-ship, helped me buy my horses and was an endless source of nomadic cultural insight.

In Kazakhstan I stayed with around seventy families, but in particular I'd like to thank Evegeniy and Misha Yurckenkov in Oskemen, Aset and his son Guanz (who generously offered me Tigon), Dauren Izmagulov and Azamat Sagenov in Atyrau. I'm also grateful to Kosibek Erzgalev, the minister for agriculture in Western Kazakhstan, and his team who helped me get my horses and Tigon into Russia. Special gratitude goes to the late Baitak in Akbakai, who passed away suddenly in 2010. Without him, neither Tigon nor my horses would have made it past our first winter on the steppe. Baitak is survived by his wife Rosa, and their son Dubek. In Kazakhstan I would also like to acknowledge my Australian friend Cordell Scaife, and his then partner Cara Poulton, who joined me for a particularly tough segment of my journey through the desert – a shared adventure that did not make the cut for this book. Sorry!

In Russia I was supported by Dr Anna Lushchekina of the Russian Academy of Science, journalist Inna Manturova, and Dr Liudmilla Kiseleva. Liudmilla, a professor of biology and an environmental activist, was unfortunately killed in a car accident only a couple of weeks before the end of my journey. I'd also like to thank Yuri Nimeevich and the Saiga protection park in Kalmykia, the Kalmykian Institute for Humanitarian Sciences, and Nikolai Vladimorivich Luti and all his crew in Timashevsk.

In the winter of 2005/2006, I travelled to Crimea to renew my Russian visa. I was hosted for a month in Sevastopol by my surrogate Russian grandmother – Baba Galya – who I had befriended in 2000 while cycling in northern Russia. Her daughter, Shura, grandchildren, Olya and Dima, and son-in-law, Sasha, kindly looked after me. Sadly, Sasha passed away in 2007. Baba Galya passed away on 24 November, 2008, just shy of her eightieth birthday.

In Ukraine and Crimea more broadly, thanks go to Ismet Zaatov, deputy minister for culture of Crimea, and Ira of Argamak Horse Centre near Feodosiya.

Thanks to Anya Summets, for her love and support, particularly during the period of my father's death. And to Vladimir Sklyaruk and his family in Kodyma, who arranged for Tigon and the horses to be looked after when I returned to Australia at the time of my father's passing. In the Carpathians, Ivan Ribaruk remains a good friend.

I was fortunate in Hungary to have broad support from many. I am indebted to Janos Loska, who singlehandedly arranged my journey across the border into Hungary, then to the Danube, and finally the special ceremony for the finish in Opusztaszer. Peter Kun, Istvan Vismeg and Tamas Petrosko also deserve special mention. But my biggest thanks in Hungary goes to Aranka Illes (and her family), who loved and cared for my horses as her own for more than ten years. At first my horses were looked after at the children's home in Tiszadob of which Aranka was director, and more recently near Kecskemet, where Aranka continues to work with disadvantaged and orphaned children.

Here in Australia I owe great thanks to my mother, Anne, for her patience and love, and for involuntarily sheltering me for the best part of two years after I returned home (and Tigon for many more). Mum has witnessed the highs and lows I have experienced while coming to terms with the end of one journey and the beginning of new challenges. Likewise, thanks go to my brothers, Cameron and Jonathan, and my sister Natalie. Family friends Graeme Cook, the Wallaces and the Nicholsons have been great supporters of our family, particularly since the passing of my father.

It goes without saying that I owe much to my father for introducing me to the outdoors, and doing everything he could to support me on my path to adventure and writing, even when it involved abandoning my law degree at university – something that did not sit comfortably with him at the time.

There are untold individuals who have been a big part of Tigon's life and mine in the past few years. There are, for example, hundreds of people who generously put

Tigon and me up in their homes as we travelled across Australia, speaking at schools, and for a variety of different events. Then there are those who helped raise funds to get Tigon home in the first place. To you all, a big thank you; you know who you are.

Closer to home, thanks go to Khorloo Batpurev, who shared her life (and house) with Tigon for many years, and to book publicist extraordinaire Brendan Fredericks, who shared many a car, bed and walk with Tigon during the first book tour.

In Mount Beauty (Tigon's primary and spiritual home in Australia) I'd like to mention the Mcilroy family, who were our neighbours, hosts and friends for six years. Tigon and I were also lucky to have the support and friendship of another Mount Beauty family, the Van Der Ploegs – who, by the way, are now owners of Ali, one of Tigon's beautiful daughters.

In 2017 Tigon and I made the big move to Melbourne to start writing this book. For a year we lived with the ever-accommodating and generous Rob Devling and Rachel Falloon . . . and Max (their fearless little canine who enjoyed many a run with Tigon and me along the Yarra River). Later I carried out much of my writing at Mycelium Studios where I found a loving and appreciative community – thank you. The last stages of this book have been written in a beautiful abode at the Abbottsford Convent, a space I have come to love, and which Tigon would no doubt have adored too. Finally, thanks to my new neighbour and friend, Isobel, and her sons, who have provided valuable feedback, understanding and friendship.

In the last year of Tigon's life I owe particular gratitude to Valeria D'Agostino. Valeria was perhaps Tigon's favourite patter of all time. She generously looked after Tigon on occasions when I was away. Valeria, thank you also for your kind heart, care and support, which have been instrumental in helping me to cope with the grief of Tigon's passing.

Through all of this time, I am thankful for the patience and belief of my literary agent, Benython Oldfield in Australia, and publisher Claire Craig at Pan Macmillan for believing in this book.

To anyone else that I have not mentioned, please know that you will forever be in my heart, and Tigon's.

Lastly, it would never have been possible to carry out this journey without the support of sponsors. I would like to thank:

Main sponsors
Iridium (Satellite Phone Communications)
Internetrix.net (particularly support from Daniel Rowan)
Saxtons Speaking Bureau
The Australian Geographic Society

Medium level sponsors

Odyssey Travel

Mountain Designs

Spelean Australia – distributors of such brands as MSR, Therma-Rest, and Platypus

Fujifilm

Inspired Orthotic Solutions (thank you to Jason Nichols)

Equip Health Solutions

Dick Smith Foods (special thanks to Dick Smith)

Minor sponsors

Baffin *Polar Proven*, Nungar Knots, Ortlieb, Leatherman, Magellan, Mountain Horse, Tour Asia Travel Agency (Kazakhstan), Tseren Tours (Mongolia), Bates Saddles, Custom Pack Rigging, Lonely Planet